# Spring's Promises
A Larry Macklin Mystery-Book 13

A. E. Howe

# Books in the Larry Macklin Mystery Series (in order):

| | |
|---|---|
| November's Past | September's Fury |
| December's Secrets | October's Fear |
| January's Betrayal | Spring's Promises |
| February's Regrets | Summer's Rage |
| March's Luck | Autumn's Ghost |
| April's Desires | Winter's Chill |
| May's Danger | Valentine's Warning |
| June's Troubles | St. Patrick's Cross |
| July's Trials | Memorial Day's Escape |
| August's Heat | Independence Day's Search |

Copyright © 2019 A. E Howe

All rights reserved.

ISBN-13: 978-0-9997968-8-7

This book is a work of fiction. Names, characters, places and incidents are the product of the author's imagination or are used fictitiously. Any resemblance to actual events, locales, business establishments, persons or animals, living or dead, is entirely coincidental.

Except as permitted under the U.S. Copyright Act of 1976, no part of this publication may be reproduced, stored in a retrieval system or transmitted in any form or by any means, electronic or mechanical, including photocopying, recording or otherwise, without written permission from the author. Thank you for respecting the hard work of this author.

# DEDICATION

For all of the doctors and staff at Florida Cancer Specialists and the Mayo Clinic Jacksonville for helping to make sure I'm still here to continue Larry's adventures.

# CHAPTER ONE

I looked at Pete Henley and shook my head firmly.

We were sitting at our desks in the Adams County Sheriff's Office on a Wednesday morning in mid-March. I was trying to catch up on my reports, but it wasn't easy while Pete and my partner, Darlene Marks, harassed me about my upcoming nuptials.

"It's the law. Florida Statute 8.4-something. You could go to jail if you don't," Pete said, looking somber.

"No," I told him. "Don't do it."

"You know Pete's not going to let up," Darlene told me.

"How can you support this?" I asked her.

"Because I'm going to be right there, sugarplum." She gave me a wicked smile.

"I'd rather go to jail," I told Pete.

"Fine. We can do it that way. We'll lock you up and hold it in the jail." He shrugged.

"This is ridiculous," I said, frowning.

"Throwing you a bachelor party is my duty as best man," Pete said smugly. "That's also stipulated in the statute."

"I can't argue with you if you're just going to make stuff up."

"Good," Pete and Darlene said in unison.

Before I could respond, my phone rang. A glance at the number told me I had to take the call.

"What's up, boss?" Lt. Johnson hated to be called that. After spending many years in the military, he still found our more laid back approach a little hard to deal with.

"There's a body for you, Macklin," he said curtly. "At the Railroad Nursery. Deputy Spears is already there."

"Thanks, boss," I said cheerily and he hung up on me.

"You shouldn't taunt him, Larry," Darlene warned me.

"He's been even more humorless than usual," I said as I stood up. "There's a body out at the nursery."

"Want me to ride along?" Darlene asked. She worked twice as hard as the rest of us and, as a result, she was always caught up on her reports.

"That or you can stay here and finish *my* reports from last week," I offered.

"Fat chance, lead bottom. Let's roll." She grabbed her notebook and phone off the desk.

"Have fun, kids. I'll be here ironing out the details of your party," Pete said with a dismissive wave at our backs.

The nursery was located just south of the railroad tracks that ran through the middle of Calhoun. Long before I was born, the nursery's office had been a depot that received lumber, grain and other dry goods shipped from throughout the Southeast. Now the ten acres surrounding the old building were filled with all manner of plants and garden supplies.

As we drove up, I saw Randy Spears's patrol car parked in the back where the nursery kept large piles of rocks, dirt and mulch. The area wasn't fenced, but a large gate blocked the access road after hours. I pulled up near the gate and we got out of the car. I could see that Darlene was already scanning for signs of anything unusual.

"What have we got?" I asked Spears as he walked up to meet us.

"Not a hundred percent sure. Definitely a dead body. A

woman. I'm leaving everything else up to you guys," he said. "I've already called Shantel and Dr. Darzi's office. And I made sure to mark my route to the body."

Darlene pulled gloves and protective booties from the trunk of my car and handed them out. Once suitably garbed, we followed Spears through the gate and along a path he'd marked off with crime scene tape.

After passing various piles of mulch, dirt and rocks, all clearly labeled and priced, we came to a large mound of red mulch. Sticking out from the pile were about eight inches of a woman's leg. I could see that she was wearing black slacks and at least one casual, low-heeled shoe. The pants were scrunched up and revealed a few inches of pale skin.

"I felt her ankle on the off chance she was still alive," Spears said with a shrug.

"Doesn't anyone bury bodies anymore?" I asked, leaning in and looking closely at the leg.

"I suppose murderers are busy like everyone else," Darlene said. Leaving the body to me, she began to walk slowly around the area, though we'd wait for Shantel Williams and her crew to arrive and make a record of the scene before we started an intensive search of the grounds for evidence.

"This isn't an indigent," I said. The pants were neatly hemmed and the sole of the shoe looked new.

I tried to think of anything else we could learn without digging the body out of the mulch, but I was stumped.

"These piles block the view from the road and the rest of the nursery. The person who dumped the body had plenty of privacy," Darlene observed as we retraced our steps back to the gate to wait for Shantel.

"As long as no one came back here. Who found the body?" I asked Spears.

"A guy who was buying some mulch. He's waiting up at the store," he said. "I talked to him and the owner of the nursery."

I'd been there before on official business back when I'd

been a rookie right out of the academy. I remembered nervously talking to the owner about a burglary while my field-training officer squinted at me, ready to pounce on any perceived faux pas.

"Is the owner's name Austin Castro?" I asked, dragging the name out of my long-term memory.

"Grady Watson. He bought the place a few years ago," Spears corrected me. "I asked him if anyone else had been back here this morning. He didn't think so, but he couldn't be sure. They try to keep an eye on the side road, but he said customers come back here all the time to look at the materials and decide what they want."

"Aren't they worried about theft?"

Spears waved his hand at a large pile of rocks. "If you buy this stuff, they send a guy on a tractor with a frontend loader to put it in your truck. It's not like someone is going to shovel much of it into their vehicle on their own."

"Depending on how dead the victim is, she could have been in the mulch since yesterday."

"The leg was air temperature when I got here."

"Our body dumper doesn't have to be a customer. Could have been an employee or ex-employee with a key to the lock," Darlene said as we reached the gate.

The crime scene van was just pulling up. Shantel climbed out of the passenger's seat, yelling for Nisha Branch to grab the cameras out of the back.

"A body in the mulch." Shantel shook her head. "We best get our pictures taken so you can get the poor woman out from under that mess."

"I'm going up to talk with the witness and the owner," I told Darlene.

Deputy Spears followed me to the nursery office and introduced me to the key players before calling dispatch and going back into service. It would be a few hours before we would need extra hands to help with the investigation. Being a small department, we all tried to work together to best utilize our limited resources.

I decided to talk to the witness first, a man in his mid-sixties. He had on well-worn jeans, a plaid shirt that was threadbare at the elbows and sturdy work boots. His face was brown and lined from years of working in the sun.

"Full name?" I asked.

"Morris Clement Byrd, same as it was when I told that deputy," he said with the practiced grunt of a professional curmudgeon.

"Yes, sir. Just crossing my t's and dotting my i's. Date of birth?"

"Long time ago," he said and gave me a look, but added, "Fifth of May, 1950."

I needed his information to run a background check. It was always a good idea to look closely at the person who reported finding a body. A surprising percentage of them were the actual killers. I hadn't gotten a good look at our victim yet, but I was confident that Byrd could move anything weighing under one-fifty.

"Why did you come to the nursery today?"

"Oh, for Pete's sake, to get some mulch. It's springtime. I always mulch the beds around my house in the spring," he grumped.

"Did you come to the office first?"

"Yep. Told them to have the backhoe meet me out there. I went on down and backed my pickup up to the pile. When I got out, I saw that leg stickin' out."

"It was in plain sight?"

Byrd looked uncomfortable for the first time. "I like to check the mulch. Sometimes it's rotted underneath or got ants in it. I took my shovel and dug down a little. I uncovered it," he admitted.

"How deep was it buried?"

"Not far. Maybe six inches."

"Did you see anyone else when you were driving back?"

"No one. And I just hightailed it back up here when I found it."

I asked a few more question, then said, "I'd like to take a

look at your truck."

"Look away," he said and I followed him out of the office.

Byrd's truck was backed up to the loading platform of the old depot, so I was able to look down into the bed of his truck. It was a classic Chevrolet C10 that was old, but not abused. There was a fine dusting of pine pollen all over the vehicle, including in the back. One glance and I knew that the body hadn't been in the bed of his truck. If it had been and he'd pulled it out, there would have been streaks and smears in the layer of pollen.

I took a few pictures of the truck, then thanked him for his time and got a grunt in reply before he drove off.

Back inside, I found the owner wearing a frown. He was younger than I'd expected, early forties at most, with a lean and lanky build and a boyish face.

"I don't know how to feel about all this," he said. "I'm Grady Watson, owner and manager." He looked confused for a moment. "Of course, the deputy already introduced us."

"What do you mean, you don't how to feel?" I asked, thinking it was an odd statement.

"I'm worried about how this will affect my business. I know that seems pretty callous since someone's dead, especially if it's one of my regular customers. That'd be awful. It's just… a horrible situation."

"I don't think you have to worry about your business. You'll probably get bonus traffic from rubberneckers coming by to gawk. Some of them may even buy something," I told him, thinking how depressing that fact was.

"I bet you're right. Again, I feel awful asking, but how long will you need to have the back closed off?"

"We'll move as fast as we can to gather up any evidence that was left behind. We should be done in a day or two. Tell me about your morning routine and make sure to include any employees."

"I've only got Carlo working for me this morning. I got here just before seven. We open early so the contractors can come in and get what they need before heading off to job sites."

"Contractors?"

"Landscapers, gardeners..."

"You unlocked the gate to the rocks and mulch area?"

"Yes."

"Did you see anything out of place?"

"No. It was just like any other day."

"Are you sure that the gate was actually locked?"

"It's a padlock. So, yeah."

"Think. Did you see anything that seemed different or out of place?"

Watson was silent for a few minutes and looked thoughtful. "No."

"What did you do after you unlocked the gate?"

"Came up here and opened the store."

"When did Carlo get here?"

"He was waiting for me when I came back from unlocking the gate."

"Does he have a key to the padlock?"

He squinted thoughtfully. "I want to say no... but he could have. I've given him the spare key sometimes and asked him to open up the back. Since it's the spare, I don't always get it back right away."

"Where is the spare key kept?"

"In my office."

"Show me."

He opened a half door behind the counter. The little office was no more than ten-by-ten. A desk, a couple of chairs and three filing cabinets barely left room to turn around. Just inside the door was a wooden plaque with half a dozen sets of keys on it. Each was clearly marked with a tag, including ones for a tractor, a lawn mower and the back gate. Both keys to the gate were on the board.

"How much security camera coverage do you have?" I

asked.

"I've got a camera on the counter and two in the parking lot."

"Show me footage from the counter."

Watson sat down at his desk. After a few taps on the keyboard and clicks of the mouse, he turned the monitors so I could see. The camera covered enough of the counter to also pick up anyone coming into this office.

"I'll need a list of all your employees and former employees."

"Whose... body is in the mulch?" he asked.

"We haven't seen enough of it to even guess. We have to wait until our crime scene techs get done and the coroner helps us dig out the body. Do *you* have any thoughts on who it could be?"

"I... no."

I thought I saw something in his eyes. "But?" I pressed.

"I really don't know. It's just that there was a woman who disappeared a few years ago. When I heard that a body had been discovered..." He frowned.

"I can tell you that this body is very fresh. If it's someone who's been missing for years, then they were still alive a day or two ago."

"Of course," he said, sounding dissatisfied.

"Who is the missing woman?"

"She worked at the Dollar Saver just on the other side of the tracks. Here." Watson walked to the front of the store and pulled a piece of paper from a collection of flyers near the door. The page showed a smiling woman with sparkling eyes and slightly crooked teeth. The photo looked like it had been taken at a party, but had been cropped to focus on Terri Miller. She'd been twenty when she'd disappeared.

"I remember. She went missing right before I moved into criminal investigations. I did some of the door-to-door interviews. The investigators were never able to find any evidence of foul play or anything else." Pete had been one of them and Miller's file was still in his box of active, unsolved cases.

"I knew her... a little bit. She liked to come over here on her lunch break and walk around, looking at the flowers. I told her if I ever had an opening, I'd hire her," Watson said with a faraway look in his eyes. "Her mother comes by every couple of months to refresh the posters."

# CHAPTER TWO

I asked a few more questions then headed back to the crime scene. Darlene was talking with Linda and Ann from the coroner's office. They were watching as Shantel and Nisha finished photographing and filming the area.

"My two favorite vultures," I said with a smile.

"Caw, caw!" Linda responded.

"Do vultures caw?" Ann asked.

"They have to make some kind of noise. Otherwise, how would they attract mates and scare off other vultures?" Linda said, a quizzical look on her face. She turned to me. "Aren't you getting married?"

"Soon."

"That'll be good. Knock you down a peg and take that smile off your face." She punched me lightly in the arm.

"Not goin' to happen. I'll be as happy on my twenty-fifth anniversary as I am today," I said with a smug expression. Linda just rolled her eyes.

"You can check out the victim now!" Shantel shouted.

We all got serious and donned protective gear before we made our way to the mulch pile.

"This seems like an odd place to leave a body," Ann said.

"I've been thinking about that," I said. "If you wanted the body to remain hidden for a period of time, yet also wanted to make sure it would be discovered before *too* much time had passed, then this would be ideal."

"Looks like a female," Linda said, stating the obvious. She took a thermometer out of her bag and pushed it into the mulch near the body. "Let's see what temperature it's been resting in. Should be somewhat insulated."

While she waited on the temperature, Darlene and I helped Ann lay out a plastic tarp.

"We'll need to transfer the mulch onto the tarp so we can sift through it for any evidence," Linda said. "Be particularly careful around the face in case there's any vomit we need to collect."

I hadn't thought of the possibility that the woman might not have been dead when she was buried in the mulch. I winced at the thought.

As carefully as we could, the four of us took small handfuls of mulch and sifted through it before moving it to the tarp, slowly digging our way down. Soon I was finding long strands of brown hair mixed in with the mulch. I carefully separated it out, trying not to pull on it.

Forty-five minutes later, we stood back and looked at the corpse of the woman. She appeared to have been in her late thirties and was in good shape. Her teeth were clean and well taken care of, as were her skin and fingernails.

"Nice clothes, and those look like gold earrings," Darlene pointed out. I knew that she was thinking the same thing I was. This wasn't a robbery gone bad, but had all the signs of a very deliberate murder.

"Her head looks slightly deformed," I said, indicating a sunken area near her left temple. "And there's a little dried blood in the hair above her ear."

"Looks like a wicked blow," Linda said, leaning forward.

"We'll leave it to you," I told her. They'd need to examine the body thoroughly, which would take a little time. "Let us know when you're ready to move her." We hadn't found a purse or wallet, but I still held out hope that there might be something underneath that could lead to a quick ID.

"Do you want to take a picture?" Darlene asked.

"Not with all the mulch still sticking to her," I said. Normally, I'd take a photo so we could show it to folks who might recognize the victim, but I wasn't going to show anyone an image of the victim with mulch stuck in her eyes. Bad enough that *we* had to see it.

Darlene and I helped Shantel and Nisha search the area for possible evidence. After a few minutes, Darlene called for me to join her by the gate. "There," she said, pointing at a spot to the right of the gate just beyond the six feet of wooden fencing that kept anyone from driving around the barrier.

I looked where she was pointing and could see that the grass had been tramped down.

"They carried the body in?" I said, letting my mind wander through the possibilities this presented. "Our victim isn't a big woman."

"A hundred-and-twenty pounds. Roughly," Darlene said.

"If they parked their car right by the gate…" I let my eyes follow the path they would have taken. "… they'd have had to carry her about fifty yards. Doable for someone in good shape."

"Probably a man."

"And since Jack LaLanne is dead, I'd say they were most likely less than sixty years old."

"Working the probabilities." Darlene looked thoughtful. "It's an interesting choice."

"They took a lot of chances. The more time you spend at the dumpsite, the more likely it is that someone might see you or that you might leave traces of yourself behind."

"The ground looks pretty soft. We need to go over the that trail carefully."

"A footprint would be nice," I agreed.

"We're ready to move the body!" Linda called.

Darlene and I watched as Ann and Linda carefully lifted the victim into a body bag that was open on the gurney. Her head, hands and feet had been bagged to preserve any forensic evidence. The bagging process was always awkward for us and undignified for the victim.

Unfortunately, there wasn't anything under the body. I stepped away and started making calls to our dispatch, the Calhoun Police Department and other law enforcement agencies in the surrounding counties. If the woman had been reported missing, I wanted to find out sooner rather than later. Every minute we went without a name for our victim was time lost in the investigation, which could mean a murderer going free.

Once I was done with the calls I joined Darlene, who was helping Shantel scour the dirt path the killer might have taken around the gate.

"Any luck?" Darlene asked.

"No. The only people recently reported missing aren't even close to our victim in age. Two teenagers, a senior citizen and a black man in his late twenties."

"Someone should be missing her," Shantel said.

"Middle class, middle-aged, no signs of drug use. I'm pretty sure we'll get a name. The only question is when," I said.

"I asked Linda to send us a picture of the victim's face when they get her cleaned up. She said they would do that as soon as they get back to the morgue," Darlene said. They would also take her prints after checking for any forensic evidence on her hands and under her fingernails.

"We found a footprint," Shantel said, pointing to an orange flag halfway along the path around the gate. "Looks to me like a rubber boot."

"Maybe all the pieces will fall together on this one," I said, trying to be optimistic. "Unfortunately, my gut is telling me that this is going to be a real whodunit. If it had been any of the usual suspects, like a husband or a lover, they would have probably tried harder to conceal the body."

"Thanks, Columbo. Why don't you start looking for some evidence?" Darlene said with a good-natured smile.

We spent another hour tagging and bagging anything that might have been left behind when the body was dumped.

"We need to start pulling CCTV footage from around here," I said as we leaned against my car, watching the crime scene van drive off.

"This is a pretty industrial area, but there's the Fast Mart and maybe some of the warehouses have security cameras," Darlene said. I could tell she was already trying to visualize the routes that the person who'd dumped our victim could have taken to get there. Darlene's easygoing façade hid a smart and calculating mind. This, combined with a work ethic that put almost everyone else in the department to shame, made her a valuable partner. Most of the time I was sure she was more important to my success than the other way around.

"This doesn't feel like a random killing," I said.

"I agree. I don't understand why the killer chose this spot or buried her in the mulch, but it feels calculated."

Both of our phones buzzed with text alerts. Linda had sent us an image of the victim's face.

"They did a nice job," I said, looking at the picture. Not only had Linda and Ann managed to clean all of the mulch off of the victim, but they'd also found good lighting so that the face looked more natural.

We started at the nursery office, but Grady Watson didn't think he'd ever seen the victim. Our next stop was the Fast Mart.

Every law enforcement officer in the county knew this store, one of several Fast Marts in the area. Its location near the railroad tracks and proximity to a lot of rental and low-income property made it a popular hangout for unsavory characters. Odds were that there was more business being conducted in the parking lot than in the store. A faint odor of urine and stale beer greeted us as we got out of the car.

"We're in luck," Darlene said, nodding toward the store.

Through the glass I saw that Zac, the son of the man who owned all the Fast Marts, was working behind the counter. He was frowning at a man in a hoodie who seemed to be having trouble counting out his money.

"Y'all are getting better. I didn't even have to call you this time," Zac said as we walked in, still giving the man in the hoodie a glare. "Please tell Mr. Choke here to count his money before coming to the counter."

Choke turned and looked at me. He'd gotten his nickname from some long-forgotten baseball game. "I got the quarter," he said, digging in the pockets of his filthy jeans.

I looked at the counter where a pack of crackers, a beer and several small piles of coins were sitting. I pulled a quarter out of my pocket and tossed it on the counter. "That's for the crackers, not the beer."

"Hey, man, thank you, Deputy Larry," Choke said through missing and broken teeth.

Zac dragged the change off of the counter and put it into the drawer before bagging the beer.

"Don't open it where we can see you," Darlene told Choke with motherly concern.

"No, ma'am," Choke said before shuffling out of the store.

"I've begged my father to sell this place," Zac said, shaking his head. "None of our clerks want to work here. Who can blame them?"

"It's a service to the community," I said and got a dirty look from Zac.

"You should be nicer to me. I voted for your father."

"We come every time you call 911," I reminded him.

"Yeah, yeah." He waved dismissively. "What do you need?"

Darlene already had the victim's face pulled up on her phone. She turned it toward him.

"Do you recognize this woman?"

Zac peered at the phone. "What's she done?"

"Nothing. Have you seen her?" I pressed.

"She's dead?"

"Very," Darlene said.

"Oh, man, let me think." He stared at the picture. "Yes, maybe. Not here, though. At another store. But, yeah. Who is she?"

"That's what we're trying to figure out. Can you remember which store you've seen her in?"

"One of the nicer ones. Maybe on the northwest side."

"The one at the corner of High and Oakland?" Darlene asked.

"I think I've seen her come in for gas."

"Who manages that store?"

"Jake, my no-good uncle." He paused. "Seriously, don't tell him I said that."

"No worries. Would you mind calling him and letting him know we're on our way." Darlene made it a statement, not a request.

"And we'll need your security footage from last night," I said.

After the video was downloaded onto a flash drive, Darlene and I headed up to the other store. It was hard not to be struck by the contrast between the two locations. The one we'd left looked like a set from *The Walking Dead* while this one was new, clean, bright and filled with people who looked like they could pay for their own beer.

A very busy young woman was working behind the counter. I caught her attention between customers by holding up my badge. "We need to speak with you for a moment."

This elicited a puzzled look from her and a glare from the customers waiting in line.

"It won't take long." I turned to the patrons. "In fact, I could use everyone's help. We're trying to identify a woman whose body was found this morning. We have reason to believe that she shopped here on occasion."

"Now who's going to help us?" Darlene prodded. The

expressions of the people in line had changed from pissed-off to confused.

"The only picture we have was taken by the morgue, but you won't see any blood or gore." I didn't want anyone claiming that we'd traumatized them.

A tall man with broad shoulders and just the hint of a beer belly came out of a door marked "Employees Only."

"You all the cops?" he asked as he walked up. I explained the situation to him.

"Okay, sure." He turned to the customers. "If you want to help these guys, we'll do it in the back corner," he said, pointing to an area of the store where you could fill out cards for the lotto, pick up a case of beer or both.

Four people followed us back. The three men and one woman looked very somber as I showed them the photo on my phone. The second man didn't have to tell me that he recognized her; I could see it in his face.

"I know her," he said slowly.

"What's your name?"

"Me? Erick Fedderman." He looked shell-shocked.

"And you know this woman?" I asked as Darlene thanked the other three and sent them on their way.

"Yeah, that's Elizabeth Collins. She lives… used to live…" He stopped, flustered. "I don't mean because she's… I mean she moved out of her house right after the new year."

"But she used to live around here?"

"That's right. Her husband and kids still do …" His eyes got wide. "Her kids. Wow! That's horrible. What happened to her?"

"What's her husband's name?"

"Ian," he said softly. "But his last name isn't Collins. It's Barton. I guess she kept her maiden name. I never asked."

Out of the corner of my eye, I saw Darlene call dispatch to get an address for Ian Barton. I looked at my watch. It was two o'clock. There was a good chance he would still be at work.

"Do you know where Ian works?" I asked Fedderman.

"He's like a sales manager for a company that builds garage doors. I don't know their name."

"Do you have his cell phone number?"

"I don't know him that well. I just saw him around the neighborhood and at get-togethers, you know."

Not getting anything else helpful from Erick or anyone else at the store, we headed over to Ian Barton's house.

# CHAPTER THREE

The house, a brick ranch set back on two acres, had plenty of curb appeal, though the dogwoods and azaleas were past their peak. Two weeks earlier the yard would have been a riot of springtime color. There weren't any cars in the driveway when we pulled in, but the garage door was closed, so we walked around a basketball hoop and knocked on the front door. Nothing. I rang the doorbell and got more of the same.

"Neighbors," I said and Darlene nodded. "It's probably safe enough for us to split up. I'll take the one on the right."

"I don't know. The squirrels could corner one of us," Darlene joked.

"Don't forget the old movie trope: It's too quiet."

"You have a point. I've worked many an hour in the seediest neighborhoods in the county, but it would be just my luck to take a bullet in this little piece of suburban heaven." Not really worried, Darlene headed for the neighbor's house on the left.

Everyone around here seemed to get along without fences, so walking next door didn't involve going back into the street. I found a well-worn path leading from the Barton property to the neighbor's house.

The house next door was of similar design, but with differently colored trim and a larger front porch. There was an SUV in the driveway, so I had reason to be optimistic when I rang the bell. Sure enough, the door was answered in less than a minute.

"I'll save us both a lot of time. I'm not buying anything or giving any money to charity," said the blonde woman who answered the door. I could hear a baby crying in the background.

"I'm with the sheriff's office," I said, taking out my ID.

"You're not selling anything?" she asked with a suspicious look in her eyes.

"I just need to ask a couple of questions about your neighbor."

"About time. They've been having parties over there almost every weekend. I've called you all like a dozen times. I didn't think you were taking it seriously. There! You can hear them now!"

I could hear the faint sound of hip hop music coming from the house on the other side. "Actually, I wanted to ask you about Ian Barton and his family."

"They don't make much noise. My son and his oldest are friends. No, it's the other neighbors that are causing all the problems." Her mouth turned down into a frown as she placed her hands on her hips. I could still hear the baby crying inside the house.

"Do you need to see about your baby?"

"No. What I need is for you to take my complaint about those people over there seriously." The frown deepened.

"I'll take care of it. Maybe I should talk to Mr. Barton. Do you have a daytime contact number for him?"

"Ian? Sure, he's pissed too." She took out her phone and pulled up his number. I copied it down.

"Thanks. I'll get with code enforcement about the noise problem." I turned and started to walk away.

"You better, Officer… What's your name?"

"Pete Henley," I said over my shoulder as I hurried

toward Barton's house.

I waited by the car for Darlene to get back. "I got his number," I said when I saw her walking up.

"You had more luck than me."

I dialed Barton's number and he answered on the third ring. "Mr. Barton, this is Deputy Larry Macklin with the Adams County Sheriff's Office. I need to speak with you. Can I meet you at work?"

"What's this about?"

"I'm sorry, Mr. Barton, but we need to meet in person." I wasn't about to tell him that his wife or ex-wife was dead when her identity hadn't been confirmed. It would be much better to show him the picture to ensure that we were talking about the same person.

"I guess you can come here."

"Where's here?"

"The Florida Garage Door Company. We're in the industrial park off of Capital Circle Southeast in Tallahassee," he said, sounding concerned.

"I'll be there in forty-five minutes."

"Call me when you get here and I'll meet you at the door. Are you sure you can't tell me what this is all about?"

"When I see you."

I put my phone away and turned to Darlene, who said, "Drop me at the office. I'll go on the assumption that Elizabeth Collins is our victim and start doing a work-up on her."

I made good time and pulled up at the garage door company in forty minutes. The man who met me was heavyset with a bushy mustache. Well dressed and groomed, Ian Barton looked like a very successful car salesman.

"What's this all about?" he asked after I'd followed him back to his office.

"We found the body of a woman this morning. I'd like to show you a picture and see if you can identify her."

"A body? Is this some kind of joke?"

"If you would just take a look," I said, turning my phone toward him.

He frowned, but stepped forward and looked closely at the photo. "No," he said in a whisper. "I don't believe it."

"You know this woman?"

"It looks like my wife," he said softly.

"Her name is Elizabeth Collins?"

"Yes." His voice sounded stunned. "What happened?"

"We don't know much right now. Where was Ms. Collins staying?" I watched him closely, trying to gauge his reaction.

"She moved out several months ago and rented a house downtown."

"In Calhoun or Tallahassee?"

"Calhoun. She wanted to stay close to the kids."

"Why did she move out?"

"Because we weren't getting along, why else?" he snapped.

"She moved out?"

He gave me an exasperated look. "Yes, she moved out. Elizabeth wasn't the… homemaker type. We decided I'd take care of the kids, so we stayed in the house and she moved out."

"She was okay with this?"

"What happened to her?"

"Until an autopsy has been performed, anything I told you would be guesswork."

"But you're here investigating her death?"

I sighed. "It looks like she may have been murdered."

"Really? That's crazy," he said, still sounding numb.

"What was the cause of your separation?"

"The kids, her work. She's a CPA. Lives in her world of numbers. The more stress at home, the more she'd stay at the office. She works in this little cave with no windows, and she spends all day going over people's books."

"So she was obsessed with her work?"

"It's just how she is… was. Elizabeth was clearly on the

spectrum. Everything in our house had to be a certain way. I was cool with it when it was just her and me, but once Ethan and Clarice came along... Kids can't be forced to be neat. She would come home and find some normal kid chaos and go berserk. Eventually she just stopped coming home."

"Did you fight?"

"Oh, yeah. I know she had... issues, but they're kids. You have to be flexible. Not her. She didn't even try." There was sadness mixed with anger in his voice. The wounds were obviously still very raw.

"Where were you last night?"

Barton looked at me and narrowed his eyes. For a second I thought he was going to blow his top, but he must have decided that there wasn't any point in being angry.

"I was at home all night with the kids."

"How old are they?"

"Ethan is five and Clarice is three."

"Where did Elizabeth work?"

"Roberts and Mann CPAs. They're on the north side of town."

"I'll need to call them." I waited while he looked in his phone and gave me their number.

I called the firm and was told that Elizabeth Collins hadn't come into work. I let them know we were investigating a body that we thought might be hers. When I asked them to lock her office and not allow anyone in until we had a chance to go through it, they weren't happy about it. I told them the point wasn't negotiable and hung up.

"What is Elizabeth's current address?" I asked Barton.

He gave it to me, along with the name of the landlord.

"And her cell phone number and carrier?" Finding her cell phone would be important for the investigation.

"Do I have to call her parents?" Barton asked after providing the additional information.

"You have a problem with that?"

"They've never liked me. Her mother is a real... battle-axe would be the most polite way of putting it. And her father is worse."

"Give me their number and I'll call them." I wouldn't mind hearing what they had to say about their son-in-law.

After a few more questions, I told him the coroner would want a formal identification of the body. He nodded grimly.

I grabbed a late lunch at a drive-through on the way back to Adams County. By the time I pulled into the parking lot of the sheriff's office, dispatch had hunted down Elizabeth's landlord, who agreed to meet me at the house in an hour. I went inside for a quick check of email and messages.

"You want to ride together?" Darlene asked, getting up from her desk after I told her we'd found the landlord.

"Perfect. You can fill me in on what you've learned."

"Elizabeth Collins wasn't dumb," Darlene said as I drove. "She graduated at the top of her class from Florida State University. And I don't mean top five; she was numero uno. Long list of accolades. I got a lot of this from Roberts and Mann's website, but I double-checked it too. She was born in West Palm Beach. Her parents are Harvey and Charlene Collins. He was a big-time real estate lawyer, but he lost his shirt and got in some legal trouble when the real estate market crashed in 2009. Apparently he'd been involved with some shady stuff to do with mortgages. He had a stroke five years ago. Couldn't get anything on her mother. Ian and Elizabeth got married when he was twenty-five and she was twenty-seven. Have a boy and girl. Credit history's good and neither of them have a criminal record, not even a traffic ticket. She drives a white BMW. I figured we'd see if it's at her house before I put out a BOLO on it."

The house was only a mile from the sheriff's office. It was a small, cottage-style house tucked between more ornate Victorian homes. There was no BMW in the driveway or parked at the curb, so Darlene called dispatch and had them enter it into the system.

Ten minutes later, Elizabeth's landlord drove up. She had

to have been in her seventies, but climbed down easily from a full-size pickup truck. She came over and introduced herself as Martha Thibodeaux.

"I met you, Larry, when you were just a wee thing. I knew your mother pretty well. I worked at the elementary school and she'd come in and volunteer when you were a student. Nice woman. I was so sorry to hear about her passing." She turned to Darlene. "And you used to work for the city police. I think you took a report when one of our other rentals was broken into."

"I remember." Darlene nodded.

"This was Lester's and my first home," she told us, jangling a dozen keys. "I'm awful sorry to hear about Elizabeth. An accident, you say?"

"Probably not," I said.

She stopped and looked at me with sad eyes and a shake of the head. "What's the world coming to? Elizabeth was quite a woman. Kind of reminded me of myself. Maybe a little more obsessive. She was the first tenant I ever had that investigated *me*." She laughed.

We followed her onto the small wooden porch. After unlocking the door, she started to go in.

"We'd rather you wait outside," I said.

"Of course. Crime scene and all that. I watched *CSI* religiously." She backed up and let us go through the door.

Inside, the front room was bare except for a sofa, an end table with a lamp and a small stack of taped cardboard boxes.

"I guess she hadn't unpacked," Darlene said. "It's going to make searching the place easy."

There were only two bedrooms and one bath and only one of the bedrooms showed any sign of use.

"I see what her husband was talking about," I said, looking in the closet. The clothes were lined up with military precision.

"Certainly appears to have been a neat freak," Darlene said, looking in the chest of drawers.

The bathroom showed a similar degree of organization.

"Wow, even the bottles on the counter are lined up evenly according to height," I said.

"This would be a hard lifestyle to maintain," Darlene admitted as she admired the towels folded neatly on a shelf.

"I'm going to find it hard to get into her mind," I said, not able to imagine being that obsessive.

"I hear you, brother."

"Have you seen any electronics?"

Darlene stopped and looked around. "No. No TV, computer, phone. Nothing."

"There's not even an alarm clock in the bedroom," I said.

"Do you think she had a thing about electricity?" Darlene asked, raising her eyebrows.

"Surely she worked on a computer in her office. And I know she had a cell phone. Besides, the husband didn't say anything about it."

"Still kind of odd."

"The place is so neat, it's not like there'd be a dust ring left if something had been stolen. I'll ask Ian about it."

"Finding her phone would be helpful."

"Pretty strange how that's become the primary source of information on victims."

"And on perpetrators. Evidence found on some dimbulb's phone has locked up more than a few bad guys."

We opened up the dozen cardboard moving boxes. There was nothing but what you'd expect to find when someone has recently moved, except for the fact that they were all packed as neatly as her closet.

Darlene had been right. It didn't take us long to finish up. Mrs. Thibodeaux locked the door behind us.

"What should we do with the house?" she asked us.

"Keep it locked up for now. We may need to get in again. If any of her family wants to enter, give us a call." Then a thought occurred to me. If the killer had Elizabeth's keys, then he would have access to the house. "Would you mind having the locks changed?"

"No. We do it whenever a tenant moves out of one of our houses." She looked at her watch. "I can probably have it done this evening. Joe's a friend of ours."

"That'd be great," I told her. Darlene and I gave Mrs. Thibodeaux our cards before driving off.

It was after five when we got back to the office. I went inside to call Elizabeth's parents. Notifying parents of a child's death was always soul-wrenching.

"Hello. If this is a sales call then you're wasting your time," Elizabeth's mother answered the call.

"No, ma'am. I'm a deputy with the…"

"I'm not contributing to any cause, thank you," she said, and I had to jump in quickly before she hung up.

"This is about your daughter."

There was a long pause. "What?" She sounded less sure of herself.

"I'm an investigator with the Adams County Sheriff's Office. I'm afraid that a body was discovered this morning and we have good reason to believe it's your daughter, Elizabeth Collins," I said as gently as I could.

"Nonsense. My daughter is fine," she shot back. "I don't know what kind of hoax this is, but it's reprehensible. I'm going to report you—"

"Mrs. Collins, have you been in contact with your daughter today?" I interrupted.

Another pause. "No. Not today."

"Would you like to try calling her and then call me back?" I offered, then asked belatedly, "Is your husband there?"

"Yes." I wasn't sure which question she was answering.

"Fine. Try calling your daughter and then call me back. I hope she answers," I told her.

"Wait. My husband says we should call your office."

"Sure, they'll patch you through to me." I gave her the number. It wasn't a bad idea to verify any call supposedly coming from a law enforcement officer.

I hung up, but only five minutes later dispatch reconnected us.

"This is Harvey Collins," said a gruff, slightly slurred voice. I remembered Darlene mentioning that he'd had a stroke.

"Mr. Collins, I'm Deputy Larry Macklin. Were you able to get through to your daughter?"

"No. What's this about a body?"

"A woman's body was discovered this morning. We've been in contact with Ian Barton and he's tentatively identified a photo of the victim as his wife, Elizabeth."

"That idiot. What do you mean tentatively?" He sounded confused and I wondered how much the stroke had affected him.

"He still needs to go down to the morgue for a formal identification. The picture was on a cell phone so…"

"I see. I wouldn't trust anything that man says."

"Your daughter didn't go into work today and there is no one at her house," I explained.

"Well… What happened to this… victim?"

"We won't have full details until the autopsy is done. We do believe that there was foul play. At the very least, the body was moved."

"Foul play," he grumbled. "Have you arrested Ian?" I could hear Mrs. Collins getting worked up in the background. There was fear and anger in her voice.

"No, sir. As I said, we aren't even sure of the cause of death yet."

I heard them argue over the phone and then Mrs. Collins was back on the line. "We're coming up there," she said. "I think it takes about eight hours."

"I'll be glad to meet you at my office in the morning."

"My husband is right. Ian wasn't any good for Elizabeth. We knew right from the beginning that the wedding was a waste of money. We'll call when we get there," she said and hung up.

I understood why Ian Barton had wanted someone else to call his in-laws. Of course, they could have been right about his being guilty. The odds certainly favored it. An estranged spouse always topped the suspect list. Plus, he didn't have much of an alibi. The two children could have easily been drugged with something as simple as cough syrup to sleep through the night, giving Ian time to commit the crime, dispose of the body and get back before they woke up in the morning. I made a note to talk to the children's teachers or caretakers to see if they had noticed any odd behaviors that might be attributable to a drug hangover.

I packed up and headed for home, hoping Mrs. Collins wouldn't really call me at two in the morning when they got to town.

# CHAPTER FOUR

The days were getting longer, so it was still daylight when I pulled up to our little doublewide in the woods. Cara had beaten me home and was out in the yard with Alvin, our Pug. He trotted over to me and wagged his curled tail as he sniffed around my pants leg.

"Sorry, little guy, I didn't run into any pups today. Not even you buddy Mauser." Mauser was my dad's three-year-old, overgrown lunk of a Great Dane.

Cara put her arms around me and I hugged her tight.

"Have a good day?" I asked.

"We saved a Greyhound that had been hit by a car. Dr. Barnhill did a great job on him, but it was three hours in surgery." Cara had been promoted to office manager at the veterinary clinic last fall, but she occasionally still helped as a tech when they were short-staffed.

"Wow."

"I thought we were going to have to call Mauser in for a blood transfusion, but we had just enough." Mauser had given blood in the past. Great Danes were ideal donors for other large dogs. "How was your day?"

"There was a body down at the nursery."

"I figured. Word got around. By noon, one of our clients

was telling the doctor about it."

"Small-town life. What's on the agenda for tonight?"

I asked because I was never sure these days. We'd made a deal to limit work on the wedding to only a couple of nights a week. A friend of Cara's from work had suggested it. He'd learned the hard way that if you didn't contain the chaos, it could overwhelm and exhaust everyone involved. Even so, I tried to avoid the details whenever possible.

"I think we're going to need to spend more time on the wedding," Cara said hesitantly, as if she were worried I might get upset.

"I'm not sure I can maintain an interest in meal plans and ribbon colors more than two nights a week," I said, hoping she'd take it as a joke, though it really wasn't.

She leaned in and gave me a quick kiss. "You've been good about everything, but April 22 is closer than you think. Most of it's done, but there's a bunch of loose ends that are driving me crazy."

"Whatever you want," I said, trying hard to be sincere. "Speaking of agendas..." I went on to tell her about the phone call with Elizabeth's parents and to warn her that my phone might go off in the middle of the night.

"I can't blame them," she said, and I had to admit she had a point.

We shared a quick dinner, then Cara brought out the wedding checklists. After much debate, and more than a little unwanted input from Cara's mother, we'd decided to hold the wedding a Crandall Grove. The large Victorian home on an old hunting plantation had been turned into a bed-and-breakfast and event venue. If the weather cooperated, we planned to hold the ceremony in a gazebo on a hill overlooking a ten-acre pond, with the reception to follow inside. Tonight, Cara wanted to finalize the menu and linen colors. I did my best to listen and give my opinions, but I could tell that she wasn't very happy with my attitude.

Once the wedding was put away, we managed to get back in sync and streamed a sci-fi movie where aliens took the form of domestic animals. Ivy, our tabby cat, watched the show with an unsettling interest.

We made love before bed and I fell fast asleep. I was surprised when I opened my eyes to see light streaming into the bedroom. Just as I swung my legs out of bed, my phone buzzed on the nightstand. A quick glance told me it was Elizabeth's parents and I mentally thanked them for waiting until daylight.

In a weary voice, Harvey Collins told me they'd be at the sheriff's office by eight and he expected me to be there. I glanced at my watch and saw that it was past seven already. Cursing under my breath, I told him I'd be there and rushed through my morning routine.

Cara was just getting out of bed as I headed for the door. "Animals are fed," I said and kissed her, receiving a blurry-eyed smile and "I love you" in return.

Harvey Collins looked like he'd answered a casting call for the lead in *Death of a Salesman*. Charlene Collins hovered behind him as though she expected him to collapse at any moment. The right side of his face still drooped a bit from his stroke.

"Good morning. I'm Deputy Macklin," I said, sticking out my hand as I met them in the lobby. Mr. Collins looked at his watch and seemed disappointed to see that I'd made it there five minutes early. He shook my hand reluctantly.

"I'm sorry that we have to meet under these circumstances," I told them both.

"We want to know everything," he said, and I saw a little of the fire that must have once been in his eyes during his legal career. I took them to our small conference room and he sat down carefully in one of the chairs, telling Mrs. Collins do the same.

I took out my phone and pulled up the picture of Elizabeth. "I'm sorry, but this is the best picture we have."

"Show me," he said. Mrs. Collins averted her eyes.

I laid the phone on the table. Mr. Collins took out his reading glasses and put them on, slowly and deliberately, before lifting the phone. For a minute I thought he wasn't going to react, then tears started rolling down his cheeks. His hand was quivering as he set the phone back down.

"That is my daughter," he said stiffly, wiping at his tears. "What happened?"

"You'll understand that I must keep most of the investigation confidential. If information was leaked, it could compromise a criminal case against the offender," I said in my most official voice.

Mr. Collins looked hard at me, then took a deep breath and glanced down at his hands. When he looked back up, there was anger in his eyes.

"Let me make one thing straight. If you screw up this case, I will haunt you in this life or the next. I want the bastard who killed my daughter to pay for it."

"Fair enough. Then I'm going to need something from you. Information. I need to understand who your daughter was. That doesn't mean just the nice things you tell people at dinner parties. I need to know any family secrets or problems that Elizabeth might have been having."

"The only problem she had was that fool of a husband. I know you need to look at the big picture first, but make sure you take a good long look at him."

As he talked, Mrs. Collins was crying softly. When he started to talk about Ian Barton, her hands began to clench and unclench.

"I will gladly listen to everything you have to say, including your feelings about your son-in-law."

"Good." He nodded. "Now… Please tell us what happened to her."

I looked over at Mrs. Collins. I didn't want to cause her any more pain. He saw me and reached out to take her hand. "It will be better if we know."

"I understand." I took a deep breath, then said, "She was found at a nursery on the south side of town. Her body had been... left there. From what I saw, there weren't any obvious signs that she had been abused physically or sexually. At the scene, we saw just a single wound to her head. From the placement and severity of the wound, my guess would be that she died quickly."

"Thank you."

"Are you up to talking about your daughter and answering a few questions?"

"Yes."

"I'd like my partner to join us. Can I get you all some coffee while I go see if she's in?"

He shook his head, but Mrs. Collins said in small voice, "Water."

I found Darlene at her desk. I wasn't surprised, as she almost always beat me to the office. I filled a cup with water from the dispenser in the hallway and we rejoined Elizabeth's parents.

After making the introductions, I told them we would be recording the interview.

"What is your understanding of your daughter's current assets?" I asked.

"She is very frugal with her money. Always has been. The man she married, not so much. However, I understand that the house they were living in was mostly paid off. She hated to be in debt."

"Any life insurance that you're aware of?"

"I don't know. I carry a policy on my wife and myself in which Elizabeth was the named beneficiary, but I don't know what she had." Mr. Collins paused for a moment. "She might have. For the kids."

"Did she have many friends? Maybe some old friends from school?" I asked them.

This time it was Mrs. Collins who answered. "Elizabeth didn't make friends easily. Even when she was a child. And now...We haven't been on the best of terms since she married Ian. He drove a wedge between us," she said bitterly.

"What sort of wedge?"

"He wasn't good enough for her," Mr. Collins groused. "But she jumped at the chance to marry the first guy who ever showed an interest in her."

Darlene and I traded glances. We were both realizing that Elizabeth's parents weren't necessarily the best judges of Ian Barton's guilt or innocence.

"Did she have any hobbies?" Darlene asked.

"She jogged. Always stayed in shape. I know she had a gym membership in Tallahassee. I don't know the name of the place, but it was close to her job." Mrs. Collins seemed to realize that she was talking about her daughter in the past tense and pursed her lips tightly.

"Did she ever tell you that she was afraid of or worried about someone?"

"I can't think of anyone," Mr. Collins answered. His wife had drifted back into the pain of her sorrow.

"Have you been on better terms with Elizabeth since she left her husband?" Darlene asked.

I saw him hesitate. He looked at his wife for a moment, but she was off in her own world. "It's been better lately. Since the separation," he mumbled. The question had clearly brought up past injuries.

"Was she angry about the separation from Ian?" I asked.

"You have to understand... Elizabeth didn't show her emotions. When she was younger, if she got upset she'd just go off to her room and work on her spreadsheets."

"Spreadsheets?"

"She had hundreds. Some of them covered sports and others had to do with grades, and she even kept data on weather and water temperature. You need to realize how unique Elizabeth was. She got a perfect score on her math SATs. Even in elementary school, she loved numbers. Honestly, we thought there was something wrong with her for a while. Like she was an idiot savant or something. But she found balance in her life."

I could tell from his tone that this wasn't the first time

he'd felt obliged to defend his daughter.

"Was she getting along well at her job?" I asked, knowing that people often let trouble in their personal lives spill over into their jobs.

Mr. Collins gave a short laugh. "She could go in there wearing a potted plant on her head and the partners wouldn't have said a word. They aren't stupid. They knew what they had with Elizabeth."

"Which was what, exactly?"

"She had several dozen regular accounts that she worked on, but what she was valued for was her ability to troubleshoot. If a company was having a problem getting a hundred-million-dollar set of books to balance, they'd just plunk it down on her desk and let her go at it. I know she cleaned up one set of books that two different firms had given up on. They'd sweated over them for months trying to find the problem, but in less than two weeks Elizabeth had cleaned them up. She was gold to that firm."

"Is there a chance she had a boyfriend?" I asked; not that we'd found anything to suggest that a man had ever been inside the house she was renting.

"I doubt it."

"She never mentioned any unwanted attention?"

"Like someone stalking her? No." He seemed to dismiss the idea out of hand. "She was pretty, but not flirty or… you know, sexy. She lived up in her head. I doubt she ever stopped thinking about numbers. Elizabeth didn't talk to people out in public. I guess you'd say she came across as… withdrawn. Now, when she was around people she knew and had a drink or two, she could come out of her shell."

"Did she drink much?" Darlene asked.

"I say it like it happened all the time, but I'm talking about only once or twice a year."

"Did she normally carry cash?"

"Maybe forty dollars or so. Enough to buy a coffee and have lunch, that sort of thing."

Darlene and I were running out of pertinent questions.

So far, there weren't a lot of trails to follow.

"We'll give you regular updates on the investigation," I assured them. "And we may have more questions for you as the investigation moves along."

"When can we… have Elizabeth?" He looked confused for a moment before pulling himself together. "We'd like to take her back home for burial."

"Mr. Collins, I'm afraid that the body will be released to her husband," I said as gently as I could.

His face turned red as his teeth started to grind together.

"No!" Mrs. Collins blurted.

"We'll see about that," Mr. Collins said. I could see the exhaustion in his face, and his words were more slurred. He looked like a man who'd run a marathon, but was determined to cross the finish line. "Our grandchildren are going back with us too."

"I can't help you there. What I will tell you is that if your son-in-law had anything to do with Elizabeth's death, we'll make sure he faces the consequences," I said.

"Damn right," Darlene added.

Mr. Collins stood up. He had to take his time straightening up before he reached out for Mrs. Collins's hand and helped her to her feet. Darlene and I walked with them to the front door.

"We need a plan, Stan," she said as we watched the grieving parents drive away.

"Yes, we do."

Ten minutes later, we were back in the conference room with our notes.

"This afternoon is fine," I said into my phone. "I'll be there." I hung up and turned to Darlene. "Do you want to join me for the autopsy?"

"No. You go on and take that one by yourself."

"We need to find out where the murder took place. I hate to think about all that forensic evidence going to waste."

"I'm afraid we're going to end up working the case backward. Once we have a suspect, we may get an idea of where the murder occurred," Darlene said. "Unless it happened in her car."

"No word on that yet?"

"No. I sat in on the morning briefing and did a show-and-tell to get everyone on board with trying to find it."

"At this point we need to expand the BOLO to neighboring states. Our killer could be halfway across the country by now."

"I did that after the briefing," Darlene said. She always made me feel a little inferior when she was keeping a dozen moves ahead of me. Of course, when she outpaced the bad guys, I never complained about the results.

"We need to establish a timeline. We need to know what Elizabeth was doing on Tuesday and who she was doing it with. Her body was found Wednesday morning at seven o'clock. Her office said that she came to work on Tuesday. According to her husband, she often worked late. Hopefully the building has security cameras. If so, we should be able to establish when she left work. Getting her phone records would also help."

"We need to ping her phone. If her husband is on her account, he can help us cut through some of the red tape with the company," Darlene pointed out.

"I'll check into that," I said, making a note.

"I'll spend the rest of the morning getting CCTV footage from the businesses on different routes to the nursery. We have an advantage there. The murderer had to have dumped the body either late on Tuesday or early Wednesday. There won't be much traffic then, especially in that part of town."

"When we get the phone or the phone records, that will help us figure out who she was interacting with in the last couple of days."

"We need to look at the list of nursery customers and staff. That's an unusual place to dump a body."

"Do we need to get some extra hands and feet from patrol?"

"Not until we know where the murder took place or we

find the car."

"I agree. It's not like there are a lot of houses around the nursery to canvass."

"And any evidence at the dump site would have been in the area we searched. I doubt the killer did much more than carry the body from his car to the mulch."

"We can go ahead and release the Elizabeth's name to the press too. That might bring a witness or two out of the closet."

We congratulated each other on our to-do lists and split up. Darlene headed for the door to start collecting CCTV footage while I went to my desk to make calls. The first was to Elizabeth's cell phone carrier to request an emergency ping of her phone. They called me back within thirty minutes to report that her phone was off the grid. I sighed, knowing it had been too much to hope for. The killer had either turned it off or destroyed it.

My next call was to Ian Barton.

"I'm at home. I couldn't leave the kids," he said, sounding confused. I couldn't blame him. How do you explain the death of a parent to children that young?

"Are you on the same phone plan with your wife?"

"Yes. We hadn't gotten around to changing it."

"I'd like you to request Elizabeth's cell phone records." I didn't want it to sound like he had a choice.

There was silence on his end of the phone.

"Is that a problem?"

"No... no. I'm just not sure how to go about it."

"All you have to do is call them and ask." Was he dragging his feet?

"Yes, of course."

"You'll do that?" I pushed.

"This afternoon."

Then my do-gooder nature kicked in. "Your in-laws were here this morning."

"Damn it," he muttered.

"You might want to try and make peace with them. Look

at your children and remember that your in-laws just lost their daughter."

There was more silence from his end of the phone, and then: "Of course. Yes, you're right."

I told him we'd be in touch.

Then I called the office of Roberts and Mann CPAs and asked that one of the partners be available that afternoon. I figured I'd look over Elizabeth's office and talk to her co-workers after the autopsy.

I spent the rest of the morning catching up on some of the other cases I was juggling. Pete called just before noon and asked what I was doing for lunch. I told him I was planning to catch something on my way to Tallahassee, and he offered to bring me a pulled pork sandwich from Deep Pit Bar-b-que. My mouth was watering by the time I hung up.

# CHAPTER FIVE

Half an hour later, I heard someone approach my desk and looked up.

"I thought you were Pete delivering my lunch," I said, grinning at Julio Ortiz. "Man, you look sporty in that suit."

Julio had been transferred from patrol to CID a month earlier after a year of hustling to make it happen.

"I bought it before I realized there wouldn't be a pay increase with the transfer," he joked.

"How many burglars have you caught?"

"I've been doing my job. You just need to convince the judges to keep them in jail. Hey, I hear you've been doing some gardening."

"Funny guy." I handed him a flyer I'd made that showed a photo of Elizabeth's car. "Keep an eye out for this. We still haven't found our victim's car. And if you hear over the radio that someone has found it, tell 'em not to touch it and call me. It could be our murder scene."

"I just came in to grab a warrant and then I'm headed out to the meth-head country club. That wouldn't be the worst place to dump a car. I'll drive around a little when I'm done."

Julio was right. The "country club" was our nickname for

a part of the county with a lot of run-down trailers and old houses on large lots. I knew more than one drug entrepreneur who worked that area. With vacant properties and dirt roads leading to nowhere, the area was ideal for drug deals and other nefarious activities.

Julio grabbed a few things from his desk and headed for the door, passing Pete and my lunch on their way in. The sight of the greasy bag and the smell of barbeque warmed my heart.

Pete waved the bag invitingly as he walked to my desk.

"Special delivery. Tips will be accepted," he said, inhaling the smells from the open bag. "I didn't get you a drink."

"No problem. I'll grab a tea from the machine," I said, standing up and setting the bag on my desk without thinking.

Pete followed me to the break room. "Any luck with the body?"

I filled him in on the victim and everything we currently knew.

"Can't you ever just get a simple drive-by shooting? I had one last month. Interviewed a few people at the scene, tracked down the car, arrested everyone in it. Done. The only hard part has been deciding which person in the car actually fired the gun. Not that it matters, but it makes the jury feel better."

"Lt. Johnson gives you the easy cases 'cause he knows that's all you can handle," I kidded him, knowing it wasn't true. Pete's manner was very deceptive. He gave off a heavy dose of good ol' boy while hiding a keen mind that took in every detail.

"Noooo, I think it's more likely 'cause he hates you," Pete joked.

While I didn't really believe our supervisor hated me, it was certainly true that he tended to give me a harder time than some of the other investigators. My tendency to ignore the chain of command and my unorthodox approach to some cases often violated his sense of order.

We both grabbed drinks from the machine and headed

back to our desks. The carnage we found when we got there left me stunned.

"Wow!" Pete said as I stared down at the remains of the paper bag that had contained my pulled pork sandwich. The bag was shredded and tiny bits of foil were strewn on the floor. "I brought you fries too," Pete said solemnly. I could see the cardboard slip they'd come in poking out from under my desk.

Fury boiled up from my stomach, producing a fire that burned all the way to my eyeballs. I glared at the foamy white drool on my desktop.

"I know who did this and I'm going to find him!" I swore, stomping my way toward Dad's office.

"What have you been into now?" I heard Dad's assistant say loudly when I was halfway down the hall.

"My sandwich!" I yelled back at her.

The sound of my voice triggered the black-and-white weapon of mass destruction. Mauser, Dad's one-hundred-and-ninety-pound Great Dane, came charging back down the hall at me.

"No! I am not your friend today!" I shouted as he galloped toward me, his drool-flecked jowls flapping.

He ran past me, only to circle around and ram into me with his usual bone-crushing greeting.

"I am not going to pet you! Come on, let's go see your owner and find out how he's going to pay me back for that sandwich you ate," I said, pushing past the canine roadblock. Mauser followed me, bumping me affectionately with every other step.

"Is he in there?" I asked Dad's assistant when I reached her desk.

"He kicked Mauser out earlier because he was being a nuisance," she told me.

Mauser just looked at us with a *Who? Me?* expression.

I stepped up to the door of Dad's office and knocked. "The Macklin Monster is running amok and eating the peasants' food," I said to the door.

"Come in," Dad shouted.

I didn't hesitate to let Mauser follow me in.

Dad frowned at us both. "He's been a pain in the ass all morning," he said.

"So you just let him run the halls?"

"This *does* bring up something I wanted to talk to you about," Dad said, ignoring my opinion on his lack of pet parenting skills.

"What?" I asked suspiciously.

"Genie and I are taking Jimmy to compete in the regional Special Olympics out on the panhandle at the end of the month."

Genie Anderson was Dad's girlfriend and Jimmy was her son. He'd been born with Down Syndrome, but now lived a mostly independent life in a group home in Tallahassee.

"Okay, that's great," I said cautiously.

"Unfortunately, that's also the end of Jamie's spring break," Dad said, referring to Mauser's usual babysitter. "He'll be down in St. Pete building houses with Habitat for Humanity. I told everyone that you and Cara would be glad to take care of Mauser and the horses while we're gone."

I narrowed my eyes at him. Dad was an expert at setting up situations where, if I said no, I'd wind up looking like an asshole. How could I say no to a young man participating in the Special Olympics or a guy building homes for the homeless?

"Do I have a choice?" I said, defeated.

Dad shrugged.

"You and Dogface owe me, then, and not just a pork sandwich. I want a twenty-five-dollar gift card to Deep Pit Bar-b-que." My face was stern.

"Done," Dad said with a smile.

Mauser burped.

"I hate you," I said into those big brown eyes.

"What's going on with the body found at the nursery?" Dad asked.

Weak from hunger, I dropped down into a chair across

from his large desk. Dad maintained a hands-off approach to investigations unless they appeared to be going south, but he liked to be in the loop on the basic facts so that reporters and the public never caught him off guard.

"Her name is Elizabeth Collins..." I went on to tell him what little we knew.

"What's your feeling?" I still found myself surprised when Dad asked my opinion about a case.

"Right now the husband is our only viable suspect. We need more information. The trouble is the woman was a bit of a loner. Her work was her life."

"Think it could be work-related?"

"I'm going to her office today after the autopsy. Honestly, I don't really know what they do or how a CPA's office works. I'd assume that even if she found dirt on someone through their accounts, there wouldn't be much point in eliminating her. The numbers would still be there so the next person working the books would find them. Certainly the person who brought the accounts to them wouldn't be the person trying to hide something."

"Maybe she was blackmailing someone?"

"That would surprise me. I saw her house. Elizabeth wasn't a person driven by greed. I'd call her more of a math monk."

"Keep me up to date," Dad said in his best *You're dismissed* voice. I stood up. "And don't forget about the end of the month."

I turned to Mauser, who was laid over on his side, eyeballing me.

"You're going to get bread and water at our place, you thief. I should have filed a report and let Julio arrest you."

The dog just closed his eyes and sighed contentedly.

I went back to my desk and cleaned up the remains of my lunch, feeling like the father in *A Christmas Story* after the Bumpuses' dogs ate the family turkey.

I grabbed a very unsatisfying burger on my way into Tallahassee. When I arrived at the hospital morgue, Dr. Darzi already had Elizabeth's body in front of him on a stainless steel table.

"You are late," he informed me when I came in.

"The dog ate my lunch."

"The victim doesn't appear to have suffered much damage in the attack," Darzi said, ignoring me and looking over the body in his usual methodical way. He always started at the head and carefully worked his way down. He looked with his eyes while his hands felt for broken bones and soft spots that the eye couldn't identify. "She wasn't a regular user of drugs. Skin, teeth, mouth, genitalia all appear well cared for."

"Was she sexually assaulted?"

"No, nor does she show signs of recent sexual activity."

After making his way down to her feet, he moved back up to her head. He gently lifted the head and worked his hands around the front and back, feeling for the parameters of the wound.

"A single blow. Delivered with a great deal of force," he pronounced.

"What caused it?"

He frowned. "A rounded object. Something cylindrical. There is only the small abrasion, so the object would be smooth, probably metal. We took X-rays before you arrived. When I've taken measurements from them, I will be able to make a 3D image of the part of the object that contacted the victim." He'd recently been using some fancy new software that helped him create 3D images based on the wounds of a victim. It could take a knife wound and create an image showing the shape and size of the blade that had entered the body.

"Is there any chance she fell and hit her head?" I said, thinking out loud.

"No," Darzi said bluntly. "Stop trying to avoid work," he added with a smile. "If she had fallen hard enough to produce this much damage, then there would have been other injuries, particularly to the neck. This was a savage blow to the head. Look at the body. There are no other signs of an attack. Your victim was taken unaware."

"You sound impressed," I chided him.

"Most of the murder victims I see in here are the work of bumbling amateurs. The bodies are broken and bruised. It is rare that one comes in with a single, precise killing wound."

"When I catch the son of a bitch who did this, I'll tell him you enjoyed reviewing his work."

"Everyone's work becomes mundane. If I'm to keep myself from becoming a burned-out shell of a man, I must look for the new and different."

"Could she have been unconscious when the blow was struck?"

Darzi leaned in and looked at the wound for another five minutes. "I doubt it. I will do some modeling of the attack, but from a cursory examination, I'd say the blow was delivered while she was standing." He waved me in closer and, with his fingers just above her skull, he outlined the area that had been crushed. "See how the wound is mostly in the front of the forehead and only extends back maybe five inches into the hairline."

We heard the double doors open and looked up to see Linda walk in, dressed for action in scrubs and protective gear.

"Just in time," he said to her. "I'm ready to turn the body over."

Together they poked and prodded the body for another half hour. When they'd finished, Darzi and Linda gently turned Elizabeth's body back over, slid her onto a gurney and covered her for the trip to the locker.

"Time of death?" I asked.

Darzi turned to one of the monitors and scanned through the notes that Linda had made at the nursery. "What is your opinion?" he asked her.

"Based on the ambient temperature, body temperature

and state of rigor mortis, I'd estimate sometime between ten the night before and two in the morning."

Darzi nodded. "I concur."

"Anything else you can tell me?" I wanted to be thorough, but I was ready to leave the morgue. I could only tolerate the place for so long before I started to get squirmy about all the dead bodies I knew were stored there.

"As I said, I don't think the victim fought back. She probably had only a split second to realize that the blow was coming. I scraped her fingernails and there weren't any significant hair or fibers." He turned to Linda again. "Did you find any hair or fibers on her clothes or body?"

"Some, but nothing that will help to find her attacker," Linda said apologetically. "Of course, if you have someone in custody, then we might be able to match it to him."

"Or her," I added.

"If it was a woman, she would have to be fairly strong. I will have a better idea of the attacker's height after we have done our modeling."

I found the offices of Roberts and Mann CPAs in an upscale Federal-style, two-story brick building. If the Ferraris and Land Rovers in the parking lot hadn't clued me in, then the large chandelier in the entryway and the reading material in the reception area would have. Their clients were wealthy. When I stepped up to the desk, I tried to look like I belonged there in my eighty-nine-dollar coat and slacks.

"I'm here to talk with Mr. Roberts or Mr. Mann," I said.

"Mrs. Roberts," the woman behind the desk said with a tight smile.

"I'm an investigator with the Adams County Sheriff's Office. I called earlier," I said, showing her my star and ID. Her façade cracked.

"Oh, I can't believe Elizabeth is dead." She put a shaking hand up to her mouth.

"Did you know her well?"

"I... No, not personally. I'm not even sure that would apply where Elizabeth is concerned." She sounded confused.

The brass plaque on the desk said that her name was Rose Teague. "Ms. Teague, what exactly do you mean by that?"

"Oh, nothing bad. Just that Elizabeth always seemed to be working. She was here when I opened the office in the morning, and she was almost always here when I locked up in the evening. What kind of personal life can you have living like that?"

I glanced up at the ceiling and saw several discreet cameras located in the corners.

"Do you have someone in charge of security?"

"We've hired an outside company for that."

"I'll need to speak with them too. Could you let Mr. Mann or Mrs. Roberts know I'm here?"

"Of course." She picked up the phone and told whoever was on the other end that an investigator from the police was here and would like to talk with Mrs. Roberts. When she hung up, she told me that Mrs. Roberts would be down momentarily. "Would you like something to drink while you wait?"

"I'm fine," I said, trying to pretend that I was in the right tax bracket to be one of their clients. I looked at the reading material on one of the coffee tables. I had a choice of *Yachting Magazine*, various Sotheby's auction catalogs or a number of financial magazines I'd never heard of.

Ten minutes later, a woman wearing a perfectly tailored aqua green suit, and with a pair of eyes that could pin you to the wall, came down the stairs. She held out her hand like a duchess bestowing honors upon the little people.

"Zeph Roberts," she introduced herself.

"Deputy Larry Macklin," I said, wondering if she expected me to kiss her hand.

"What terrible news about Elizabeth. It's a blow to us both personally and professionally," she said, looking theatrically sad. "We'd like to do anything we can to help."

"We appreciate your cooperation," I said. "First, I'd like to see Elizabeth's office."

"About that. I'll need you to sign our standard privacy and non-disclosure forms," she said, looking me square in the eye and putting her hand out to Ms. Teague, who managed to materialize the forms out of thin air.

"No, ma'am, that's not the way this works." I'd taken the time to get a search warrant before I came over. I'd had to work hard to come up with a list of items we were searching for. Judges wouldn't just let you go fishing. I pulled the warrant out of my pocket and handed it to her.

"Of course, this is just a formality. I can assure you of two things. One, I have no interest in anything that doesn't have to do with the murder of Elizabeth Collins. Two, you shouldn't worry that I'm going to glance at a financial spreadsheet and gather any vital information. I promise you, I know nothing about accounting. If it comes down to that, we'll call in a specialist, and there will be much more paperwork for your lawyers to look over."

My monologue seemed to assuage her concerns a bit. She even gave me a slight upturn around the lips. "Very well. I'll have to remain with you at all times."

"That will be fine."

I followed her up the stairs. The place was over the top when it came to decor. Everywhere I looked there were cushy, overstuffed chairs and sofas, gilt-framed landscapes and vases you could hide in.

"Her office is down here," Roberts said, striding along in her high heels. She stopped at a door with a brass sign on it that read "Elizabeth Collins, NO ADMITTANCE without prior approval."

"She didn't like being disturbed." Roberts stated the obvious before unlocking the door and pushing it open.

I stepped through the doorway and entered a room that stood in stark contrast to the rest of the building. A plain wooden desk dominated the center of the office. On the desk were three top-of-the-line monitors arranged in a semicircle and facing a chair that looked like it could have come out of a spaceship. The walls were lined floor to ceiling with shelves filled with painfully neat stacks of financial books and folders. As Ian had mentioned, there were no windows.

"She insisted that we brick over the window," Roberts said as if reading my mind.

"How often did you come to see Elizabeth when she was working?"

"Never. Elizabeth got very... nervous if anyone else was in here."

"No one except Elizabeth came in here?" I asked.

I could tell that she was thinking about her response. Finally she said, "She had one real friend here. Not that she had any enemies, either."

The mention of a friend sparked my interest. "Friend?"

"Our office steward," Roberts said through pursed lips.

*Office steward? What the hell does an office steward do?* I wondered. I figured I could ask this steward when I interviewed him.

I walked slowly around Elizabeth's office, looking for anything that seemed out of place. It was a waste of time. There wasn't anything that wasn't directly related to her work. No pictures, no funny cartons, no motivational posters, no personal touches whatsoever. There weren't even any drawers in the desk. Just a keyboard, a mouse and a generic mouse pad.

To my surprise, Roberts waited patiently for me to finish. "I could have told you that you wouldn't find anything in here that would help with your investigation. But you had to discover that for yourself."

"I try to be thorough in my work. Though I can't say I'm as meticulous as Ms. Collins appeared to be."

"She was unique. Elizabeth craved challenges. We have one employee who spent half his time hunting up the toughest accounts available, just so we could keep Elizabeth interested in the work. We were able to bring in accounts that are more suited to firms five times our size because of her. It will be a significant blow to lose her."

"Would you say that it was well known how important she was to you?"

"What are you suggesting?"

"Could someone have killed Elizabeth in order to damage your firm?"

Roberts seemed taken aback by the idea. She stared at me for an uncomfortable amount of time before answering.

"The possibility exists. We were constantly fending off efforts by other firms to recruit her. Her abilities were admired by a number of people in the business."

"I would like you and Mr. Mann to come up with a list of businesses that might want to see your firm hurt, and also any disgruntled employees or former employees."

"You don't need to concern yourself about current employees. If we had even a hint that one of our employees wished to hurt the firm, they would be terminated immediately."

The way she said "terminated" sent a chill down my spine. *I'm sure she just means fired*, I told myself.

"I'd like to talk to the office steward." I was still wondering what this person did.

"This way," Roberts said, locking Elizabeth's office door behind her.

We went back down the stairs and, when we reached the ground floor, we turned away from the front entrance. I followed her through a very nice office kitchen to a room next to a rear exit. The plate on the door read "Mr. Rex Tindall, Office Steward." Roberts rapped twice on the door.

"Come in," a voice called.

"It's me, Mr. Tindall," Roberts said instead of opening the door.

A moment later the door was opened by an older man wearing a blue polo shirt and Dockers. "Sorry, Mrs. Roberts, I'm not used to you knocking on my door," he said with a grandfatherly lilt to his voice.

"Quite all right. This is an investigator from Adams County. He's here looking into Elizabeth's death. We'd like you to answer any questions he has."

"Of course." The man looked stricken at the mention of Elizabeth. "Come on in," he said, stepping back from the door.

I walked in and looked to see if Roberts was going to follow me, but she turned and took up a position beside the door. "I'll be here when you're done," she told me.

# CHAPTER SIX

The room was fifteen feet square. Like Elizabeth's office, the walls were lined with shelves. However, these shelves held various manuals and parts for a variety of items. Some looked like plumbing, others electrical. On a table beside a desk was a vacuum cleaner laid out like a patient in an operating room.

"You're the office steward?" I asked.

Tindall touched the side of his nose and said in a low voice, "Janitor. But that's too low brow for this place. What happened to Elizabeth? I hear things, but people love to exaggerate."

"She was killed. It's early days in the investigation."

He sat down on a corner of his desk and shook his head sadly.

"That doesn't make any sense. Why would anyone kill her? I know lots of folks get killed, but look at the way they lived… Elizabeth, though?"

"Y'all were friends?"

"I'm not sure I'd say that. We talked some. I thought a lot of her." He lowered his voice again. "She was the only person around here who didn't act like they got a stick up their butt." He nodded toward the closed door.

"What'd you two talk about?"

He lifted his shoulders, then let them drop. "Nothing in particular. The weather, her kids. Sometimes she'd ask my advice about fixing something."

"Did she like do-it-yourself projects?"

"Not really, but she had a way of looking at things. If she could turn a problem into numbers... Well, hell's bells, she had it in a second." He snapped his fingers for emphasis.

"Did you ever go over to her place to help her fix something?" I tried not to make it sound like an accusation, but it was.

He looked disappointed in me. "No."

I decided to level with him. "Mr. Tindall, as you probably know, Elizabeth was a very private person. She had very few relationships. When someone is murdered, you have two choices. Either it was done by someone they knew or by a stranger. Nine times out of ten, it's someone they knew. So we start there. So far, I can count the number of people that Elizabeth associated with on one hand. You're one of them. You can't blame me for asking the questions that I have to ask. If I can eliminate you as a suspect, hurrah! That makes me just as happy as putting you in the category of possible suspects."

He nodded. "I want the person who did this to her to be punished."

"Good. So where were you on Tuesday night and early Wednesday morning?"

"I was at home with my wife. We watched TV for a while and then I went out to my workshop and did some carving. Went to bed around midnight." He gave me his wife's name and number.

"When you and Elizabeth were talking, did she ever mention anyone she was having problems with?"

He put his hand over his eyes and appeared to be deep in thought. "No. She was upset about the marriage being on the rocks, but she blamed herself for that."

"How so?"

"Elizabeth wasn't stupid. She knew she was hiding out up in that windowless office of hers. She just couldn't help it. I told her that she couldn't fight her nature. In her head, she saw herself as an involved mother. You know, taking the kids to soccer and music classes, that sort of thing. The truth was, she couldn't handle the chaos that kids bring. Me and my wife had three children. Two boys and a girl. Before the kids were born, our house was neat as a pin. Both of us worked to keep it that way. Then the kids come along and for twenty-five years you couldn't walk through a room without tripping over some piece of junk or another. Chaos. Just comes with the territory. Now that we finally got them all out on their own, our house and yard are tidy again."

For just a second. I wondered what Cara's and my life would be like with kids tearing through the house. I told myself not to start projecting into the future.

"I just want to be clear. There was no one that Elizabeth ever complained about?"

"She just seemed kinda sad. Sort of afraid of the world outside of that office."

We talked for a few more minutes before I left and was escorted around so I could talk to some of the other employees. I wanted to make sure that everyone was on the same page when it came to Elizabeth and her office relationships. They were. They almost never saw her. She kept to herself. Period.

"I want to talk to whoever is in charge of your security," I told Roberts when I was done interviewing employees.

"We contract with a corporate security firm, Silver Security. I'll need to give you authorization, otherwise they won't talk to you." She hit a speed dial number on her phone.

After identifying herself and entering a code into her phone, she explained the reason for her call.

"I am authorizing you to share with—" She held out her hand and I placed one of my cards in it. "—Deputy Larry Macklin with the Adams County Sheriff's Office any security videos and information regarding who entered and exited the building for a period beginning a week ago and ending today." There was a pause. "Yes, I will forward an email to that effect." She hung up and gave me a *Does that satisfy you?* look.

"Thank you," I said. Without another word, she showed me to the door.

I hadn't told her, but it was a spot of luck that they used Silver Security. I knew a former deputy for Adams County who had gone to work for them. I was pretty sure he was still there.

I called their office from my car. "I'd like to speak with Andrew Reyes," I told the woman who answered.

Andrew had joined our department a couple of years before I did and had left to work for Silver Security three years ago. I'd run into him a couple of times since then.

"Hey, old buddy," Andrew said. "Let me guess. You want to know if there are any openings here."

"Nope."

"I heard you're getting married. Time for you to get a real job. I'm tooling around right now in a company-supplied Range Rover, living the high life. Odds of being shot are very low."

I explained why I was calling.

"Cool. Let me check the clearance and I'll meet you somewhere for dinner. My treat."

The burger at lunch hadn't quite hit the spot, so the offer was tempting. I called Cara to make sure she didn't have any special plans for dinner and then called Andrew back. We met at Backwoods Crossing, a restaurant on the east side of Tallahassee that specialized in farm-to-table fare.

I got there just after he pulled into the lot. Andrew climbed out of the Range Rover dressed in casual, but expensive, business clothes. He'd always been a natty dresser.

"Larry! Good to see you." We exchanged manly handshakes that stopped just short of being painful. "I heard your dad won reelection. He deserves it."

We sat down and got our orders in before getting down to business.

"Let me be a selfish prick and say I'm glad that she didn't get killed at Roberts and Mann. That wouldn't have looked good."

"We don't know where she was killed. That's one of the reasons I want to see the security footage."

"It didn't happen at the office. After I heard about her death, I had one of our tech guys pull up the footage and watched her drive out of the lot Tuesday evening."

"That was quick."

"The software we use has an automated search function. And it's been programmed to recognize the employees of all firms that we work for. So all he had to do was query the last time that Elizabeth Collins was at Roberts and Mann. The footage of her getting into her car and driving off came right up."

"I'm both impressed and a little terrified of Big Brother."

"That ain't nothin', son. The software is constantly monitoring all of the offices we provide security for and it has disturbance recognition capabilities. If a camera picks up an argument that gets a little heated, or someone carrying an item that the software thinks might be a weapon, then the feed goes live in our office so that a tech can decide if something bad is going down or if it's a misinterpretation. The software has a ninety-five percent success rate interpreting situations.

"Now, when we get a new client, it might take a month or so to help the software interpret the new situations. About a year ago, we were hired by a company that manufactures parts for heavy machinery. It took a while to persuade the software that all the huge guys carrying large pieces of metal around weren't dangerous."

"Brave new world," I said, a bit awestruck.

"No more having some nine-dollar-an-hour guy in a faux cop outfit sitting at a desk of monitors all night. We're able to provide high-end security for over fifty businesses, some not even in this city, with two guys on duty at night. And nothing gets past them. They've tweaked the software to give false positives rather than take a chance of us missing something."

"So what do *you* do?" I said, intrigued in spite of myself.

"The majority of my job is to design the layout of the cameras and alarms. I also testify in court, which is usually when we've caught a bad guy. Though there are a number of cases where we get called in on a civil matter. Like if someone is suing one of the companies. We get subpoenaed to provide video evidence one way or the other, and they always need someone to testify to the validity of the footage. Just the usual questions: Was that all of footage? Do we constantly monitor the business? Etc."

I was quiet for a moment and he smiled.

"Go ahead and ask," he said. "I don't mind."

"It's really none of my business."

"I make one-fifty per year, plus a bonus that's about a quarter of my salary."

"No kidding?" I said, breathing a little faster.

"And I'm not playing Russian roulette pulling cars over."

I had to restrain myself from asking if there was an opening.

"We need to talk about Elizabeth," I said just as the waiter brought our food. Once we'd taken the edge off our hunger, I continued, "I'd like to get all the footage of her from Monday morning through when she left on Tuesday."

"There's actually a camera in her office."

"Really? They seem so uptight about the confidentiality of the books."

"And we accommodate that paranoia. The cameras in the offices only focus on the people, everything else is blurred out. Roberts and Mann even hired an independent tech company to look at our software. They wanted to make sure there wasn't any way of unblurring the footage."

"So why exactly are the cameras in the offices?" I was

trying to suss it all out.

"It is possible someone could make it all the way into a person's office and then attack them. Also, and more commonly, it protects people from claims of sexual harassment or other liability claims."

"How much does a company like Roberts and Mann pay Silver Security?"

"I can't tell you that, but I can say that every company who uses us for a couple of years ends up saving money in the long run. When a liability suit can run into the tens of millions, it's not hard to prove that we're saving the companies money."

"When can I get the footage?"

"If you want, we can drive over there when we're done. One of our geeks will be there. He'll put it on a flash drive."

When were ready to leave, Andrew pulled out his Silver Security Visa and paid for the meal, leaving a generous tip. I couldn't help but wonder what it would be like to have some real cash flow and to work for a company that had top-dollar perks.

I followed Andrew to his office and we parked in front of a large, nondescript steel-and-glass building with a small sign identifying it as the headquarters of Silver Security. The lights in the parking lot illuminated the dozen cars still parked outside. I looked up and saw cameras mounted all around the building.

Andrew swiped a keycard on a pad outside the main door, and then placed his hand on a biometric scanner at the inner door. Once inside, he directed me to a kiosk where I had my picture taken and my right hand scanned before a plastic visitor card was issued by a machine. The card had my picture and a magnetic strip on it that Andrew said was imbedded with a ton of information about me.

I had two thoughts. One was that the whole thing was creepy as hell, and the second was that municipal buildings, such as jails and courthouses, would be well served by this type of high-tech equipment—though Lionel West, our IT guy, didn't agree with me. I remembered a discussion I'd had with him a month earlier when construction was wrapping up at the sheriff's office. I had suggested that we should install more sophisticated security, but Lionel thought it could become a crutch that made people complacent. His argument was that, if employees believed they had a super-sophisticated system that couldn't make mistakes, and then they saw someone in the building who shouldn't be there, they'd assume it was fine because they'd made it past security. He went on to explain that the more complicated a system was, the more likely it was to have a vulnerability.

Andrew and I rode down in the elevator to the basement.

"All of the electronic hardware is located in the basement because it's easier to heat and cool. The basement is kept at a constant seventy-two degrees and has a backup generator for the backup generator."

When we stepped out of the elevator it looked like we'd walked into a modern hospital. The hallway was glaringly white.

"Who do you get to clean for you?" I asked, realizing a possible vulnerability.

"We pay our janitors more than you make," he said matter-of-factly. "They have to pass a rigorous background check and undergo weekly drug tests."

A third of the way down the hall, we stopped at a door marked "Surveillance." We both had to slide our keycards to enter the room.

"Why can't I just follow you in?" I asked, still trying to find a flaw in their defenses.

Andrew pointed to the camera above the door. "The camera will only let the person whose image is on the swiped card enter the room. If you tried to slip in with me or force the door, a very, very loud alarm would sound and, within two minutes, someone armed would respond."

I took him at his word.

Inside was a large, comfortable space where a tall, olive-skinned woman was walking along a wall filled with monitors. Every few steps, she'd stop and take a closer look at one of the screens. Through an open door, I could hear the distinct sounds of a pinball machine.

"Hey, Andrew," the woman said without turning away from the monitors.

"Hey, Bebe." To me he explained, "We always have two people in here. They do twenty-minute shifts watching the monitors."

A young man in his twenties came out of the back, chewing on a pretzel. "Andrew, what's up?"

"How long before you're up?"

"Five minutes."

"Zeke, this is Larry, an old friend from my days on the street."

Zeke came over and shook my hand.

"He needs some footage. We'll wait for Bebe."

We spent the next five minutes watching the monitors.

"See, that red light means that the software has detected unusual activity." He pointed to one of the monitors where a new image had come up, a flashing red dot in the corner.

"It's BS. Those two roughhouse all the time," Bebe said as we watched two guys pushing and shoving each other in a cafeteria. There was no sound, but after a minute, one them fell to the floor. For just a second it looked serious, then he started laughing and the other guy put out a hand to help him up. "Too much testosterone." She clicked a button and the red flashing dot went away.

"I'm up," Zeke said.

Bebe relaxed her pacing and came away from the wall of monitors. Before it was her turn again, I had a flash drive loaded with all of the footage of Elizabeth since Monday.

Andrew escorted me back to the parking lot, using the time to try to recruit me. I took his card, but told him I'd probably just muddle along working for the sheriff's office.

It was dark and the roads were quiet by the time I headed home. When I opened the door, I found Cara nestled on the couch with Alvin.

"Long day?" Cara asked, wiping at her eyes.

"You were napping," I said in mock accusation.

"Never!" she said, pretending to be scandalized.

"Would you be willing to take a polygraph test?"

"Nope. Besides, y'all don't use polygraph tests."

"You're right. Dad hates them and hates the way law enforcement uses them. They aren't reliable. No one who knows anything about the law would agree to take one. It's crazy that law enforcement agencies still judge people who won't take one."

Cara came over to me and we wrapped our arms around each other.

"You're kind of cute when you get all righteous and start preaching."

"You do realize I'm slowly going to become my dad over the next twenty years?"

"That's okay. I like your dad. What about me becoming my mother?" Cara asked.

"No, no, that's not going to happen. I think you take after your dad," I said. Her mother was very earthy and just a little crazy.

"You might be right. Of course, that means I might go berserker and pillage some small, defenseless village." Her dad had more than a little Viking blood under his grey hair.

"I'll take my chances." I gave her a kiss and savored the moment, feeling very close to her.

"Tomorrow needs to be a wedding prep night. Sorry."

"I can live with that," I said and gave her another hug. "Would you still love me if I was bringing home six figures?"

She squinted at me. "Are you going to start taking bribes?"

I told her about Andrew and Silver Security.

"Being safer is tempting, but I can't see you going all corporate," she said after a long moment of thought. "Besides, I think you're doing the job you're supposed to do. No, we'll just stay poor."

"Deal."

## CHAPTER SEVEN

When I got to the office on Friday morning, I was beginning to feel the case sliding into neutral.

With some cases, it was possible to achieve and maintain a momentum that carried the investigation along at a steady pace, day after day, all the way to the finish. Not this one. I had a number of people to interview and leads to follow, but all of them seemed like side trails, not the main road to a solution.

"We can bring the husband in," Darlene said in a way that suggested she didn't really support the idea.

"Not now. If we're gonna go there, we should wait until we have the full autopsy report and have finished reviewing all the CCTV footage from the roads leading to the nursery."

"I've collected about fifty hours' worth from a dozen stores and businesses."

"I'll split it with you."

"It'll still take some time to go through. Especially since we don't know what we're looking for."

"Her car, for one thing. But you're right. The killer might have used their own car to dump the body."

"Where *is* her car?" Darlene asked, sounding frustrated.

"Maybe it was a car jacking. They kill her, dump the body

and take off with her car. They could be halfway across the country by now."

"Maybe. If that's the case, then it's going to be solved by shoe leather. Ours or some LEO in another county or state."

I snapped my fingers. "You're gonna hate this, but there's more camera footage we need to collect. The time stamp on the video from Silver Security shows Elizabeth driving out of Roberts and Mann's parking lot at seven on Tuesday. We need to get any CCTV footage we can of the vehicle from that point on. If she went straight home, then we should be able to pick her up on a couple of cameras. From her office, there's only one route that makes sense."

"Any chance she picked up some guy in Tallahassee to bring back to her place and he killed her?"

"Unlikely, but who knows. Motive is thin on this one."

"You said that this could be an attack on her firm?"

"Possible. They are certainly playing in the majors, at least for Tallahassee, and Elizabeth was one of their MVPs."

Darlene shrugged. "That sounds like a promising motive... at least as good as anything else we've got. I think we should dive into employees past and present that might hold a grudge, and any rival companies."

I told her what Zeph Roberts had said about the amount of time they would keep an unhappy employee.

"Then we're talking past employees. The way you describe her, it sounds like Roberts could piss someone off pretty easily."

"In the right circumstances, I think she could be cold and brutal," I agreed.

Darlene looked thoughtful. "Any chance Roberts and Mann has a motive for getting rid of Elizabeth?"

"She was very valuable to them. However, maybe something had changed to make her less of an asset and more of a liability. It would be interesting to see what past employees have to say about the firm."

We spent another hour in the conference room, working out a plan that would allow both of us to work on the half dozen other cases on our desks. I didn't have any other murders, but I had a couple of aggravated assaults, an assault on a law enforcement officer and an attempted murder by some idiot kid throwing a knife at another kid.

I ran into Pete on the way back to my desk.

"Just the man I wanted to see," he said with a huge smile on his face. "Here are the dates. Pick one." He handed me a piece of paper with four dates on it.

"What's this?" I asked suspiciously.

"Those are the dates when the venue I've selected for your bachelor party is available."

I looked at the paper and back at him. "You aren't going to let this drop, are you?"

"No way, little buddy." The smile had turned into a somewhat menacing grin.

I took a deep breath. "If I've got to have a bachelor party, let's get it over with. March 31." I handed the paper back to him.

"Can do," Pete said cheerily.

He started to walk off and I stepped in front of him.

"Seriously, I don't want this to get crazy or creepy."

"Trust me."

"Please don't say that."

He relented and put his hand on my shoulder. "There are breaks on this train. Darlene and Sarah are helping with the planning. No naked women and plenty of designated drivers."

I stepped out of his way. The fact that Pete's wife would be involved made me feel marginally less paranoid.

"Be there or be square," Pete said as he walked off.

"You're enjoying this way too much!" I shouted to his back.

Back at my desk, I put in a call to the CPA firm and asked that Zeph Roberts call me back as soon as possible. My phone rang as soon as I hung up. Momentarily impressed at her responsiveness, I answered the call and was a little disappointed to hear Deputy Matti Sanderson on the other end of the line.

"There's been a little disturbance. Since the two parties are fighting over who is going to get the body of your victim, I thought you might be interested."

"Where are you?"

"At the husband's house. The victim's father and mother confronted him. We got the situation under control and have an ambulance on the way. Nothing too serious. The father ended up on the ground with a leg injury."

"I'm on my way," I told her and headed for the door. I saw Darlene pulling out of a parking space and waved her down. I hopped into her car and explained as she drove.

"I knew this might happen," I groused.

"Grief and anger are very closely related. I've been to four—no, five funerals where fights broke out."

"I remember Dad responding to a shooting at a funeral back in the early '90s that left three more people dead."

Two patrol cars and an ambulance filled the driveway when we showed up. Sanderson had Ian Barton boxed in at his front door while another deputy, Andy Martel, was talking to the Collinses at the back of the ambulance where Hondo Valdez, an EMT and Darlene's boyfriend, was working over Mr. Collins's leg.

"Let's go talk to Ian first," I said.

"I'll be curious to see where this leads," Darlene said, nodding at Hondo as we made our way past the ambulance to Ian.

"He's at my house!" Ian told Deputy Sanderson through clenched teeth. "My kids are in the house."

"He's saying you pushed him," Sanderson said calmly while making notes on her pad. She looked up as we walked over. "I'm going to leave you in the care of these two investigators. No decisions have been made yet whether to charge you or not. So go ahead and tell them your side of the story." She flipped her pad closed.

"It's not my side of the story, it's *the* story," he argued as she turned to walk away.

"Tell it to them."

"Ian, what's this all about?" I asked, starting with my best sympathetic tone of voice.

"I tried to meet them halfway. But those sons of bitches want to take my kids," he said angrily, and I saw him start to edge toward the ambulance.

"Stop," I told him. "Look over here." I moved to the side so he could look at me without having the Collinses in his line of sight.

Reluctantly, Ian shifted around and stopped staring at his in-laws.

"Tell us what happened, from the beginning."

"Harvey called and said they wanted to come over to see the kids." He took a deep breath. "I thought, all right, that might be good for Ethan and Clarice. They don't really understand what's going on, but they know something is wrong. Maybe seeing their papaw and mamaw would distract them. I was being stupid. When I opened the door, I stepped out to talk 'cause I wanted to go over some ground rules. Last thing I wanted was to upset the kids more. I started talking and suddenly he interrupted me and said they were taking the kids back to West Palm with them. No way that's going to happen." Ian's agitation rose as he told the story, until he was almost shaking with fury.

"Take some deep breaths," Darlene told him.

"I'm fine," he said after a minute, sounding better. "I told him to leave. Instead, he got up in my face. When I turned to go into the house, he was so close to me that he stumbled back and fell. I never laid a hand on him."

"Have you all decided on funeral arrangements for your wife?" I asked.

"What, with them?" he said acidly, pointing over his shoulder. "Forget it."

"She's their daughter. Remember, we talked about this."

"I hear you, but they aren't being reasonable."

"Listen to me. You need to remain calm and rational. Incidents like this aren't going to look good if your in-laws get you in front of a judge who's going to decide the custody of your children."

From the look on his face, I didn't think he'd even considered that he might have to fight for his children in court.

"No way," Ian said, looking as confused as a fish out of water.

"He's reading from the gospel." Darlene backed me up. "Walk into court with a charge or two and the judge won't look kindly upon you."

Ian took a couple of deep breaths and paced around the small porch.

"I see your point," he muttered nervously. "I really didn't push him."

"We'll go talk with him. Let's see if we can work this out here and now. But be prepared to bend a little," I said sternly.

"They're not going to take my kids."

"I'm not talking about them taking your kids. Let me talk to them and see what we can work out."

Ian nodded.

"Stay with him," I told Darlene. For now, there needed to be a least one or two people between the combatants.

I walked over to the ambulance. "How are you doing, Mr. Collins?" I asked, addressing the question to Hondo as much as Mr. Collins.

"I'll live," Harvey Collins grumbled.

"It's probably just a sprained knee, but he should go to the hospital and have it X-rayed," Hondo said.

"I'm not going to the hospital."

"Harvey, you need to get it X-rayed," Charlene Collins said, tears running down her face.

Mr. Collins huffed and waved his hand in irritation. "Have you arrested him?" he asked me, glaring toward Ian.

"You don't want us to do that."

"I damn sure do."

"Do you love your grandchildren?" I asked. "Because

right now they need some stability in their lives, and that's going to require all of their loved ones to come together for at least as long as it takes to bury their mother."

Elizabeth's parents both looked at the ground.

"But he killed her," Mr. Collins muttered.

"All the more reason you want to leave him out of jail for the time being so we can investigate her death and his possible involvement without being distracted by this kind of crap." I'd worked up a good amount of righteous indignation.

"Harvey?" his wife asked.

I let the silence draw out as he considered the situation.

"All right," he snapped.

"I'm going to have our victim advocate work with you all to negotiate the funeral arrangements. Agreed?"

More silence.

"Yes," Mrs. Collins said, sounding more assertive. "Now let's take you to the hospital and have your leg looked at," she told her husband, who looked deflated now that his anger was gone.

"It hurts like hell," he muttered.

"Carol isn't going to thank you for this," Darlene said when I told her what I'd discussed with the Collinses. Carol Buford was the head of our all-volunteer victim advocate group. We didn't have the money to employ a full-time victim advocate, but Dad had scrounged up enough of a salary for a part-time position. Carol was married to a deputy and was great at recruiting and training volunteers.

"I thought about that right before I threw her under the bus," I said. "I'll give her a call and warn her."

I turned back to Ian. I could tell that he was mentally and emotionally exhausted. I decided to take advantage of his condition. First I explained what I'd discussed with his in-laws, then casually slipped in my request.

"Mind if we come inside and look around?" I asked innocently, knowing that he wasn't in the state of mind to make a clear decision.

"I guess," he said without even asking what we were looking for. I also had a few questions I wanted to ask him, but I was going to wait until we'd had a look around. I didn't want him to get mad and kick us out too soon.

"I really don't know what I'm going to do," Ian said as we entered the house. "Excuse me. I have to go check on the kids. I put them in the bedroom." He headed for the back of the house while Darlene and I wandered through the living room.

The house was clean with a healthy smattering of kids' toys and clothes. On the mantel above the fireplace were several family pictures, many that included Elizabeth. I looked in the kitchen. There were dishes in the sink, but no more than you would expect from a one-parent household in the midst of an emotional crisis.

Darlene was reading book titles on the living room shelves when I came back in.

"Looks just like you would expect," I said. "Any books on how to bludgeon your wife?"

"His reading material is a little heavy on espionage, but I won't hold it against him. It's his computer search history that we really need to look at."

"Not sure we can push him that far," I said, just before Ian came back into the room carrying his youngest child.

"They all right?" I asked.

"How can I tell?" he said as Clarice buried her dark head in his shoulder. "Ethan is curled up on his bed playing with his dinosaurs."

"Did you and your wife have life insurance?" I asked.

He gave a sad little laugh and rubbed Clarice's back. "Funny story there."

"How's that?" Darlene asked.

"A couple of months ago, Elizabeth and I sat down to go over our finances and figure out who was going to pay for what. The way our policy was written, we were each other's beneficiary, but if something happened to us then the money went to the kids, with my parents being their guardians. That was something we'd decided years ago when Ethan was born. It made sense 'cause my parents are younger and healthier than hers. But with the breakup, she wasn't happy about my parents being the guardians. We got into an argument about it."

Ian shook his head and swayed from side to side, soothing Clarice, who'd turned to look timidly at us. "So stupid. Both of us were irritated and I suggested that we just get rid of the policy we had. Then we could each get a policy on ourselves and name whoever we wanted to handle the money for the kids. Elizabeth agreed. I called up the next morning and canceled the policy. About a month later, I had a new life insurance policy on myself naming my kids as beneficiaries and my parents as the trustees. I don't think Elizabeth had gotten a new policy. When I asked her about it, she just said she was working on something. Whatever that meant."

"Are you sure she didn't have one?"

"She didn't make financial decisions rashly. If we were going to buy a car, it would take her six months even though we had the money sitting in the bank. That was just more trouble caused by her love of numbers. She loved doing all the research and number-crunching, but it took her forever to make a decision."

"What about her assets?"

"You don't honestly think I…" He looked down at his daughter and lowered his voice. "…did something for the money? Get real. Yes, most of her money will come to me. I'm still her husband and the truth is, after the argument over the insurance, I think we both just kind of ignored the money subject. Most of our finances are still tied together. Like this house. Both names are still on the mortgage."

We asked a few softball questions before leaving.

"Do you believe him about the insurance?" I asked Darlene when we were headed back to the office.

"That would be a stupid lie. I don't think we're looking at a money motive for him."

"I agree. I'd bet she brought home more money than he did. So he could probably count on child support from her since she walked out on him and the kids."

"He kills her, he loses out financially," Darlene agreed.

"If he killed her, it would be the standard ex-husband motive—anger, hurt, possessiveness."

"Unless we find a boyfriend or girlfriend of Elizabeth's that we don't know about, we can rule out jealousy. I'm liking him less and less for the murder," Darlene said, shaking her head as she pulled into the sheriff's office parking lot.

## CHAPTER EIGHT

"Get up!" Cara said, throwing a pillow at me.

"I don't want to be a crime fighter today," I groaned and rolled over.

"Fine, but you have to call in sick. I'm not doing it for you." She had already taken her shower and dressed.

"I don't want to do that either," I said, squinting at her through one eye.

"Then you have to get your butt out of bed. Is this what married life is going to be like?"

I threw one foot out of bed and let it drop to the floor. "I'm up," I joked, then swung the other leg out. "See?" I sat halfway up, then fell back onto the bed.

"What's up with you today?"

I sat up for real this time and tried to pry my eyes all the way open. "It's the Collins case." It had been over a week now and we'd gotten exactly nowhere. We had no decent evidence nor a good suspect.

"You've had plenty of cases that you couldn't solve right away."

"Ouch!" I said, reaching for my heart.

"I didn't mean it like that."

"I know. I don't expect a murder case to be solved in a

week, but to not even have a good working hypothesis is daunting."

"Now I know you're awake if you're using fancy words like 'hypothesis' and 'daunting'," Cara mocked me.

I tossed a pillow at her.

"Could it really be just a random killing?"

"See, that's what's bothering me. It doesn't *feel* random. Maybe if she'd been stabbed in the back and left on the street."

"Don't most serial killers pick victims they don't know, and don't a lot of them dispose of the body somewhere other than where they were killed?"

I stood up and headed for the bathroom. "That's true, but they usually have a sexual or sadistic reason for killing. Elizabeth didn't show any signs of being abused in any way."

"Haven't found anything on the CCTV footage?"

"Not yet. And there's only so much of that we can watch each day before our eyes fall out. Right now all we have is a possible shoe print, which means less than zero until we have a suspect. We're still waiting on the lab reports and, on top of all of that, we still haven't found her car." I crammed my toothbrush into my mouth

"I've got to go," Cara said, blowing me a kiss as she headed for the door.

Half an hour later, I was walking to my desk when my phone rang with a call from Dr. Darzi.

"We've been working on our 3D model of the wound and the attack on Elizabeth Collins. I think you are looking at a classic lead pipe. Or something very similar. The diameter of the weapon is approximately two inches."

"Good. Anything back on the lab work?"

"Nothing beyond the basic information I was able to get right away. She wasn't drunk or under the influence of any common drug. And now we can assume she was standing on her own two feet. I'm sorry I can't be of any more help."

"No, I appreciate the information from the modeling."

Darlene walked over as I hung up with Darzi.

"Let's go see Shantel and look at the evidence we picked up at the nursery. Maybe we missed something the first time around," she said after I shared Darzi's report. "Though I'm pretty sure we would have noticed a lead pipe. Does anyone still use lead pipe?" She was clearly as frustrated as I was.

"Nah. Maybe it was copper."

We headed for the evidence room and the new lab. Most of the renovations that had been started before last year's hurricane had finally been finished.

"When do you get the new flooring?" I asked Shantel, who was at her desk reading emails and eating a pastry.

"Another week. Everything else is pretty much done, thank goodness."

"We wanted to look over the items we picked up at the nursery."

"I heard you still haven't solved that one."

"It's worse than you think," Darlene admitted.

"Not a clue," I chimed in.

"Well, you can't look at 'em 'cause I don't have 'em. I sent almost everything we picked up last week to the state crime lab," she said, clicking icons on her computer. "Look. I mapped out the route that the killer, or whoever dumped the body, probably took if we're right about him going around the gate."

"I'd bet money on that part," I said, looking over her shoulder at the computer screen where she'd pulled up a map of the nursery, marked with red X's.

"So I looked back at where all of the evidence was found and anything, and I mean anything, that was found within ten feet of that track, I sent it in."

"Dad's going to love that." Money was always a concern in a small department, and tests from the state lab weren't cheap. It was tough trying to solve murders while continually running into financial roadblocks.

"We were lucky he was able to get that grant for the construction," Darlene said.

"It drives me crazy having to explain to victims that we

aren't going to send the window screen from their burgled home out for DNA testing," I said.

"And if we did, they'd expect the result back in a week." Shantel shook her head.

"*CSI* effect," I agreed. "I appreciate you sending all those items in."

"Don't bother checking your email for a while. I told them it wasn't a rush job. The lab is good about putting the rush on when we need it. I don't want to wear out our welcome."

"That's fine. Like the rest of this investigation, it's just a fishing expedition anyway."

Darlene and I turned to leave and Shantel said to my back, "I'm looking forward to your bachelor party."

I raised my hand and waved it in the air, "Glad someone is. See ya."

"Wouldn't want to be ya," she lobbed back.

Two hours later, both Darlene and I got a text from Pete: *You're gonna want to see this.*

"Where are we going?" Darlene asked once we were in the car and I'd called Pete for directions.

"The Highway 14 bridge over Little Kono creek."

"He said there's a body?"

"Specifically, a body that was assigned to him. I'm not sure why he thinks we need to come out there," I grumbled. The Collins case had me behind on half a dozen other cases. I didn't need to be running all over the county looking at Pete's problems.

"He didn't give any hint about why he wanted us to look at it?"

"He was being very cagey."

I parked near Pete's car and the crime scene van on the shoulder near the bridge. Darlene and I got out and walked to the middle of the bridge. Looking over the side, we could see Shantel and Nisha down below, taking pictures. I leaned forward a little and could just make out the body of what, from twenty-five feet up, looked to be a female who had been in the water for a while.

Pete was standing on the southern end of the bridge.

"We can't work your cases and ours," I groused, trying to make it sound like a joke, though I wasn't kidding.

"We'll see whose case this is," Pete said with raised eyebrows.

"Give," I prodded.

"Trust me. Just go through the scene with me," he said, his serious tone making me curious.

"Let's hear the man out," Darlene said diplomatically.

"Okay, I'll play. Who found the body?"

"Found the car first. That's it in the pull off," Pete said, pointing to a newer Toyota sedan. It was parked in a spot frequented by old folks who liked to fish. Many times I'd driven by and seen several of them lined up near the bridge, sitting in old lawn chairs with coolers beside them, watching their lines bob in the water.

"The body was down there?" I asked, gesturing toward the creek.

"Right. The car was unlocked and had been sitting there for at least a day. He found it." Pete pointed over to an elderly gentleman whose gray beard highlighted his dark brown complexion and who was sitting sideways in the driver's seat of a Chevy pickup that had been new when Clinton was president. "He saw the car yesterday and figured it had broken down. But since it was fairly new and was still here this morning, he took it upon himself to check it out. The keys were in the ignition and a purse was in the passenger seat in plain view. That's when he called us. We were lucky he checked it out before someone decided to steal it. While he was waiting for us, he looked around a little and found the body of a woman in the water under the bridge."

"Cause of death?"

"No idea yet. We haven't moved the body. But it was

obvious to Deputy White that she was definitely dead."

"Do you know who the victim is?"

"I know whose car that is and whose purse was in the passenger seat. Until we turn the body over and look at her face, I'm just guessing that they're one and the same."

"And?" Darlene pushed. Even she was showing signs of impatience.

"Her driver's license identifies her as Beth C. Robinson. Here's where things get interesting. While I was waiting for Shantel to show up, I did an online search. The 'C' stands for her maiden name, Collins."

I perked up. "Beth Collins?"

"Wait, there's more. Beth is short for Elizabeth."

"How old is she?"

"Thirty-five."

"Seriously?" I said. "We have two people named Elizabeth Collins, both the same age, who've died in Adams County within a week or so of each other?" What were the odds?

"What's her address?" Darlene asked, being a bit quicker on her feet than I was.

"It's a Tallahassee address. Up in Killearn," Pete said, referring to large area on the north side of Tallahassee that encompassed dozens of neighborhoods and thousands of homes.

I was just getting ready to ask when he expected someone from Dr. Darzi's office to arrive when I saw the coroner's van pull up behind my car.

"I'll be interested to find out what killed her," I said, as much to myself as to Pete and Darlene.

"Bet you're glad I called you now."

"I'm not so sure about that. I don't know what to think right now. We don't even know for sure if this is a murder."

"If it is, then there aren't many similarities between them," Darlene mused.

"All three of you. This must be a very special body," Dr. Darzi said as he came over to us.

"And we have the doctor himself," Darlene said with a smile.

"Deputy Henley," he nodded at Pete, "said this might be a rather unusual case. Besides, my choices were to come out here or go to the monthly hospital administrator's meeting. Sunshine or boredom. The choice was not difficult."

"He can come on down if he sticks to the path closest to the bridge and goes straight to the body," Shantel shouted from under the bridge. "I'm done with the photos."

"Go on, Doc, we're all dying, pun intended, to find out what happened to this woman," Pete said.

"Unfortunately, I came by myself. If one of you would be so kind as to assist?" He pulled a protective suit from his satchel and held it out.

"Large. I take an extra large, at least," Pete said after looking at the label on the suit.

I took it and began to climb into it.

"I would have done it, sweet pea," Darlene told me.

"I don't want to wait to get a look at her," I said, still trying to understand what this new victim might mean to our current case. I just couldn't believe that it was a coincidence.

I led the way with Dr. Darzi right behind me. It was a little tricky climbing down the damp and muddy embankment wearing paper booties.

The body was lying face down in about six inches of water. The creek was twenty feet wide at this point and maybe six feet deep in the middle. We were lucky that it had been a dry spring so far. After a lot of rain, I'd seen the creek as high as the bridge and spreading out through the bottom land in all directions.

"I'm going to take her temperature," Darzi said. "Help me with her skirt."

Darzi had already laid out one thermometer to get the ambient air temperature. I helped him with the victim's clothes, doing my best to avert my eyes while he took her temperature. With that indignity done, he ran his hands over the back of her body.

"No obvious wounds here. Let's turn her over."

I wondered why we'd bothered with the paper shoe covers as I watched them come apart in the ankle-deep water while we shifted the body. Overall, it wasn't the worst corpse I'd seen pulled from the water. The March air was cool and the worst of the insects were still dormant.

Darzi leaned in close and began running his hands over the dead woman while I stared at her face and tried to determine if she was indeed Beth Robinson. Wet hair and a little bloating didn't help, but I was reasonably sure that it was the same woman as the one in the driver's license photo Pete had shown to us.

"There is a contusion on her head and her neck is damaged, perhaps even broken. No other exterior wounds."

"What's your guess?" I pushed. One of the things I liked about Darzi was his willingness to take a guess instead of always making me wait for the results of his official examination. Of course, it helped that I'd never broken his trust by taking his guess as anything more than that.

"Considering where the body was found, It's possible that she fell, jumped or was pushed from the bridge," he said. "If we are lucky, I might be able to give you odds on which it was."

"Time of death?"

"Now you are going too far." But he smiled at me. "There are too many variables here for me to give you a guess on that. How long has the body been in the water? Has it moved at all? How much sun has it been exposed to? You are going to have to wait until the autopsy. I will tell you this: she has not been dead for more than twenty-four hours."

I didn't take a picture of the body. Any photo I got wouldn't be useable except as a psychological bludgeon against a suspect.

Just as I was starting to wonder if Darzi expected me to help him move the body to the van, he relieved my fears. "Don't worry. The redoubtable Linda and Ann will be here shortly. Your assistance will no longer be required."

"Not that I wouldn't…"

He waved his hand and I turned away gladly. I tried not to be squeamish, but bodies that had been lying in water bothered me in a primal way. It hadn't helped that last year we'd had to deal with a body that had been sautéed in a hot tub. Visions of that horror still popped up in my nightmares.

"The rules are no bodies after Wednesday," Linda said, passing me as I headed up to the road.

"What can I say? I'm a rule breaker," I threw over my shoulder.

"Yeah, I can tell you're a wild one," she tossed back with more than a little sarcasm.

When I got to the top of the hill, Pete was helping Shantel photograph the car. They appeared to have it under control, so I looked around for Darlene. I found her walking the ditch, searching for evidence to tag.

"What do you think? Any connection to our case?" I asked as I fell into step beside her and dropped my eyes to the ground.

"If so, the purpose of the two crimes seems to be different," she said, her words measured.

"Indicated by the difference in MO. Though they both appear to have been killed by blows to the head."

"The first body was concealed, at least for the short term."

"This body is under a bridge," I pointed out, not disagreeing but playing devil's advocate.

"True, but the car was left in the open. It was meant to be found."

"Agreed. Also, this murder, if it *was* a murder, seems more ambiguous, at least at first glance."

"Two women with the same name and roughly the same age."

"They don't look that different either."

"No, I guess they don't. Both have brown hair. Approximately the same height. Same ethnic background…

Do you think the first murder could have been a mistake?" Darlene wondered.

"Or was this some weird murder-suicide? Maybe this Beth was mentally unstable. She meets another Elizabeth Collins and thinks she's some strange doppelganger. So she kills her, but once she realizes what's she's done, she comes here and throws herself off the bridge."

"That's only about a twenty-five-foot drop."

"Take a header and it will do the job," I pointed out. "The proof is in the body."

"There's something here," Darlene said softly, and I followed her gaze only to realize that she was talking metaphorically.

"So what do we do? Get Pete to turn it over to us?"

"We're just assuming there's a link between the two cases." Neither of us wanted to take on more work at the moment.

"Maybe the lieutenant will let us shift some of our current cases to Pete or someone else," I suggested hopefully.

"Or we can just let Pete investigate this case while we investigate Elizabeth's murder. We can meet up and compare notes regularly."

"That makes sense. Hopefully we'll know soon whether there is a solid link between the two." I took one of the evidence markers from Darlene and marked a cigarette butt in the dirt.

"Let's head back to the car and see what they've found."

Pete was standing by while Shantel dusted down the inside of the car, occasionally pointing out something for Pete to bag.

"Did you find a phone?" I asked.

"It's here on the floor," Shantel said from inside the car. "I'm dusting it now. There are some smudges and one good print."

We waited patiently until she'd finished and handed the phone to Pete. Carefully, Pete touched the home button. We let out a collective sigh when the phone lit up without a lock screen. There were a dozen missed calls and several messages. Pete went to her recents and there were dozens of calls and messages, most of them from Mom and Bob. Next he checked her text messages.

"Don't keep them to yourself," I said, and he tilted the phone so we could all see the screen.

There were messages from various people. Several of them were from someone named Mia, asking where Beth was and what she should tell her patients. The last few were from Mom and Bob, both asking where she was.

"Scroll back through the Bob ones," I told Pete.

The messages they'd swapped the day before involved plans for her to pick up Tyler who, from the content of the texts, must have been her child. "Bob's a husband or ex-husband?" I wondered out loud.

"One way to find out," Pete said. He tapped Bob's number into his own phone and waited. The call was quickly picked up by a man who sounded upset. Pete held it away from his ear so Darlene and I could hear the conversation.

"Hello?"

"Bob?"

"Who's this?"

"Do you know someone named Beth Robinson?"

"What's happened to her? Who is this?"

"I'm Deputy Pete Henley with the Adams County Sheriff's Office. What's your full name and your relationship to Beth?"

"It's Bob Harper. I'm her friend, and I watch her son for her sometimes. Please tell me what's happened." He sounded hysterical.

"We thought you might be her husband," Pete said. I knew that he didn't want to deliver the news to one of Beth's friends before he'd told a member of her family.

"No, she doesn't have a husband. She did, but he's been dead for years." We could hear him start to cry.

"I'm sorry, but we need to speak with a member of her

family."

"Her mother," he managed to say. "Just tell me if she's alive."

"I'll call you back after we've spoken with her mother," Pete said, being as gentle as he could under the circumstances.

He hung up with Bob and immediately dialed Beth's mom.

"I knew it," she said. "I knew something awful had happened when Bob brought Tyler over and Beth didn't answer my calls." The woman sounded very tired.

"One of our investigators is going to come talk to you. Is that all right?" Pete asked. He caught my eye and I nodded

"I'll be here," she said, and gave him her address.

After Pete hung up, he turned to me. "You don't mind going and interviewing her?"

"Not at all. I want to know if there's a link between our two Elizabeths. It's too weird." I shook my head in bewilderment.

"In for a penny, in for a pound. I'll stay here and help with the evidence collection. Maybe I'll see something that harkens back to the other crime scene or to our Elizabeth," Darlene said.

## CHAPTER NINE

Shelly Collins lived in Southwood, a development that was attempting a "live here, work here" approach, mixing homes, state office buildings and shopping. In my opinion they got an "E" for effort.

She opened the door wide, pausing to wipe her eyes before inviting me in and leading me to the living room. Obviously an attractive woman in her youth, her features now were deeply carved with grief.

"I don't know how I'm going to get through this," she said softly. As if on cue, a young boy about six or seven years old came charging into the room and threw himself at her legs. "Of course I have to survive for this rascal." She mussed his hair.

"Where's Mom?" the boy asked, leaning against his grandmother and looking up at me. I thought about Elizabeth's kids and decided that the person who'd killed two mothers needed some swift justice.

Shelly hugged the boy to her. "This is Tommy."

Before she could say anything else, there was a knock on the door. She looked down at the boy and said, "Mrs. Evers from next door wanted to know if you'd come over and watch a movie with her two boys?"

"What movie?" he asked.

"Let's go find out."

At the door, she whispered quietly to the young mother and the two women embraced. Mrs. Evers put on a huge fake smile and told Tommy that her boys had several movies they could pick from. Tommy didn't need much more encouragement before he left the house in her care.

"I don't know when I'll tell him." Shelly dropped down on the couch and buried her face in her hands. "Have to be strong," she said, mostly to herself.

"Do you have any other family close by?" I was worried for her.

"A sister up in Albany. I tried to call her, but... it would make this more real. My husband died in a car accident the year before Beth's husband passed away. Now this. Poor Tommy."

"I'm sorry, Mrs. Collins. We don't have a lot of information at this point, so I'm going to have to ask you some questions."

"I don't care. Ask whatever you want, but first tell me what happened to Beth."

"As I said, it's early yet. If I knew anything for a fact, I'd tell you. There will be an autopsy tomorrow. We'll have a better idea after that. But the more information you can give us now, the sooner we'll have answers." I paused to let all this sink in and she nodded. "When was the last time you heard from Beth?"

"Yesterday afternoon. She called just after she got off work at Dr. Forsyth's."

"What did she do?"

"She's a dental hygienist."

"She called you?"

"That's right. We just chatted for a bit. She said she was running some errands before she headed home."

"When did you find out that she didn't make it home?"

"Bob called when she hadn't picked up Tyler at the usual time."

"What's Bob's relationship with Beth?"

"He's a teacher at Tyler's elementary school. They became friends… and… I don't know, went out a couple of times. He's very nice, but they didn't really hit it off as a couple."

"Who broke it off?" I asked, my interest piqued. The jilted lover was always one of the top five suspects for a murder.

"I think it was mutual. Beth wasn't ready for a serious relationship after her husband…" Shelly's eyes lost focus as she thought about her daughter's life. I'd seen that look before. It was the moment when people realized that someone they'd loved had become a part of the past.

"Can I get you something? Water?" I asked.

She waved my question away and continued. "Besides not being ready for a long-term relationship, Beth and Bob didn't have the same interests. I don't want to make him sound boring, but Beth liked to be outdoors and have fun when she wasn't working. Bob tends more toward books and music."

"Did Beth ever mention meeting anyone else named Elizabeth Collins?"

"No, not that I remember. Collins isn't an uncommon name. I've met another Shelly Collins."

"Did she ever use a CPA?"

"Maybe. Even though we were very close, I don't know much about her financial business. I do know that she got a small insurance payout when her husband died."

"Can you think of any reason she'd drive to Adams County after getting off work?"

"No."

"Had you noticed anything different about her in the last couple of weeks? A change in behavior or attitude?" I asked, ticking off the standard questions when someone died under mysterious circumstances. I could see a flicker of something in Shelly's eyes. "You remember something?"

"I… maybe…" A range of emotions, from sadness to

guilt, crossed over her face.

"Just tell me," I urged gently.

"A few days ago, maybe a little more, I noticed that she seemed distracted. I asked her what was wrong, but she just said it was nothing. You know how people do when they don't want to talk about something. I would have *made* her talk to me if I'd thought she was in any kind of trouble. But Beth spent a lot of her time worrying about others. You should understand, she was very outgoing and really cared about people. She did a lot of volunteer work as well as taking care of Tyler. I just figured she was worried about a friend or someone she was trying to help."

"What type of volunteer work did she do?"

"She taught adult literacy at the library and helped them with book drives and that sort of thing. She'd take Tyler with her sometimes and do readings in the children's section. I know I'm sounding like a broken record, but Beth loved helping people. That's how she looked at her work. Her original degree was in business, but she wanted a job where she felt more like she was making a difference in people's lives, so she went back to school to become a dental hygienist. I know how this sounds. I'm not trying to make her out to be a better person than she was." Shelly needed me to understand her daughter.

"She sounds like a wonderful person."

"Most children are selfish creatures. Beth was an exception. I never knew a time when she wasn't concerned about other people. I took her to a neighbor boy's birthday party when she was about the age Tyler is now. There was a young boy there who was quiet and shy. He didn't want to play any of the party games. So Beth just sat and talked with him all afternoon. They looked at books while the other kids ran around. You know, they still kept in touch. That was my daughter." Shelly began to sob uncontrollably.

I fetched a glass of water from the kitchen and sat with her until she was able to regain a semblance of control. I managed to gather a little more information about Beth's life and friends, then told her I'd have someone from the coroner's office call her when the autopsy was completed. I gave her my card and made her promise that, if she didn't hear from them or needed anything at all, she'd call me.

Back in my car, I called Pete and gave him the CliffsNotes version of the interview.

"We're finishing up here. Shantel had the car towed back to the office so she can go over the inside with a fine-tooth comb. So far, no smoking gun," Pete told me.

"So where does that leave us?"

"Okay, in all seriousness, I wasn't really trying to rope you all into helping with this case."

"That train has left the station," I assured him.

"Do you want to do any more interviews before you head back over here?"

"I'm going to swing by and talk with Bob Harper." I tried not to think of the backlog of other cases waiting on my desk.

"Perfect. I've already called the Tallahassee police and asked them to secure Beth's house and seal it up with crime scene tape until we have a chance to get a look at it. We'll meet when you get back to town and see where we go from there."

Shelly had given me Bob's address. He lived only a block away from Beth, so I drove by her place first, just to see what it looked like and to make sure it was locked up. The bright yellow tape across the door was in stark contrast to the wholesome atmosphere of this neighborhood full of family homes.

I thought about calling before I pulled into Bob's driveway, but there was a lot to be said for getting a candid reaction from a witness or suspect. I had to knock twice before he opened the door. His eyes were red and swollen. Paired with a curly but receding hairline, he looked like a very sad Art Garfunkel.

"Deputy Larry Macklin," I said, holding up my ID.

"You're here about Beth. Come in. I can't believe it. I just can't."

The Garfunkel comparison was given more credence when he ushered me into a small living room that was full of musical instruments. He cleared sheet music off of a chair for me, then dropped down onto the couch.

"You were watching Tyler yesterday?" I asked him.

"He rides home with me and my daughter most days."

"Can you walk me through yesterday afternoon?"

"I taught school until three, then Tyler and Willow came to my classroom. They fed the gerbil and turtle while I did some paperwork. I guess we left around four. We stopped to pick up some groceries, then I dropped Willow off at her mom's house and Tyler and I came back here."

"What time does Beth usually pick up Tyler?" I asked, trying to see Bob as a crazed killer. It wasn't possible. I couldn't even see him as a cold or a passionate killer. The man exuded calm.

"By six. Always by six or she calls."

"When did you get worried?"

"Soon after six. Being late wasn't like her. When I didn't get an answer to my phone calls or texts, I called Shelly."

"When?"

"About six-thirty. She hadn't heard from her either. She called around to a few people, including the dentist and some of the other people Beth works with. They all said that she'd left right after work. When Shelly told me this, I took Tyler over to her place. On my way, I drove by the dentist office to see if her car was still there."

"Did you leave after you dropped Tyler off at his grandmother's?"

"No. Good grief, I couldn't just leave her worrying about her daughter. I stayed there with her while we tried to figure out what to do. We called both hospitals and the police."

"Did you or her mother report her missing to the police?"

"Not the first time we called. She just asked them if there'd been an accident. I guess it was around ten that we went ahead and reported her missing. An officer came out and took a report, but he said that since Beth was an adult and there wasn't any reason to believe she was in danger, all they could do at that point was to put out a 'be on the lookout' notice. Shelly was real upset about that."

I was quickly making notes so that we could put together a timeline on Beth's disappearance. "How long did you stay at Shelly's house?"

"I left about one o'clock when she insisted. I know it's hard for some people to rest if they have company. Also, I was hyper as all get out. I knew something had happened to Beth. When I left her house, even though it was late, I drove around to every place I could think of where Beth might have been."

"Where'd you go?"

"You know, the Publix where she shopped, the gas station, the library. I *almost* drove over to the Adams County library 'cause she also does some volunteer work there, but since she only does that on weekends, I didn't see the point."

I'd perked up at the mention of Adams County. The answer to why her body was found where it was could go a long way to finding out what had happened to her. And the fact she'd been to Adams County increased the possibility there might be a link between Beth and Elizabeth Collins.

"Did she have any other reason to go to over there?"

"I think she liked getting out in the country. Sometimes she'd take Tyler on the drive with her."

"Why did she volunteer in Adams County?"

"She does… did a lot of volunteer work with the Leon County library. Apparently they shared a booth or some sort of display at a street fair a while back. Beth said she got to know some of the people from Adams County and they invited her over to Calhoun. She was like that. Always trying to help people. If she liked you, she'd do anything for you." Tears ran down his cheeks and he wiped at them with his sleeve. "She was the best," he said, then completely broke down.

Feeling awkward, I waited for him to regain control of his emotions.

"Was there more than just friendship between you and Beth?" I finally asked.

Bob looked at me for a second, then shook his head. "I thought we might... have had a romantic connection when we first met, but we didn't like the same things. There wasn't any spark. Beth was a nurturer with a very free spirit. I'm a nurturer too, but I'm a homebody all the way. After I get done teaching, I just want to hang around the house and play music. She always wanted to be doing something."

I asked a few more questions before leaving, but I didn't learn anything else. Bob only seemed interested in canonizing Beth. *Was she that good?* I wondered. It was the rare person who was really as golden as they appeared.

I called Pete to let him know I was making one more stop before heading back to the office. As soon as I'd heard that Beth volunteered at the Adams County Public Library, I realized I had a possible source of unbiased information. Eddie Thompson, who'd served as my confidential informant before cleaning up his act and severing his ties with Adams County's underworld, was now working at the library.

"I'll be there in half an hour," I told him after calling to make sure he was there.

"But—"

"Don't worry. I'm not going to talk you in to doing any of my dirty work," I assured him.

"Okay." Eddie's tone made it clear that he didn't trust me.

"Just hang tight," I said, not wanting to tip him off about the real reason I wanted to talk with him. It wouldn't help if he started discussing Beth with anyone else. Whether they knew it or not, most people changed their opinions of someone once they learned that the person had died.

Witnesses also tended to alter their accounts to match the rest of a group, if given the opportunity to share experiences. It was always best to do interviews cold before too much word got around.

My last call was to Cara to let her know I'd be running a little late that evening.

"While you were in Tallahassee, did you think to go by and get measured for your tuxedo?" she asked me.

"I could just wear my dress uniform," I offered hopefully, though I already knew that option was off the table.

"You know that was one of the compromises we made with my mom to keep her away from most of the planning," Cara reminded me.

"I know."

"If you really don't want to wear the tux, I'm sure she'd be glad to see you in a traditional Tibetan Zhuigui. Or, if you remember, she *did* suggest a nudist wedding," Cara said evilly.

I cringed and sighed. "I'll get by the tux shop soon. I promise."

# CHAPTER TEN

It was late afternoon by the time I got to the library. The building, a beige-colored block structure, had been built when I was in middle school. I'd spent many hours there, studying and using their computers.

I found Eddie behind the main desk, checking out books for an older woman who was wearing too much perfume and jewelry. Her necklaces alone must have weighed three pounds. The two of them were all smiles and discussing the beautiful spring weather. I struggled to be patient.

"Can we go somewhere and talk?" I asked Eddie, once the woman had finally put her Lawrence Block books into an oversize canvas bag with a pair of cute puppies painted on the side and headed for the door.

"I'll have to get Jessie to watch the desk," Eddie said, looking unhappy about the prospect. "I'll text her."

"Where is she?"

"Re-shelving."

A few minutes later, a young woman in her early twenties, with alien green hair that was growing out brunette, came around a corner pushing a cart half full of books.

"You rang?" she said cheerily to Eddie. She glanced at me and looked thoughtful.

"Watch the desk for a minute," Eddie said, for some reason looking very nervous.

Jessie stared harder at me. "Introduce me," she said to Eddie, her voice excited.

I looked at Eddie, who seemed mighty uncomfortable. "Just watch the desk."

"Eddie," Jessie said, sounding like a mother reprimanding a wayward child.

Eddie let out a huge sigh. "Jessie Gilmore, this is Deputy Larry Macklin."

"A detective. Excellent!" she said, her eyes bright and a frighteningly wide smile taking over her pixie face.

"In Adams County, we're called investigators," I told her, amused.

"Being a detective would be so cool," she said, staring at me like I was a rock star. Her focus was disconcerting.

"Nice meeting you," I said to her, making "follow me" gestures at Eddie.

"You shouldn't have made eye contact with her," Eddie whispered to me as we walked outside the building.

We sat down on one of the concrete planters that flanked the door. The air was cool and dry, the last vestiges of a North Florida winter. I explained to Eddie why I was there and he shook his head sadly.

"How well did you know Beth Robinson?" I asked him.

"She was really nice. You know, I get looks from people sometimes, what with all the bad stuff my family has done. And then it came out in the trial that I was estranged from them because of the cross-dressing... Some people just act funny around me. Not Beth. She even gave me rides home sometimes." He looked up at me. "Geez, what about her kid?"

"He's with his grandmother," I reassured him. "Did she ever seem worried about anything?"

Eddie looked thoughtful. "No, not really. I guess she seemed... just busy. Distracted. She helped out here and with the library in Tallahassee and she worked as a... you know, one of the people who clean your teeth at the dentist."

"A dental hygienist. Did she talk about any relationships?"

"No. Well, maybe. Someone at her office..." Eddie sounded vague.

"Who?"

"No." He shook his head. "I just remember her saying something about a date with a co-worker. We'd been talking about Rita Vila, the head librarian here. She'd been over at Adams County High, but she had to come here after she married a science teacher and couldn't work at the school anymore. I guess the school board has a rule about married people working at the same school. Sounds stupid to me. You can be having an affair no one knows about, but if you get married, boom, you're out on your ass." Eddie stopped, looking like he didn't know where he was headed with the story.

"So Beth and you were talking about it?" I said, trying to lead him back on track.

"Right, right! She said it could be awkward being in a relationship at work. So I asked her if she knew that from personal experience. That's when she kind of smiled. I asked her for details and she said she didn't kiss and tell."

"You didn't get any more?"

"It's not like we were best friends or anything. Besides, I could tell she didn't really want to talk about it."

"Do you think she was trying to hide something?"

"Maybe. Like maybe it was something she felt she *needed* to hide. I thought she might be dating a married guy, something like that."

I'd found Eddie's evaluations of situations and people to be surprisingly spot-on in the past. *But if Beth was killed because of an affair, how does that help us with Elizabeth's case?* I wondered. *Are their names really just a coincidence?*

"Did you see anyone hanging around the library who looked suspicious? I mean, other than yourself."

"Ha, ha, funny guy." Eddie glared at me. "I don't know. There are always some weirdos that come in. Most of them are just homeless folks who don't have anywhere else to hang out. Mrs. V. usually gives me the job of pushing the stinky ones out the door. I point them to the First Baptist Church; they've got a shower in the basement and a second-hand clothing store. Dan, the minister, will usually give the homeless clothes if they need them."

"But no one was hanging around Beth? Or talking about her?"

"She'd be here on Saturday mornings reading to the kids in the children's section. Mrs. V. doesn't let adults stay long in there if they aren't with a kid. So, no, no one was hanging around her."

"Did Beth ever come to the library in the middle of the week?"

"Not that I remember."

"Was she here this past Saturday?"

"No."

"Was that unusual?"

"Not really. She just came when she could."

"Who else around here regularly talked to Beth? Rita Vila must have."

"Yeah, she approves all the volunteers and makes them go through a background screening."

"Anyone else?"

Eddie hesitated.

"I need to talk to anyone who might have information," I pushed.

He sighed heavily. "Jessie sometimes helps with the readings on Saturday morning."

"Why'd you hesitate?"

"She's just…"

"I noticed she was a bit… excitable. Are you sweet on her?" I asked.

He clenched his jaw shut.

"You are," I ribbed him.

"I am not. She's... infuriating."

"I need to talk to her."

"You'll regret it," Eddie said, standing up.

"Just send her out." I was amused that Eddie found someone annoying. Usually with Eddie, it was the other way around.

A minute later, Jessie came bouncing out the door. "Eddie said you wanted to talk to me." Her eyes were practically twinkling.

I explained why I was there. "He said you helped Beth out with the children's reading circle on Saturday mornings."

"Absolutely." I thought the big smile on her face was inappropriate when talking about a murder victim she'd known and worked with.

"Did she ever talk about her personal life?"

"She told me that she was having sex with someone at her office," Jessie said with a conspiratorial smile.

"Who?"

The smile dropped from her face. "I couldn't ever get it out of her."

"What did you think of Beth?" I asked, changing tack.

"She was really nice. Absolutely doted on Tyler. Of course, he's sweet as can be." She paused. I let the silence grow until she finally continued. "I guess you must think I don't care that Beth was killed. I do. I... I just love mysteries. The thought that I'm involved in one is just... wow!"

"This isn't a game or a TV show. Beth is gone. Tyler lost his mother." Even as I scolded her, I had to admit that her reaction reminded me of the interest I'd had in the murder cases Dad investigated when I was growing up. I'd read about the cases in the paper and try to overhear Dad talking on the phone or with other deputies. Without responsibility to the victim and the family riding on your shoulders, it was easier to distance yourself from the human side of the equation.

"I feel awful that she was murdered. I want to help, that's

all," Jessie said.

"The best way you can help me is by telling me everything you know about Beth and anyone she came in contact with."

"She talked to a bunch of people every time she was at the library, but there were only a few of us that she spent time with. Eddie, Mrs. Vila and me, that's all. You need to find out who she was having an affair with."

"We will," I said, taken aback by her insistence.

"I can help."

"How?" I asked doubtfully.

"I can be your CI. Eddie doesn't want to do it anymore." She stuck her chin out at me.

"Eddie had the ability to get into the… seedier areas of town. You don't look like you've spent much time on the streets."

"I've got eyes and ears." She leaned in conspiratorially. "And I'm smarter than Eddie."

"Eddie's not stupid." It felt strange to defend him.

"I want to help with the investigation," she said as though that settled the matter.

"And I've already told you how you can do that."

She gave me a disgusted look.

Reluctantly, I gave her one of my cards and told her to give me a call if she remembered anything else. As I left the library, I couldn't help but wonder what was up with the odd young woman.

Pete and Darlene met me in the parking lot of the sheriff's office, where we each summarized our day's efforts.

"So far, I haven't found any connection between Beth Robinson and Elizabeth Collins," I said, concluding my narrative of the interviews.

"I hate to leave it at coincidence." Pete frowned. "But we can't get bogged down looking for a link that might not exist."

"Maybe we *should* look at Beth's murder as a standalone," Darlene said. "The affair at the office has promise. Maybe the lovers were meeting over here. Things went bad and he killed her."

"Or it was someone angered by her affair," I said.

"Such as his wife," Pete finished. "The old motives are the best motives."

I glanced up at the setting sun. "I don't think we're going to solve this tonight."

"Meet in the morning?" Darlene asked.

"I'll bring donuts," Pete offered.

When I opened my front door I was greeted by the aromas of Italy. We usually took turns providing dinner and Cara had outdone herself that night with spaghetti and garlic bread.

"I think there's a bottle of red wine in the cupboard," I suggested.

"Already on the table," Cara said, offering her cheek for a kiss before she put the bread in the oven. "And the kids have been fed."

I looked down to see Alvin splayed out on the floor while Ivy was conducting her usual after-dinner grooming session.

"Tell me that life won't change after we get married," I said as I carried our salads to the table.

"It *will* change. That's what life does," Cara said in a tone that was several degrees more serious than I expected.

I turned and looked at her. "Is something wrong?"

"There's still so much to do before the wedding."

"I know I haven't been pulling my weight."

"You're trying," she said as she took the bread out of the oven and transferred it to a plate on the table.

I held up my hand. "I solemnly swear to do what I'm told. I will try on a tux tomorrow. I'm thinking about going back over there to interview Pete's victim's co-workers."

"Why are you investigating *his* murder?"

I explained about the two Elizabeths.

"That's a little freaky."

"Weirder things have happened."

"So you'll get measured for your tux tomorrow?"

"You have my word. What else isn't done?"

"We still need to finalize the menu for the rehearsal dinner with Mary at the Palmetto. We need to talk to the minister. I told you he called on Monday. And what are Pete and your dad going to wear?" Cara was practically vibrating with a nervous energy.

"Don't worry, we'll get it all sorted. You know, if I wore my uniform, then Dad and Pete could do the same," I suggested and knew right away that I'd made a mistake.

"You *know* that's not an option, but y'all need to figure out something soon." Her voice had risen several octaves into what I knew to be dangerous territory. Cara seldom showed the fiery temper frequently associated with redheads, but it was there and I'd learned not to rouse it.

I reached out and took her hand. "We could just go down to the clerk's office and get married," I said, trying to lighten the mood, but once again my comment misfired.

"I don't need any more options!"

"Let's eat and we'll talk after dinner," I suggested.

"I'm not hungry."

Cara walked away from the table and dropped onto the couch in the living room. I looked at my plate of spaghetti with no interest, weighing the pros and cons. If I didn't eat the food she'd prepared, that wouldn't be good, and she wasn't in the mood to talk anyway. So I methodically ate my dinner and cleaned off the table, then cautiously approached the couch.

"Can I sit?"

Cara had been lying on her side with her feet up on the couch, but she sat up at my question. I sat down next to her and pulled her into a hug.

"I don't want you stressing out about the wedding."

"Then do what I ask you to," she said into my shoulder.

"Sorry."

I thought about pointing out that I was dealing with a

couple of strange murder cases. However, that wasn't fair. It was my job. Cara had her own job. Some jobs were more time sensitive and mission critical than others, but in the end they were just jobs. If I was run over by a car tomorrow, someone would step up and take my place. Also, I knew that I'd been putting off some of the chores she'd given me even when I had more time. If things were getting down to the wire now, I was to blame for it.

"I didn't mean to spoil dinner," Cara apologized.

"I think we've just established that it's my fault you're stressed out," I said, giving her a squeeze. "The spaghetti was great."

She gave me a soft punch in the gut and got up to get her own plate and bring it back to the couch. Alvin jumped up next to her and managed to con her into sharing her garlic bread. We passed the next hour streaming a comedy about a vampire living in Alabama, before Cara left to take a bath.

I sat back down at the kitchen table and opened my laptop, spending the next hour making notes on both cases. When my phone rang, I looked at the caller ID and frowned.

"Mr. Griffin, what's up?" I hoped that Eddie hadn't gotten into trouble. Eddie rented a garage apartment from Albert Griffin, Adams County's unofficial historian, and I couldn't think of any other reason he'd be calling me at ten o'clock at night.

"I heard about the two Elizabeths."

"What?"

"The murders."

"What did Eddie tell you?" I was puzzled because I hadn't told Eddie anything about the first murder, so how could he have put it together?

"Nothing really. I heard about the first one from a friend who spends a lot of time at the nursery. Eddie mentioned the Beth he knew. I made a few calls and connected the dots."

"Do you have some sort of information for me? Did you know one of the victims?" I couldn't figure out why he was interested.

"I don't know anything about these murders, but I wanted to make sure you knew about the two Marys that were killed in Houston."

"What?" He had my full attention now.

"It was back in 2000. I don't think they have anything to do with these murders, but there are things you might want to consider."

"Okay, why don't you come to the sheriff's office in the morning? We're going to have a meeting around nine. That way you can give all of us the information at the same time."

"Right. I'll be there with bells on," he said cheerily.

*What other craziness are we going to have to deal with?* I thought, shaking my head.

# CHAPTER ELEVEN

"We have a guest speaker," I told Pete and Darlene as I ushered Albert Griffin into the conference room on Friday morning. True to his word, a dozen confections from the Donut Hole sat on the table in front of Pete.

I didn't have to make any introductions. Darlene knew Mr. Griffin because they were both active members of the Adams County Historical Society, while he and Pete had been gossip buddies back in the day when they both used to hang out in the mornings at Winston's Grill.

"I don't mean to impose on your investigation. I just heard about two Elizabeths being murdered and I couldn't help but think about the murders of two Marys in Houston," Mr. Griffin explained.

Pete and Darlene looked at each other and then at me. I knew what they were thinking.

"I didn't tell him about the cases. He figured it out himself." They were both still a bit suspicious of Eddie and probably assumed I'd told Eddie and that Eddie had blabbed it to Mr. Griffin.

"I keep my ear pretty close to the ground," he said with a good-natured smile.

"So what do these Mary murders have to do with our

cases?" Pete asked.

"I don't think they're related. I just thought they might make an interesting case study for what you're dealing with," Mr. Griffin said a little defensively.

"Hey, I'm open to any help we can get," Darlene said.

"Go ahead and fill us in," I told him.

"These murders took place in October of 2000. They made the papers around here because one of the victims had a sister in Tallahassee. Mary Henderson Morris was the first victim. She was forty-eight years old. Her body was discovered inside her burned-out car on the same day she was reported missing."

"How was she murdered?"

"They couldn't determine the cause of death. The body was burned too badly. What was puzzling was that she didn't appear to have any enemies. She worked at a bank and was well liked by everybody. Her husband seemed above suspicion.

"The next day, a call came in to the *Houston Chronical*. The caller said, quote, They got the wrong Mary Morris, unquote. No one thought much about the call until October 16 when Mary Lou Morris was found beaten and shot in her car less than twenty-five miles from where the first Mary was found."

"The details are different, but it does seem like a strange echo of our case. Were there suspects in Mary Lou's case?" I asked.

"Several, including both her husband and a strange admirer from her workplace. I think it was difficult for the detectives to ignore the coincidence of the two Marys, even though Houston, at the time, had a very high murder rate. There were something like three hundred per year in the city."

"And with the first Mary's murder not having any good suspects, it would be tempting to believe the caller who said that she was a mistake," Darlene said, reaching for a donut.

"Of course, the husband or some other suspect in the

second murder might have heard about the first murder and decided to call up the paper saying it was a mistake, just to confuse the issue and use it as a chance to kill Mary Lou Morris."

"That would be a great way to muddy up the waters," I mused.

"If the first murder was a mistake, then why call the newspaper and tell them? Definitely sounds like a play by someone wanting to kill the second Mary," Darlene said.

"There's always the Terminator explanation," Pete said.

"I'll terminate you," Darlene said, tossing a napkin at Pete.

"You'd want my marksmanship skills if there was a cybernetic assassin roaming the county." Pete threw the napkin back at her.

"The Houston detectives *did* entertain the possibility of a psycho killer picking Mary Morrises out of the phonebook," Mr. Griffin told us.

"Serial killers don't choose their victims by their names. That's the stuff of Agatha Christie," Darlene said.

"The bottom line is Houston never prosecuted anyone for the murders. They were featured on *Unsolved Mysteries* and the 'Murders of the Two Marys' are still heavily discussed on amateur sleuth forums."

"Great, let's hope they aren't talking about the two Elizabeths ten years from now." Pete frowned.

"The detectives didn't appear to make a lot of mistakes with the two cases. There just wasn't much clear evidence. There *was* one contradiction which seemed to point a finger at Mary Lou's husband. He had reported that his wife's ring was missing, but months later someone noticed that his daughter was wearing the same ring. He claimed they had found it weeks after the murder and he'd just failed to notify the police that it wasn't missing anymore."

"Hmmm," Darlene murmured with narrowed eyes. "I think I'd have gone after him pretty hot and heavy over that slip up."

"The problem was, he had a solid alibi for the murder. But another odd thing was that he made a four-minute call to her phone after it was determined she would have already been dead. He said he'd just let the phone ring for that long, hoping she'd pick up, but the phone carrier countered that it wouldn't have shown up on the records if no one had picked up."

"I assume the detectives looked into the hired killer angle. That might fit with the first murder being a mistake," I said.

"They looked into that possibility. In fact, they liked it because of the husband having a motive, but also a solid alibi. Needless to say, nothing came of the hitman theory."

"Hired killers are one of those tropes that, while they do happen, the murders seldom go off without a hitch," Pete pointed out.

"The trouble is, who has hundreds of thousands of dollars to pay for a good hitman? Pay five thousand dollars and you get a five-thousand-dollar hit that lands you and the triggerman in jail," Darlene said.

"Exactly," I agreed.

"Hitmen are for the Mob and drug dealers, not common folk," Pete said.

We thanked Mr. Griffin for his time, but I think we all believed his story hadn't added much to the investigation.

"We need a game plan or we're going to end up on unsolved mystery websites," I said after he was gone.

"I think we should each specialize," Pete suggested.

"I thought that's what we were doing with Larry and me concentrating on Elizabeth's murder and you working on Beth's," Darlene said.

"Someone should work on finding the connection between the two," Pete said.

"If there *is* a connection," I pointed out.

"So why don't *you* work on finding it?" Pete said, giving me a lopsided smile.

"What if there isn't a link between them?"

"We have to look at the possibility. Even if it's just to eliminate it." Darlene was clearly on Pete's side.

"Traitor," I said, giving her the stink eye.

"Why don't you want to work on it?" Pete asked.

"It just seems nebulous."

"It gives you free rein to explore both murders," Darlene said.

"Maybe." I was afraid I'd end up spinning my wheels or duplicating work they were doing. "If we go ahead with this plan, I want open lines of communication. I don't want to be ringing up a witness right after one of you interviews them."

Pete held up his phone. "I'm always a text away. We can have a group text to keep each other in the loop."

"I hate group texts," I mumbled.

"Then it's settled," Pete said with a smile.

"I'm going back to Tallahassee today. I want to interview Beth's co-workers and follow up on the rumor that she might have had a relationship with one of them," I said, remembering that I also needed to add a tuxedo fitting to my list. Thinking about the wedding and worrying about Cara, I glanced at Pete and had a brilliant idea. At least I thought it was brilliant. I made a note to corner him when we were done.

"I'll check with Dr. Darzi. If the autopsy is today, you might as well sit in on it too," Pete said. "I'll also make sure we get a sign up at the bridge, asking anyone who might have seen something to come forward. Maybe we'll catch a break and a driver will remember seeing something. And I'll interview her neighbors and friends to see if someone was stalking her."

"I'm going back over Elizabeth Collins's possessions, and I'll check in with her ex to see if he's made any progress getting the phone records," Darlene said.

We went over a few more details before the meeting broke up. I followed Pete to his desk. "How's Sarah doing?" I asked casually.

Pete looked at me. "She's fine. Next week is spring break,

so she and the girls are trying to figure out what to do with their time off." He hesitated for a moment, then asked, "Why?"

"Cara is stressing about the wedding prep, so I thought I might ask Sarah if she'd be willing to help out."

"Perfect timing. With the week off, the girls will probably pitch in too," Pete said. "She'll be home by four this afternoon. You can stop by and ask her when you get back from Tallahassee."

I gave him a pat on the arm. "Thanks." I was happy to think I'd worked out a solution to the wedding stress. As soon as I got measured for a tux, everything would be back on track.

"Let me call Darzi's office about the autopsy before you leave."

After a few minutes of chitchat, Pete was able to report that the autopsy had been scheduled for the afternoon. I could head over to Tallahassee, talk to the people at the dentist's office, get measured for my tux and then catch the show at the morgue. Perfect.

The office of Dr. Brant Forsyth, DDS, was in a large, single-story brick building that included an optometrist and a chiropractor. Inside, the place gave off the standard air of efficiency you'd expect from a dentist's office. There were a couple of people waiting patiently in the reception area, browsing on their phones. When I walked up to the receptionist's counter, the young lady slid aside a glass partition.

"Are you a new patient?" she asked, looking at me with an open expression.

"No," I said and showed her my badge. "I'm an investigator with the Adams County Sheriff's Office. I'm looking into the murder of Beth Robinson."

The receptionist physically recoiled, putting her hand up to her mouth. I felt a twinge of guilt as the young woman started to cry.

"I've been trying to hold it together," she said, attempting to choke back her sobs.

Another woman walked up from the back and gave me a dirty look before kneeling down next to the crying receptionist.

"This man just showed up. He's here about Beth," the receptionist managed to explain. From the look she gave me, this didn't change the other woman's opinion of me one little bit.

"Go on in the back. I'll take care of this." She helped the young woman up and gave her a gentle push toward a back hallway. The folks in the waiting area had stopped looking at their phones and were watching us.

"You really have some nerve." The woman, whose name badge read "Nicky Trent," pinned me down with angry eyes.

"I have a job to do," I said, trying to stand tall against her piercing eyes.

"You don't seem to be very good at it," she shot back.

For a moment, I thought about pointing out that all I'd done had been to explain why I was there. What else was I supposed to do? But I didn't see any point in trying to defend myself. I wasn't there to win friends. "I need to talk to everyone who knew Beth," I stated in a manner I thought wouldn't allow for argument. I was wrong.

"Today isn't the right day for that," Nicky said curtly.

"We can't hold up the investigation just to give everyone time to get comfortable with the idea that a co-worker has been murdered," I said, putting some grit into my words. I wasn't used to receiving this kind of resistance from friends of a victim.

Nicky Trent just stared at me, letting an angry silence grow. Eventually, she broke off her gaze and said, "Fine. I'll inform the doctor." Without another word, she turned and strode down the hall.

Dr. Forsyth, a tall, thin man in his late forties, came out next. He looked uncomfortable and, twice in short succession, ran his hand through his short blond hair. "You're from the police?" he asked.

I showed him my badge and explained again where I was from.

"I don't have a lot of time. I'm rendering a crown for a patient. Come on back to my office."

He opened the door that led from the reception area to the exam rooms. As we passed one of the exam rooms, I saw a dental hygienist working on a patient. I could just see a patch of green hair turning to brunette and paused a moment to stare. I could see the patient's reflection in a mirror, but it still took another second for my mind to register what I was seeing. When it did, I felt my blood pressure soaring. What the hell was Jessie doing here? *You better not be interfering in this investigation*, I thought. But I knew that was exactly what she was doing.

I tried to put the interloper out of my mind and focus on my interview with Dr. Forsyth. He ushered me into his broom closet of an office.

"Not much room, I'm afraid. I tried to make sure we had as much space as we could for the patients." He pointed to a chair and squeezed around his desk to sit down. "I can't believe that someone would hurt Beth. She was a such a sweet person."

I looked at him to see if there might be any underlying meaning to his comment. I did notice that he was wearing a wedding ring.

"How long had she worked for you?"

"Since she graduated from her dental hygiene program. I guess it's been almost eight years now." He looked appropriately upset. "She was an excellent hygienist. Could have been a dentist if she'd wanted to go back to school. I talked to her about it a couple of times. She always told me she'd wasted enough time in school. She'd gone to college right out of high school, then went back a few years later for her certification as a hygienist."

"Recently, had you noticed her acting any differently?"

Dr. Forsyth looked thoughtful. "Maybe. She was a pretty bubbly person. It's hard to quantify, but she did seem quieter this week."

"Any change in her routine? Coming in later? Leaving earlier?"

"No. She was always very punctual. Never stayed late. She was always in a hurry to see her boy."

"Any problems with anyone in the office?"

"Good grief, no. She got along with everyone."

"Was she especially close to anyone?"

"I don't know. I think she and Mia went to lunch together a lot."

"Mia?"

"She's our main receptionist," he said and I winced, thinking of the woman at the desk who had fallen apart.

"Mia seemed very upset."

"She has been ever since we heard about Beth. I tried to talk her into taking a few days off, but she took it upon herself to reschedule all of Beth's appointments with our other two hygienists."

Mia sounded like my best bet to learn about Beth's relationships. I hoped I hadn't burned my bridges with her.

"Have you seen anyone odd hanging around the office?"

"No."

"Any odd phone calls?"

"You'd have to ask Mia."

"No one has reported anything strange in the last month?"

Dr. Forsyth seemed to think about the question for a moment before shaking his head. "Nothing."

Next I moved on to the two hygienists. Mrs. Eve Colleen was exactly what you would expect central casting to send you if you asked for a middle-aged nurse who was all business. She had thin lips and dark eyes. I asked her the same questions I'd asked the doctor and her answers were almost the same.

"Was there anyone in the office Beth didn't get along

with?"

She looked me square in the eyes and said, "No. Everyone thought Beth was great."

Glenn Webster was a petite young man with effeminate mannerisms. Again I went through the same questions and received the same answers, until I asked him if Beth got along with everyone.

"I hate to be a tattletale," he said, leaning forward and his face breaking into a mischievous smile, "Beth and Eve have had words." His eyebrows went up.

"About what?" I asked, barely able to hide my surprise at this deviation from the script.

"Eve thought Beth was stealing her patients. See, about a year ago, Eve had surgery. Some woman's thing. Anyway, Mia split up her appointments between Beth and me. Almost all of the patients that Beth did a cleaning for made their next appointment with Beth and not Eve. Eve was very upset."

"Who do you think was to blame for the patients changing over?"

"They just liked Beth more. I mean, look at her…" Glenn seemed to realize what he'd said and looked chagrined and sad for the first time. "Look, I don't mean anything. Beth was pretty, perky and a darn good hygienist. I just think the patients liked her better."

"Maybe Mrs. Colleen didn't see it that way?"

"No." He heaved a big sigh. "Eve might have been jealous of Beth 'cause she was pretty, perky and a darn good hygienist."

"Were words exchanged about the poached clients?"

"I heard Beth and Eve have some pretty heated discussions. Once in our little break room and another time out in the parking lot."

"How long ago did these arguments take place?"

"The one in the parking lot was about a month ago." Glenn squirmed in his seat. "I really shouldn't have said anything. I can't see what it could have to do with Beth's death. I'm an awful gossip." He looked down at the floor.

"You're fine. I need information if we're going to figure out who killed Beth. I take everything I hear with a grain of salt," I reassured him.

"This is all just crazy. Poor Beth. And her son. What's going to become of him?" Glenn's eyes teared up.

"He's safe with his grandmother. If you think of anything else, please give me a call."

When I finished with Glenn, I considered confronting Eve Colleen about her conflict with Beth, but decided to keep it as an ace in the hole. I didn't think for a minute that an office tussle over clients had been the motive for this murder, but I might be able to use her white lie to shake more information out of her when I had a better idea what I was after.

Mia was the last of the office personnel that I talked to. Talked at was more like it. She made it clear she thought I was a jerk for surprising her at the front desk, and that she didn't want to humor me by answering any of my questions.

"I'm trying to find out who killed your friend," I argued after receiving several one-word answers to my questions.

"You aren't going to find them here," she sneered.

"I need as much information about Beth as I can get."

"You're just looking for people to harass. Somebody out there," she pointed to the window, "killed Beth. Everyone here loved her." More tears.

I appreciated her grief. What was pissing me off was her inability to see that any information I could gather was important to solving the case.

"Eliminating everyone here as a suspect will go a long way toward moving the investigation along," I said, trying to reason with her.

"Fine! No one here is guilty! You can take my word for it." She clamped her mouth shut.

"At least tell me if you've noticed anyone hanging around the office. Maybe in the parking lot," I urged.

Stubborn as mule, she kept her mouth firmly closed, but

she did allow herself a slight headshake. I gave up.

I looked around for Jessie as I made my way back to the reception area, but she'd long cleared out of the exam room. I was looking forward to catching up with her and giving her a good dressing-down. The last thing we needed was a loose cannon mucking up the investigations.

I had reached the front door when Dr. Forsyth caught up with me. "Let us know when you learn something about Beth's murder," he said with genuine concern in his eyes.

"I will," I assured him.

# CHAPTER TWELVE

Once outside, I noticed a note had been slipped under my wiper blades. I could practically feel the steam coming out of my ears as I read it: *Meet me in the Publix parking lot. J-CI.*

"CI my ass," I muttered.

The Publix was across the street. Grinding my teeth, I got into my car and drove over to find Jessie sitting in a blue Dodge Dakota. I had to tell myself several times not to go ballistic as I walked toward her truck. She smiled and gave me a quick wave. I stopped at the driver's door and knocked on the window.

"Get in," she said after rolling the window down a couple of inches.

"You need to stay away from our investigation," I said firmly, ignoring her invitation to get in the truck.

"You don't want them to see us talking, do you?" Jessie asked, glancing over at the dentist's office across the street.

"Frankly, I don't give a damn. You aren't—"

"How far did you get with Mia?" she interrupted.

"None of your business. Nothing about this investigation is any of your business."

"She sure was P.O.'d at you. I bet she didn't tell you much."

"How dense are you?" I said, perplexed at her attitude. She seemed able to completely disregard my fury.

"She's a friend of my sister. Mia and I are going out to a club next Saturday. I bet I can learn a whole bunch about her relationship with Beth. Get in and we can plan what I should ask her."

Unbelievably, I found a part of myself listening to her. I took a few deep breaths and tried to think this through. The woman was clearly off her rocker, but she had a valid point. It was possible that she could become a worthy successor to Eddie, who had never been tied down tight.

*No*, I told myself. *The risks are too high.*

"You are not to meet with Mia," I said, staring hard at her.

She had the gall to smile at me. "Eddie gave me your cell phone number. I'll text you with anything I find out." Jessie started the ignition. "You won't regret this." She almost drove over my feet as she pulled away.

I was too stunned to come up with a response. Even more angry than before, I stomped over to my car and got behind the wheel. "This isn't over," I said to no one.

On the way to the menswear shop to try on tuxedos, I went over a dozen different responses I might have tried. I deemed all of them inappropriate or unproductive. I had come to realize that it was going to take a targeted response to shut Jessie down. I just had to figure out the right one.

Getting measured for my tux left me feeling out of my element and uncomfortable. I survived, but the experience actually left me looking forward to my next meeting at the morgue.

"I thought this was the big man's case?" Dr. Darzi greeted me.

"We're doing our casework family-style now," I said, still feeling irritated at Jessie and awkward from the fitting.

"It doesn't matter to me." Darzi turned to the body of Beth Robinson, which was laid out on the stainless steel table beside him.

I walked up and took a position across the table from him. I wondered if this was the same table that Elizabeth Collins had been on.

Dr. Darzi managed to combine a respect for the deceased with scientific detachment. "I always start at the left side and move down the body left to right. Never covering more than six inches at a time," he'd once told me. "Being methodical is the key to being accurate."

Today was no different. He started at the top of the head and moved slowly left to right.

"Here are several fractures to the skull." He left the table and started to wheel over a portable X-ray machine. I'd seen him use it a few times. Within seconds of taking the images, he'd be able to look at them on the monitors mounted on the wall.

"I've got that!" Linda jumped up from the desk where she'd been typing notes on another case. On her way over, she automatically replaced the protective garments she was wearing with new ones. *How many of these paper suits do they go through every year?* I wondered. Of course, I'd seen the bill they sent to the sheriff's office.

"Take your time," Darzi said to Linda, leaving the machine where it was. "I'll continue examining the body. We can take the X-rays before we turn the body over. Why don't you load up your fall simulations? Larry might like to see them."

I watched in silence as he poked, prodded and photographed different parts of Beth's corpse. Linda fiddled with a laptop, then rolled it and the X-ray machine over to us.

"The doc was referring to a simulation program I found. I've loaded it with the data from the crime scene. Watch."

I looked up at one of the monitors while Linda clicked keys on the laptop. It displayed a rough mock-up of the bridge and creek. "I took measurements of the guardrail and the height of the bridge." She clicked a few more keys and a featureless female figure appeared at the railing of the bridge.

"I ran half a dozen scenarios. We'll have to wait until the autopsy is complete and match the data from the victim to the simulated injuries of the various scenarios."

I watched as she made the figure suffer through different permeations of falls. There were ones where the figure jumped, fell forward or fell backward. Linda hit a few more keys and another figure appeared on the screen, proceeding to shove and throw the woman figure off of the bridge. On the right of the screen, as each scenario played out, was a list of possible injuries and their severity.

"Pretty cool, right?"

"I'm impressed," I agreed.

"Do not stroke her ego. There are days she can barely fit her big head through the doorway," Darzi joked gently. "We are ready for the X-rays."

They performed a strange dance around the body, moving the machine so it would take images of the head from different angles. When they were finished with the front of the skull, they turned the body and repeated the same routine with the back of the head.

Linda rolled the X-ray machine away while Darzi stared at the monitors and clicked through the images.

"Interesting," he said as he clicked. "There." He walked up to the monitor and circled an area with his finger for my benefit. "This indicates a blow to the head that would have been damaging enough to incapacitate her, possibly even kill her."

I tried to figure out exactly where the fractures were. "Is that the front of the skull?"

"Correct. Also, look at the length. Fractures here to here." He ran his finger along the monitor. "I doubt that was from a rock. Now over here," he pointed to another image on the monitor, "this damage. That could have resulted from landing on the rocks in the creek."

"So you're saying that someone hit her with an object before she went off the bridge."

"Yes. It is very sad, but I think Linda wasted her time

with the computer graphics. Simple forensics tells us that someone clubbed her with a blunt instrument before she fell, or was tossed, from the bridge."

"Ah, contraire! My work was *not* wasted. We can now show that the damage from the blow couldn't have resulted from falling off the bridge. Some prosecuting attorney is going to be very grateful for my hard work," Linda scoffed.

"Maybe your salary can come out of his budget," Darzi said. He was back at the exam table, running his hand slowly down Beth's back.

"Do you think these injuries are consistent with the head wound that killed Elizabeth Collins?" I asked.

"I can't say for sure until I've done precise measurements. But I don't see anything now that would exclude it. I'll do the same 3D modeling that I did with Elizabeth Collins. A comparison should be conclusive."

"Besides the fact that they were both clubbed in the head, can you think of any other similarities between this body and that of Elizabeth Collins?" I asked, receiving the same skeptical look from Darzi and Linda.

"Pull Elizabeth Collins's records," Darzi said to Linda, deciding to humor me.

Linda went back to her laptop, but in the end the only thing that was similar appeared to be the weapon used. Nothing else suggested that the same killer was involved, or ruled it out as a possibility.


Once I was back in Calhoun, I stopped at Pete's house.

"What brings you around here?" Sarah Henley said with a wide smile. Physically, Sarah and Pete were opposites. He was tall with too much gut, while she was short and fine-boned. Both shared the same good natures and big hearts.

"I have a favor to ask of you. Cara is pretty worked up about the wedding preparations. Her mom and dad are busy with some things down at their co-op in Gainesville, which honestly is probably for the best. Her mother in particular tends to stress Cara out more than help. What I was hoping is that you might offer to assist Cara with some of the planning," I explained, with what I hoped was a humble and desperate expression on my face.

To my surprise, Sarah's smile faded as she pinned me down with narrowed eyes. "I will not," she stated, leaving me stunned. I had thought she might waffle a bit or make some excuses about being busy at work, but I never anticipated a flat-out refusal.

"Oh, well…" I stammered, my mouth hanging open a bit.

"Larry Macklin, you should be ashamed of yourself. Cara is perfectly capable of planning that wedding by herself. If she's stressed out, it's because you aren't involved enough in the process." Her eyes softened a little. "That's what every bride wants. She wants her future husband to act like the wedding is as big a deal to him as it is to her."

I cringed a little inside. As soon as she spoke the words, I knew that she was right and I had been acting like a jerk.

Sarah saw the look on my face. "And don't give me any crap about the planning being girly. Cara doesn't care one bit whether you pick the green or the blue, or the chicken or the beef. She just wants you to be there with her. If you don't care about the ceremony that's going to bind you both together for the rest of your lives, what hope does she have that you'll care about your *life* together? Before the wedding, men worry about how married life is going to change them and their lifestyle. Women worry about whether they're marring the right guy. So they look for signs. Signs like whether he's spending time with her, or whether he's interested in what the ceremony will be like." She leaned back with her arms crossed on her chest.

"I get it," I said, feeling like a ten-year-old whose mother has explained why they have to walk down to the light to cross the street. I drove away from the Henley house an older and wiser man.

"Your wife is tough," I told Pete when I found him at his

desk.

"Like I don't know that. Sarah doesn't let me get away with anything."

I filled him in on what I'd learned that day. I debated telling him about Jessie, but decided to keep it to myself for now. With some luck, maybe I'd be able to head her off at the pass.

I spent an hour sorting through some cases that were in my inbox before leaving the office. I called Cara. "I'm heading home."

"I'm going to be late. We just got a call that one of our clients' dogs was hit by a car. They live out in the country, so they probably won't be here for another twenty minutes."

"I hope it's not too bad."

"Me too. It's a really sweet black Lab named Boris." I could hear the emotion in her voice. I forgot sometimes that her job could be as demanding as mine. That thought made me even more determined to follow through on Sarah's advice.

I got home and fed Alvin and Ivy before mixing up a salad and seasoning the two steaks I'd bought on the way. I put the steaks in the refrigerator so they'd be ready to put in a frying pan when I was sure Cara was on her way home.

Cara finally walked through the front door three hours later. "Wow, I needed this," she said, smelling the food and giving me a quick hug. "I'll change and be right back."

"Was the Lab okay?"

"A broken leg, but he'll be fine," she said from the other room.

"I got fitted for my tux," I said after we'd both taken the edge off our hunger.

"Good. There's something else we need to do," she said, her voice telling me that it was another thing I wasn't going to enjoy.

"Oh?" I said, trying to be open to whatever it was.

"We have to meet with Reverend Pritchard."

"I thought you already met with him?"

"And he agreed to do the service on the condition that we meet with him together as a couple. I think it's a pretty standard condition."

"Sure," I said, remembering what Sarah had told me. "I guess we can do it anytime."

"He's free in the morning."

"Tomorrow?" I said, just managing to keep the reluctance out of my voice.

"Yep. It's Saturday and we both have the day off." Cara knew she'd set up the classic ambush.

"You got me."

"It won't be that bad."

"He seems like a nice enough guy."

"You've been to his church?"

"With Dad. First Presbyterian is one of the churches he circulates through regularly." Dad went to church almost every Sunday, and seldom to the same one in a month. It helped him keep up with what was really going on in different communities throughout the county. "When Mom was alive, that was the church we went to. Of course, there was a different minister then."

Cara smiled at me and moved her chair closer. We finished the meal side by side.

# CHAPTER THIRTEEN

We were on our way to the church by nine-thirty Saturday morning.

"I want to take part of the afternoon to talk with Eddie."

"About that woman?" Cara asked. I'd given her a brief recap of my encounter with Jessie.

"Exactly. You can ride along if you want."

When we pulled up at the church, I thought about how much it looked like a time capsule. While there had been restoration and maintenance work done on the building and grounds over the years, everything still looked exactly as it had when Mom and Dad had brought me to Sunday school.

"This building was built in the 1870s after a fire destroyed the original church."

"It's classic," Cara said, looking at the muscular white columns that held up the roof over the brick building.

"We could always get married here," I suggested.

"Are you kidding? The contract is already signed with the Grove! Besides… I know it's chancy to have an outdoor ceremony, but it's probably safer than taking Mom and Dad inside a traditional church," she said with a grin, only half joking.

Walking to the church office, we saw Reverend Pritchard

dressed in jeans and helping several men manhandle a deep freezer into the kitchen at the back of the dining hall. I trotted over, but I was too late to help much. Several of the men were familiar to me. They all knew Dad, and I got pats on the back and handshakes.

"Sorry about that," Pritchard said, wiping his hands on his jeans. "Come on back to the office."

The small room was filled with three large bookcases stuffed randomly with books on religion, community, psychology and relationships. Most of them looked like they'd been loaned out several times. Here and there around the room were children's drawings and various odds and ends that spoke of special moments in Pritchard's time as the church's guiding hand.

"Marriage," he said solemnly, once we were all seated. "It's a big deal. But I can see that you aren't children. I know you a little bit from your visits to the church with you father." He nodded at me, then gave Cara a big smile. "And I know *you* as Annabelle's favorite vet tech."

"Annabelle is his Collie," Cara informed me. "She's a very serious dog."

"You're right about that. She thinks more than a dog should, and I'm afraid she's a bit judgmental when it comes to people. I've lectured her several times about it. At least you've passed muster with her." He paused for a moment before continuing in a serious tone. "I don't really like to marry people I don't know. Of course, what goes on between a couple in private is much different than their public persona. Still, I have more confidence when I've spent time with them. Honestly, when you called I almost didn't agree. However, you're both well known in the community. After a few discreet inquiries, I felt better about performing the ceremony. Still, with every couple I like to sit down and talk to them about their understanding of the institution of marriage."

I must have looked a little stunned. I hadn't expected this to be much more than a meet-and-greet, but now we were getting a lecture on what it meant to be married.

"You do understand that it's an institution?" the reverend asked me. He must have thought my expression was in response to what he'd been saying and not my overall surprise at the nature of the meeting.

"Well, I guess..." I stumbled over my thoughts, uncomfortable with the teacher singling me out.

"We could love and have children without ever involving the church or state. Many people do. But you've come to me wanting the church and state to legalize the bond between you. Why? What does this mean to both of you?"

I wanted to bolt for the door. I felt like a kid showing up to class unprepared on test day. So I did the only thing I could think of and turned to Cara, as though the question had been specifically directed at her. She looked at me with a *don't-throw-me-in-the-fire* expression, then turned to Pritchard.

"I think I want the marriage to be... official because I want everyone to know that we're a family," Cara said, sounding only a little uncertain.

"A good answer," Pritchard commended her. "It's a recognition of your commitment to each other in front of your friends and neighbors and the church. When you are married, like with any institution, there are expectations about how you will behave toward each other, and as a couple in your community."

The question-and-answer session went on for a while. Before it was over, Cara and I were acting like fifth graders trying to beat each other out with the right response.

"There's one last thing I want to talk to you about," Pritchard said, an amused smile still on his face. "Our congregation has many members who are first responders... and I've spent time counseling them about their relationships. Both of you are in jobs that can be extremely stressful. What I want you to think about is creating a home that is a sanctuary of love. A place where you both feel safe. Where you can talk about your stressful jobs and receive love and approbation from your partner. It takes hard work to create a home that feels safe and that you long to return to every day. Think about what it feels like to be received into your partner's warm embrace. Remember that feeling and try to make your home just as warm and inviting to each other in the future as that hug is to you now. Inviting God into your home is important. He is someone you can both turn to when it's difficult to talk to each other."

"I've seen how hard it is for some of my fellow deputies to be in a relationship," I said, reaching out and taking Cara's hand. "So I appreciate what you're saying. I think we can do this."

"I *know* we can," Cara said, squeezing my hand.

Pritchard looked back and forth between us and a smile spread across his face.

"One more bit of advice, and this comes from my own experience as a married man. Practice forgiving. It's not an easy skill to master. In a marriage, there will be times when your power to forgive is the only thing that can save your union." He put his hands down on his desk and stood up. "Now for the commercial. Coming to church and being a member of our family can be an asset as well. Eleven o'clock every Sunday, rain or shine."

Back in the car, I leaned over and gave Cara a kiss. "We fooled him," I said, and got shoved back onto my side of the car.

"You're bad. I was surprised you didn't burst into flames in there." She laughed.

"We were just in the office. If we'd gone into the sanctuary…" I made incendiary motions with my hands.

"Start the car, silly."

As we rolled out of the parking lot, I turned to Cara. "I'm glad we came and talked with him," I said seriously. "The size of the commitment we're making to each other scares the hell out of me when I think about it. It's good to know we aren't alone."

"You know what's funny? Sometimes when I look into the future of our lives together, I can see us facing tough times, but we're always there for each other, so it's all right." Cara leaned across the seat and put her head on my shoulder.

When I pulled into the library's parking lot, I looked around nervously for Jessie's truck. Relieved that it wasn't there, I parked the car. We found Eddie shelving books in fiction. I let him finish replacing a hefty book by Stephen King, then tapped him on the shoulder.

"I want to talk to you about your little friend."

"*My* friend? I explained all that to you. And she's already told me that you've got her doing undercover work or something," Eddie said with a shake of his head. "I told you to be careful."

"I *don't* have her doing anything for me. She hasn't given me the chance to—"

"Hey, soon-to-be Mrs. Macklin," Eddie cut me off and turned to Cara. "I haven't gotten my invitation yet," he said with downcast eyes.

"I'll give you an invite…" I said threateningly.

"Larry!" Cara chastised me. "We *should* invite him. I'm pretty sure he's helped save your life a time or two."

"That's right!" Eddie piped up.

"Fine. You'll get an invitation," I conceded. "But right now I need to know everything you've got on Jessie."

"You're getting your former CI to rat out your current CI. That's very meta."

"Let me be crystal clear. She is *not* my CI."

"Not what she says," he shot back.

I gripped my hands into fists in frustration. The problem was that, while I absolutely did not want Jessie interfering with the investigation, I was interested in spite of myself to see if she could learn anything from Mia. The receptionist had taken such a dislike to me that I didn't stand a chance of getting anything from her. When I ran it all over in my head, it did kind of sound like I wanted Jessie to act as a CI.

"Never mind that. I just need to know more about her," I

told him.

"If you're going to raise your voice, then we better go in the back," Eddie said, sounding like a schoolteacher.

I thought of a few snappy comebacks, but just bit my tongue and followed him into a small meeting room.

"While you boys talk, I'll check out the new books," Cara said with a smile and a wave.

"Tell me anything you can about Jessie," I told Eddie once we were seated at the table.

"Don't be pushy. I really don't know that much. She lived in Virginia for a while. Her father was in the Navy. Apparently a real asshole."

"Both of you had assholes for fathers. See, you *do* have something in common," I said brightly.

"Yeah, right. Anyway, they moved to Jacksonville at one point. That's how she got to Florida. Her dad was assigned to the Naval Air Station. I guess she was in her teens when she ran away. Got caught, ran away again. Got in trouble. You know the drill."

"See, you're made for each other."

Eddie's face turned red. "Knock it off," he said it with enough heat to make me feel bad for teasing him… but not that bad.

"Go on."

"She told me she went straight at some point and found herself in Tallahassee. People helped her out. She went to Tallahassee Community College, blah, blah, blah."

"Why is she so interested in this case?"

"She did know Beth a little. I mean, I want to see the asshole who killed her caught too." Eddie was serious.

"Understood. But this whole CI thing…" I noticed Eddie's face turning red.

"I might have made too big of a deal about being a CI," he said, looking sheepish.

"Thanks a lot," I sighed.

"She's really interested in true crime. Reads about it all the time and when she first started working here, I… maybe

I might sorta like her."

"So you used your work for me to talk her up and now I'm stuck with her."

"I didn't know how crazy she is. I've never known anyone so… excitable. Sometimes she's like a meth-head who's downed a case of Red Bull. Crazy."

"Meth? Do you think she does drugs?"

"She's clean. She says she used a lot when she was younger, but I think that's mostly talk," Eddie said. *That's something at least*, I thought.

"What's she do when she's not working here?"

"Goes to Tallahassee and listens to bands. Reads books."

"You follow her on social media?"

"She's not into it."

"Seriously?" I wasn't sure I'd met a person her age who wasn't glued to their phone, Twittering, Instagramming or whatever.

"I said something once and she got real defensive."

"Seems odd."

"I knew a guy. I just cross-dress, but he was into the drag thing. I met him online. He was pretty out there, kind of like Jessie. I don't remember what it was all about, but some people started picking on him and it blew up until he just shut his accounts down. That's the vibe I got from Jessie."

"Where's she live?"

"She's got a room in a house with two other girls. It's behind the Supersave."

The neighborhood behind the supermarket was made up of several modest starter homes that some folks had kept and rented out after they'd graduated to a higher standard of living. I decided to drive by the area first chance I got. I also wanted to run a full background check on Jessie. If she was going to provide me with any useful information, I needed to know how reliable she was.

"Eddie, I need you to think. Is there anything else you know about Jessie that might be important for me to know?" I stared hard into his eyes, trying to impart how important the question was.

"Like what?" he said in a small voice.

"Like... I don't know... Have you seen her with any shady people? Or with more money than you think she should have? Come on, Eddie, you know what trouble looks like."

"No, she just talks a lot and is real excitable."

On that note, I rejoined Cara at the front desk where she was checking out a few books. "Find out what you needed to know?" she asked me.

"Maybe."

"You seem mighty worked up about this woman."

"She's just driving me crazy."

"You worked with Eddie. I'd think you could work with anyone," Cara said, not without a considerable amount of truth.

"Jessie is a loose cannon."

"Then why are you dealing with her at all?" Cara asked as we got into the car.

"Maybe loose cannon was the wrong analogy. A loose cannon can only do damage. Since we don't have any strong evidence, it feels like the investigation, or investigations plural, is in danger of getting away from us. Jessie has a tie to someone at Beth Robinson's job so, who knows, maybe she'll luck into something," I said, turning in the direction of the Supersave.

"So what you really don't like is that you don't have any control over her," Cara observed with stunning accuracy. I looked at her and nodded.

"I guess you're right. With Eddie, I always knew that I could wave a little money in front of him and he'd listen to me. With Jessie... not so much."

"You're going to have to make up your mind. Do you trust her? If you do, then you have to let her do her thing."

"That's easy to say when you're talking about painting pictures or planting a garden. Someone acting as a CI can get killed. I need to know that she'll listen to me if things get dangerous." Which was all true. Half of my concern was my inner control freak coming out, but the other half was genuine concern for Jessie's safety.

I took a left, went two blocks and took a right. Halfway down the block, I saw Jessie's truck parked behind a Prius in the driveway of a small, concrete block house. The yard was neat and the house looked well kept.

"Her place?" Cara asked, watching me stare at the house.

"Yep." The way someone lived could be a big clue about their personality.

I sped up and headed back to the main drag.

"What's the verdict?" Cara asked.

"No red flags."

"You expected to see a bong in the window?"

"You'd be surprised," I said, just as my phone rang. I hadn't put it on the dash mount and fumbled with the case attached to my waist for moment before I could answer. "Macklin."

Nothing. I looked at the number and saw that it was from dispatch. After a couple more useless hellos, I ended the call and hit redial.

"Adams County 911. What's your emergency?" I recognized Marti's voice.

"Hey, it's Larry. I just got a call from you?"

"I transferred a call. It came in on the non-emergency line. A woman who wanted to talk to someone investigating the Beth Robinson and Elizabeth Collins murders."

"She said that? Mentioned both murders?"

"She did."

"What was her name?"

"Didn't say. I asked twice."

"There wasn't anyone on the line when I answered."

"I can give you the number she called in from."

I pulled to the side of the road to write the number down. Marti read it off.

"Is there a recording of the call?" I asked.

"No, since it didn't come in as an emergency."

"If she calls back, please do your best to keep her on the line."

"Ten-four."

I hung up and tried the number. There was no answer and voicemail wasn't set up. I had a bad feeling about the whole thing.

"A tip?" Cara asked.

"Maybe." *If I hadn't fumbled the phone when I answered it, would the caller have still been on the line?* I wondered.

"If it was important, they'll call back," Cara said in her best supportive voice.

"I hope so," I said, trying to ignore the possibility that I'd just missed a big break in both cases.

# CHAPTER FOURTEEN

When I got to the office on Monday, Darlene was already at her desk, pounding away at the keyboard.

"You're making the rest of us look bad," I said, peering over her shoulder. There was a pile of reports on the left side of the desk and a much smaller one on the right.

"I've been here since five trying to clear out as many reports as I can. I'm going to spend most of the week on the Elizabeth Collins case."

"My goal for the week is to find that elusive connection between the two cases. So send me copies of any information on Elizabeth Collins. I'll tell Pete the same for Beth Robinson. Plus, I've got some angles of my own to explore."

"Go get 'em, tiger."

I told her about the call I'd received Saturday afternoon.

"Interesting that, whoever she was, she linked the two cases," Darlene said thoughtfully.

"My thoughts exactly."

I'd almost put my butt down in my chair when I got a text from Dad reminding me that Cara and I were going to have Mauser as a houseguest starting Thursday. I texted back a thumbs-up.

I sat down at my desk and sorted through a pile of reports from the previous week that still needed my attention. One was a domestic that had not-going-anywhere vibes coming off of it. Deputy Teresa Pelham had taken the report and she was very good at writing between the lines. What came through was that she was not happy neither party had been interested in pressing charges. Also salted throughout her narrative were hints that she thought the couple was involved in illegal drugs. *Great*, I thought, setting that one aside.

Two others were interesting because they appeared to be connected. Both hit-and-runs, they had occurred about the same time and in the same part of town late Wednesday night. One of them didn't involve anything other than property damage. That wasn't something an investigator would normally follow up on, but the second, more serious report was. Several young men had been hit by a vehicle and, while no one had been killed, three of them had been taken to the hospital for their injuries. Lt. Johnson must have had the same gut reaction I did when he assigned the cases to me.

I made a note of the address of the domestic abuse call and contact information for the hit-and-run witnesses. I needed to follow up with interviews soon.

"Hard at work?"

I looked up to see Pete holding out a greasy bag.

"I need everything you have on Beth Robinson's case."

"Can do," he said as I opened the bag to reveal two sticky, glazed donuts.

"You know how much this plays into the cop stereotype, right?" I asked, taking one out.

"I'm a living caricature." Pete smiled as he quickly devoured his donut. "I came in yesterday after church and made copies of the reports I've gotten so far."

He went to his desk and returned with a four-inch stack of folders. I started sorting through them, only to watch the pile grow as Darlene added reports of her own.

"My desk isn't big enough," I muttered as I tried to spread everything out.

I thought about using a table in one of the conference rooms, but that wasn't a long-term solution. The rooms were in constant use for interviews and meetings. Then I had a better idea and headed back to the new evidence area.

"Hey, trouble," Shantel said good-naturedly as she sat at a computer station, logging in evidence. She was taking individually labeled bags out of a large box and meticulously typing the information for each one into a database. "I've tried to talk your dad into letting us get a bar code system for logging evidence."

"How'd that go?"

"He pulled out the budget and showed me how much has been spent building all of this." She waved at the new space, which included a large, climate-controlled evidence room, several cold coolers, a reception area, open work space and three offices. "And he also reminded me that I've put in a request to have Marcus hired back full time."

Marcus Brown had worked alongside Shantel for several years and they'd made a great team. Unfortunately, his wife had taken a good job in Tallahassee and he'd gone to work for the Florida Department of Law Enforcement. But, after only a few months, he'd realized he'd made a mistake and asked to come back to work for us. With our budget stripped by the hurricane, the best Dad could do for now was let Marcus do some part-time work as an independent contractor while keeping his job at FDLE.

"What's the plan for that?"

"Your dad says we can hire Marcus full-time as soon as the new budget year starts in October."

I walked over to the wall of offices. The first was for Shantel as head of the department and it was already furnished. The second was being outfitted for Lionel West, our forensic IT guy. The third would eventually serve as an office for Marcus.

"You aren't using this space yet, right?" I asked casually.

Shantel stopped typing and looked over at me. "What are you thinking?" she asked suspiciously.

"I just noticed that you aren't using this room right now."

"That's going to be Marcus's office," she said firmly.

"He won't need it until October," I said, looking at the empty room. It was the perfect size for a couple of white boards and a large table.

"That doesn't have nothin' to do with that room. Get your head out of there."

"I just want to use it for a few weeks. Maybe a month."

"Oh no you don't. I know how things work around here. Once someone moves in, they never move out."

"Come on. It's not like I'm gonna put my desk in here or anything. I just want to lay out the evidence from the two Elizabeth cases."

"No way, Jose. Marcus is excited about having an office. I let you use it and every deputy in the department will be moving their stuff in there."

"It can be our little secret," I suggested.

Shantel huffed. "Since when have there been any secrets around here?"

"I know of one. At least it's a secret from the brass," I said, raising my eyebrows.

She frowned. "What?"

"A certain ankle weight."

"I don't know what you're talking about." She clenched her teeth and I thought I could see a flush of red beneath her mocha skin.

"I promise you'll get the room back."

She just looked at me, her mouth still clamped shut.

"Don't make me lay it all out. Blackmail is an ugly thing."

"You know the neighborhoods I have to work in," she finally said.

"I sympathize with you. But I don't think the brass, including my dad, would feel comfortable with you carrying a gun on the job."

"I've got my concealed carry permit."

"Oh, okay, that's fine then. I'll let Dad know," I said lightly.

"This is low, Macklin," Shantel said, giving me her dirtiest look.

"I need a place to lay out all the evidence relating to the two cases so I can work on making some connections."

"If there *are* any connections," she shot back.

"True. But I won't know if there are or aren't until I have a chance to spread everything out, map the cases out on a couple of white boards and look at them side by side."

"I'm in the crappiest neighborhoods in the county, wearing a polo shirt that has 'Sheriff's Office' written all over it, and I'm not allowed to carry a gun," she grumbled.

"And yet you do. Our little secret," I said, tapping the side of my nose.

"You're a mean one, Macklin," she said, making it sound more like a compliment than a complaint as she relented. She opened a drawer and retrieved a wire ring with two brand new keys hanging from it. She took one off and handed it to me. "That's *my* room and this is a one-month loan," she said pointedly.

I took the key, then raised my hand in a two-fingered Boy Scout salute. "Word of honor."

"We'll see what that's worth. I'm bringing a designated driver to your bachelor party on Friday and it'll cost you a fortune in booze."

"You've always been my bestie."

"Don't push it," she said with just a hint of a smile.

I spent the rest of the morning scrounging up the white boards and a table, then moving the files I had so far into the room. I wrote Beth Robinson's name on one of the boards and Elizabeth Collins's on the other, then I listed each person's known friends and hang-outs. The first thing that stuck out was that Beth's board was full, while there was a lot of extra space on Elizabeth's board.

I was organizing the reports on the table when Darlene came in.

"Nice work, Miss Marple," she said, admiring the white boards. "What's got Shantel's nose out of joint?"

"She's not very happy about me using this room," I said, and gave her a quick review of how I'd conned Shantel into it.

"Everybody in the department knows she's got that gun in her ankle holster," Darlene said.

"You're probably right. But the department has plausible deniability as long as no one shoves it under anyone's nose."

"She's got a point too. The tech team shows up at a crime scene and an hour later all the LEOs have gone off to attend to other business, leaving them alone in Crack Town at three in the morning."

"You're preaching to the choir. And, honestly, I'd trust Shantel with a gun before I would some of the LEOs I know."

"No connections yet," Darlene said, looking back at the boards. "Are those *all* of Elizabeth's friends and family?"

"And co-workers. She didn't get out much."

"How many degrees of separation are you going for?"

"What?"

"You've got Beth's people on this board and Elizabeth's on this one. No repeats. But maybe the connection is secondhand. Elizabeth's boss knows Beth's friend or something like that."

"True. We probably need to shoot for one degree. Everybody knows everybody around Tallahassee. If I looked hard enough, I could probably link everyone on the two boards using just two degrees of separation."

"You've got a point. Anything beyond one would be meaningless," Darlene agreed.

My phone rang with a call from dispatch

"You handling the Detrick domestic?" the dispatcher asked me. I groaned inwardly, knowing where this was going. "They're at it again. Moody is on scene."

"Tell him on I'm on my way," I said, irritated but trying not to lay too much of my mood on to the messenger.

Half an hour later, I was talking to a drug-addled twenty-something with bad teeth and wild eyes while her partner sat in the back of Deputy Ronald Moody's patrol car.

"Why you take drugs doesn't matter," I told her after she'd gone into a fifteen-minute review of her last eight years, starting with a softball injury in high school that had resulted in her first Oxy prescription.

"You can't take Nate to jail," she said. It was a phrase she'd put on repeat.

"If he hit you, then you need to file a report," I said for the fifth time.

"We just messed up," she moaned.

Deputy Moody left his charge and came over to us. He was one of the department's older deputies and looked like a black version of Santa Claus, but without the beard.

"Same old shit," he said after he'd pulled me away from the woman, who was now crying softly and hugging her knees.

"They're the classic drug couple, clinging to each other as they swirl down the drain," I said, frustrated.

"I pulled enough drugs off of both of them to put them away for a while. Don't think they can make bail," Moody said without enthusiasm.

"We do that, then they'll have time in jail to get sober. I don't see any reason to keep pushing her on the domestic complaints." The only reason they'd been fighting was because of the drugs. Their affected minds couldn't come up with any coherent plans that stretched more than an hour into the future. Their cravings and frustration had led them to strike out at one another.

"Waste of everyone's time," Moody said. His eyes reflected the pity he felt for them.

"Every once in a while, one of them makes it out alive."

Moody raised his eyebrows. "Not many. Gator Jones. He's the only one I can think of. Thought that dude would end up behind a dumpster with a needle in his arm for sure."

"He works for the Council for Hope now."

"Seen him yesterday. Dude is respectable." Moody looked at the man in the back of his patrol car. "Guess you never know."

We spent an hour getting them booked into the jail, then Moody and I hit the taco truck downtown for lunch.

"I thought you were a confirmed night owl?" I asked him as we ate our way through a tray of tacos and chips. Until recently, Moody had been one of the field training officers on the night shift.

"Kids are all in college now. They were the reason I started working nights. Momma and I agreed that one of us would be home all the time for them. She worked days, I worked nights. Twenty years of passing each other at the door."

"Must have been rough."

"Not that bad. Felt good that we were taking care of business, you know? I think the kids appreciated it. Didn't always show it, but there were a few times when one of them really needed Momma or me and they didn't have to go hunting for us. Not that I'm down on what other families do. We're all just tryin' to get by. Now both girls are in college and Ken is taking business classes and HVAC. He's got this five-year plan to have his own business."

"Nice."

"Anyway, a couple of months ago, I realized I didn't have to spend all my time in the dark."

"You like working days?"

"Yeah. I'm less likely to trip when I'm chasing some lowlife across somebody's yard." He chuckled.

"When's the last time you chased someone?" I asked, causing him to break out in a full-throated belly laugh.

"You got me! Ten years ago, I figured out that if I was an FTO then I could have someone young and gung-ho to do the legwork. Which reminds me, I need to tap the sergeant and see if I can get another trainee."

"Dad's put a freeze on hiring until the new fiscal year."

"Man, that's months away. I need a runner now," he said, only half kidding.

For the rest of the week, the Collins and Robinson cases got lost in the shuffle of our everyday work. I'd filled up my white boards and watched as the pile of reports from Darlene and Pete kept growing. I managed to find a couple of tenuous links between Beth and Elizabeth, but they all appeared very benign. Otherwise, I didn't have much time to spend on the cases.

Thursday dawned clear and cool, a perfect spring day in North Florida. Or at least it was perfect until I remembered that I needed to pick up Mauser in the afternoon.

Pete came by my desk just as I was finishing up reviewing reports from the night before. "Have you heard from your new CI recently?" he asked. I'd finally decided to mention that new development to Pete and Darlene as my concern about Saturday night continued to increase.

"Don't call her that. I'm still trying to figure out how to talk her out of her plans." Then I remembered something I'd meant to ask him about. "I was going through the reports on Elizabeth's murder yesterday… Did you ever think to see if there might be a link to that missing girl, Terri Miller?"

Pete frowned. "I can't see any possibility of that. The only connection I can see is that Terri spent time in the area where Elizabeth's body was found." He paused. "I'm afraid the Miller case is going to be the one that haunts me. More than four years I've had that report on my desk. Every month or so I try to find a new angle to explore. Drives me crazy. She just disappeared. Went out one day intending to go to the store and, poof, she was gone. Less than two blocks. Middle of the day and no one saw anything."

"I remember when it happened."

"She looks a little like my Jenny. And Jenny's getting close to the age that Terri was when she disappeared." Jenny was Pete's oldest daughter. "I think about that every time I talk to her parents."

"Every investigator has one of those cases."

"I know. I just pray that I can find her before her parents pass away and I'm in a retirement home."

"Anytime you want me to look through the case file, I'd be glad to. Fresh eyes and all."

"I may take you up on that after you get back from your honeymoon." He seemed to shake himself mentally, like a bear coming out of a mountain stream. A smile appeared on his face. "Are you ready for tomorrow?"

"What?"

"Your bachelor party. You better not forget."

"I'll be there," I said resignedly.

"You bet you will. We're picking you up," he said with a mischievous smile.

"That's not necessary," I assured him. I didn't know what he had planned, but he was scaring me.

"Forget it. We're picking you up so there won't be any 'I can't drink' nonsense from you."

"I'm not a big drinker."

"That's what's going to make it all the more fun," he promised.

"Now wait a—" Before I had a chance to finish, Lionel West joined us with an excited look on his dark face.

"Sorry it's taken me so long to get to it, but I've finally gone through Beth Robinson's phone. There's some good stuff on it," he said to Pete. "One thing in particular you both might be interested in."

"Lead on," Pete said and I followed them back to the glorified broom closet where Lionel currently worked.

"When are you moving into your new office in evidence?" I asked.

"I've still got the guys putting in the outlets and fiber optic cable. They were supposed to be done two weeks ago. You know, Shantel really isn't thrilled about you moving into that other office."

"I haven't moved in. I'm just using it for a little while."

"That's not what she said." He picked up Beth's cell phone. "I downloaded what I could off of it. We were damn lucky she didn't use a passcode to lock her phone. Texts, contacts, all that stuff, I've put it in a shared folder. What I couldn't do is get her Facebook password. But," he held the phone up with a grin on his face, "she was already logged in. You can scroll through it on the phone."

"Excellent," Pete said with eager eyes. He reached for the phone, but Lionel held it back.

"Big warning. If for any reason it logs out of Facebook, then you're done. Finished. You won't be able to get back in."

Pete got a concerned look on his face.

"So we can't close the app?" I asked.

"You can close the app, but if the phone goes dead or gets turned off, you won't be getting back in. Also, you could be screwed if Facebook or Apple does an update. As a precaution, I did turn off all the automatic updates."

"Let me see it." Pete held out his hand.

"Just remember that this is your only shot," Lionel said, then passed the phone to Pete.

"My eyes are getting old. I hate looking at things on a phone screen," Pete muttered as he began to scroll through Beth's Facebook page. "At least she was old enough to still be using Facebook. My daughters have already moved on to some new thing and informed Sarah and me that Facebook is for old people."

"Luckily, I never got on it," I said.

"We all know you're no fun," Pete said. "We'll need to write down all of her friends. This is going to be tedious as hell."

Pete started to explain how Facebook worked, but I held up a hand to stop him.

"I'm not completely ignorant. Cara uses it. She keeps up with all of the clinic's patients and her friends from school. She shows me posts all the time. Especially all the cute animal photos and funny memes."

"That's good, 'cause we're going to have to scroll through Beth's news feed regularly. It's not like you can get a list of all the posts she's liked. Checking it constantly is going to be the best way to see what she was following, what might have been going on in her life and who was in her inner circle. And we need to look at all of her messages."

"I might be able to find a way to print out her messages," Lionel offered and Pete handed him the phone. "I can screenshot her friends list as well." He tapped on the phone. "She had two hundred and thirty-two friends. As well as…" More tapping. "Ten unconfirmed friend requests, most of which look like spam."

We left the phone with Lionel, who said he'd have the printout in an hour, after which we could come get the phone and scroll through Beth's feed to our heart's content, or until we screwed up and the phone logged out of Facebook.

By four o'clock, I'd received half a dozen texts from Dad reminding me that I needed to pick up Mauser. I headed on out to his property, knowing that he wanted to get on the road.

"Hey, champ, you ready for the big game?" I asked Jimmy, who was waiting for me in the front yard.

"Champ!" he shouted, coming over to me and giving me a bear hug. His excitement was infectious. I heard the door open and Mauser came tearing across the lawn toward us. Jimmy started chasing him through the yard.

"Jimmy, you better slow down! You're going to be worn out before you even get to the games," Genie shouted cheerily as she carried a suitcase toward Dad's truck. Dad was right behind her with a large cooler that he seemed to be having trouble carrying.

"You know, they probably have food and drinks where you're going," I told him and received a dirty look in return.

"Don't start with me," he said, though there was only a little grumble in his tone. "You can carry Mauser's luggage out to the van."

I had already transferred the stuff I'd need for the weekend from my car to Mauser's old minivan. The elephant-dog was too big to fit in a regular vehicle. Anytime I took him anywhere, it had to be in his van.

"How much... Never mind." I'd started to ask how much stuff one dog needed, but I knew better. Ten minutes later, I'd put Mauser's toy bag, food bag and treat sack into the van. "Spoiled animal," I told him as he supervised my work.

There was one last set of hugs all around, then I loaded Mauser into the van and Genie, Jimmy and Dad packed themselves into his truck.

"Give it your all!" I told Jimmy through the rolled-down windows.

"I'll bring back ribbons!" he assured me, while Dad and Genie smiled and laughed. Not for the first time, I thought about how good Genie and her son were for Dad.

"If anything from your bachelor party ends up on the Internet, I'm going to hold you personally responsible," Dad said, his tone half serious.

"Pete's in charge," I said defensively.

Dad just pointed a finger at me and backed out of the driveway.

The reception at home was mixed. Alvin let out one of his few barks and ran through Mauser's legs excitedly, while Ivy took her place on the back of the couch and frowned down at the pair. For his part, Mauser only had eyes for Cara. They were old friends and he never seemed to hold her job at the vet against her.

After dinner and watching the animals settle in, I turned to Cara. "I'm going to ask you something that I never thought I would."

Cara looked at me from her side of the couch. "What?" she asked cautiously.

"Show me the ins and outs of Facebook."

"What?" she repeated, sounding shocked.

I explained the situation. "Pete and I are going to take turns watching Beth's page."

Cara chuckled and grabbed her phone. A brief demonstration of the various features quickly brought me up to speed. Though I had to agree with Pete on one thing. "This would be so much easier to read on a laptop screen."

"You need good eyes and small fingers," Cara said.

"I guess I should be glad we have what we have."

"You can find out a lot about someone from their Facebook page," Cara agreed.

Later, as we were lying in bed, I told her what Pete had promised. "They're driving me to my bachelor party."

"How wild is this thing going to get?"

"I won't let it get too out of hand."

"I wouldn't think that Pete would either. I mean, there's not going to be… strippers or anything, right?"

"Are you going to have strippers at your hen party?"

She hit me with a pillow. "You know I'm just having a little bridal shower at the office."

"I'm having the same thing, only at some venue that Pete's picked out and with a bunch of deputies. And no strippers. Though there are going to be plenty of women from the office. Shantel and Darlene will be there."

"I trust Shantel. I'm not so sure about Darlene."

"You got a point. Word has it that when she gets a few under her belt, she can go pretty wild."

"Now you're making your party sound more fun than mine," she said, poking me gently in the ribs and leaning in for a kiss.

## CHAPTER FIFTEEN

Just before noon on Friday, Pete and I were in my war room, talking about Beth's Facebook page. Pete had taken the phone home and spent most of the evening following her feed.

"I've started prioritizing her friends list. Reading through her messages, I could figure out which ones she'd had contact with recently and which ones are just one-offs or old friends from her past." He paused, looking at the phone. "It's just frustrating how this case seems to be losing all its momentum."

Pete's unflappable good humor seemed to be slipping. I thought about the Miller case and wondered if Pete was letting his frustration with one case bleed into another.

"You've had cases that simmered on the back burner for a while, but you've always managed to turn up the heat," I said, proud of my metaphor.

"Not always," he said, looking at the notes he'd made on the printouts Lionel had given us. "Remember Terri Miller."

"You said it yesterday. They are two different cases," I reminded him.

"And the Robinson case is even *more* exasperating."

"How so? Other than the fact we have two dead

Elizabeth Collinses."

"It lacks a… I don't know. It just feels like I haven't come to grips with anyone who could be a solid suspect."

"There's always the dentist's office. Jessie might turn up something," I said, hating myself for being willing to hope that wild card might actually learn something.

"I should have interviewed her coworkers." Pete saw my eyes narrow and held up his hand. "Not that I don't trust you. I just think it might have helped me feel like I was on solid ground."

"I can see that. Beth was definitely involved with someone at her job, but I don't know who. If Jessie doesn't give us anything, then we'll go in loaded for bear and see if we can shake things up."

"Can do. She's seeing this friend of Beth's tomorrow?"

"They're going to a club in Tallahassee."

"I'm already looking at expanding the interviews to all of her friends and the people she did volunteer work with. That will take some man hours. Just covering all the people she interacted with at the libraries will take a chunk of time." Mentioning time caused him to look at his watch. "Crap. I've got some errands to run. Tonight is your big night, you know." He winked at me.

"Don't do that."

"What?"

"The winking. It's creepy."

"Ahhh, you better loosen up before this evening," he said, handing me Beth's phone and heading for the door. "Tonight." His last comment was directed at Shantel, who seemed to have forgiven me for my intrusion into her space.

"Wouldn't miss it," she said without taking her eyes off of her monitor.

The thought of the bachelor party made me shudder. I didn't like being the center of attention.

I spent the next hour going through Beth's Facebook feed. Being a dental hygienist, a chunk of her friends were in the teeth business. Who knew that there were so many dental memes? Another portion of her feed focused on Florida State sports, with basketball and baseball dominating. Beyond that were dozens of posts from friends and relatives describing trips for fun and business. Cara had explained that the feed was run by some secret Facebook algorithm, which left me wondering what I was missing. Of course, that's why Pete and I had been spending so much time obsessed with the feed. I understood what Pete was feeling. Work came easier if you were sure you were making progress.

I was on my way to lunch when I was stopped by Randy Spears, who had been the responding deputy on the hit-and-run with injuries.

"Any luck identifying the vehicle involved?" he asked me.

"No. Did you see the other report?"

"The one about the parked car that was hit?"

"Exactly, a mile away and around the same time. Trouble is, we managed to get some paint scrapings off of the car. Whatever hit it was grey. Your victims described a car that was dark, possibly black, dark blue or green."

"Then there were two cars involved?"

"Or they aren't related. I pulled some security camera footage, I just haven't had the time to review it."

"I can do it," Spears volunteered.

"Works for me. There might be some other cameras I missed. Lionel has the footage."

"I'll check it out."

I called Cara and found out that she was getting ready to take her own lunch break. "Let's do it up big. I'll meet you at the Palmetto."

"You need to have a good meal since you're going to be drinking all night," she joked.

"Don't remind me."

Fifteen minutes later, our orders were in and we were grabbing homemade biscuits out of the basket the waitress had left on the table. In addition to the Mediterranean specialties that she'd opened with, Mary had recently added some Southern comfort foods to the menu.

"Is the clinic still in one piece?" I asked. Cara had taken Mauser to work with her that morning.

"He is being very well behaved. We have the one exam room that we don't use much. It has a Dutch door, so we put him in there and left the top half of the door open. He loves it. Everyone who walks by gives him a treat and makes a fuss over him."

"That boy is such an attention hog. Sorry to leave you alone with him all evening."

"Have fun tonight," Cara encouraged me.

"I will, though it seems odd that I feel like I'm doing it more to make Pete and the gang at work happy."

"Just be glad you have good friends."

I reached out and took her hand. "I *am* looking forward to marrying you."

"You should be." She laughed. "I really appreciate how much help you've been over the last week with the last of the planning."

"Just made me realize all the work you'd already done."

"It'll be here before you know it."

"When are your parents coming in?" My stomach lurched as I thought about them visiting again. The last time Henry and Anna Laursen had been in town, they'd brought their yurt and had camped out in our front yard for weeks.

"Don't sweat it. They are coming in at the last minute and can't stay long. The co-op is keeping them pretty busy right now."

"That's good news," I said, perking up.

"This is where I'm supposed to say they aren't that bad. Though I have to admit, that last visit wore me out."


The rest of the afternoon was spent trying to tie up some loose ends on various cases. I didn't make a lot of headway. People were always hard to track down on a Friday.

I stopped by Dad's to feed his horses, Finn and Mac, then headed home. Already tired and trying to psych myself up for the evening's festivities, I drove slowly with the windows rolled down and enjoyed the beautiful spring afternoon. Our twenty acres was about five miles from town, but the area was rural with a capital "R." I pulled into the long driveway leading to our house at the center of the property and stopped to open the gate.

As I got out, I thought I saw another vehicle disappear down a small dirt track on the property across the street from mine. It was odd, because I knew that the drive led to nothing more than a cleared area where Mr. Mitchell, the property owner, parked when he came out to hunt in the fall. I waited for a moment to see if whoever it was would come back out. They didn't. Maybe Mitchell was putting out corn in the feeders or setting up game cameras. Or both. I remembered him showing me a picture that one of his game cams had caught a couple of years ago of a black bear sleeping under the corn dispenser.

I decided I was being paranoid and drove the rest of the way up to the house. As I climbed up the steps to my deck, my phone rang.

"We'll be there at seven to pick you up," Pete said, sounding like his old self. One of Pete's superpowers was the ability to leave his work at the office.

"Really, you don't have to. I can drive myself to the party," I assured him.

"Not gonna happen. See you at seven."

Cara opened the door and the visiting house bear came charging out. He almost knocked me down as he headed for the yard, circled the trees a couple of times and came galloping back.

"Slow down or you're going to hurt yourself!" I yelled as he took the steps two at a time. Back on the deck, he bounced up and down on his front paws, crushing my feet in the process.

"See, Alvin, this is how a *real* dog greets his owner," I said to the Pug, who was standing calmly beside Cara with a bemused look on his smooshed face.

"I'm happy to see you too," Cara said, pulling me into a hug.

"I'm glad you don't run out in the yard and try to knock me down," I told her. "Where's Mauser's leash?"

"Inside," she said, a little puzzled. Most of the property was fenced, so we only put him on a leash if we were going to take him for a walk in the woods. Of course, he was never outside unsupervised. We'd agreed long ago that he wasn't trustworthy enough.

"I'm going to take him for a walk." As soon as I said it, I knew I'd have to tell Cara why. "I saw someone pull onto the Mitchell property. I just thought I'd take a walk and make sure no one's up to any funny business."

"You don't need to take Mauser for that," she said.

"If it *is* Mr. Mitchell, then he'll get a kick out of seeing Mauser and I won't feel like a spy."

"I'll come along too," Cara said.

I thought about trying to talk her out of it, but I knew there wasn't any use. "Sure."

Five minutes later, we were walking on the trail around the perimeter of our land. "I'm sure it's nothing," Cara said.

"You're probably right," I said, as Mauser tried to drag me over to a palmetto bush to sniff where a raccoon or coyote had been.

From the southeast corner of our property, we could see the dirt track onto Mitchell's land. I knew he had enough money to put in a real driveway and I'd asked him once why he didn't do it. He'd explained that if he put in a road, then he'd have people dumping garbage on his land, planting "happy weed," as he called it, or coming in to "neck."

"Stay back," I said, reining Mauser in. I thought I could see the glint of metal up by the road. "Take him." I handed Mauser's leash to Cara.

"Be careful," she whispered, sounding worried.

"Hey, I'm a cop," I said, trying to keep the mood light, but feeling for the Glock on my side all the same. I took out my star and hooked it onto my belt in plain sight.

I made my way slowly across the road and onto Mitchell's land. As soon as I could see the vehicle, a blue Dodge Dakota, my blood pressure rose. I gave up being stealthy and stomped the rest of the way down the trail.

Jessie wasn't in the truck.

"Where are you?" I shouted, trying to keep the anger out of my voice. I didn't want to sound so mad that she wouldn't come back to the truck. I didn't have time to chase her through the woods. "I know you're here, Jessie. Do you want me to have your truck towed?" I yelled.

I heard movement behind me and turned to see Cara and Mauser coming down the trail. "I could hear you yelling and figured it was safe."

"I don't know. This woman is crazy." Just then I caught a glimpse of acid green in the corner of my eye and saw Jessie slinking her way back to her truck, her eyes downcast.

"What are you doing here?" I asked, barely keeping my voice level.

"I..."

"What?"

"Wow, that is some dog!" She walked over to Mauser, who was now totally exhausted after his exciting day. He gave her a little wag of his tail as she approached.

"Forget the dog. I'm asking you what you think you're doing. You followed me, didn't you?"

"I was just practicing," she said softly as she scratched Mauser's ears.

"Look at me," I scolded her. "Practicing what?"

"Following people." She still refused to meet my gaze, focusing on Mauser, who happily accepted her attention.

"You're insane," I told her, for which I received a frown from Cara. "You can't go around following people. Particularly not me!"

She shrugged.

"I don't think I can trust you. I want you to call off the meeting with Mia from the dentist."

Finally, she looked up. Her face was flushed. "No!"

"I'm telling you, call it off!"

"I will not! You'll see what I can do." She started to move toward her truck, but I stepped in front of her.

"I don't know what you think you're playing at. You aren't Nancy Drew. You could get hurt sneaking around spying on people."

Jessie looked past me to her truck. "I'm sorry. I didn't mean to…" I think she wanted to say "spy on you," but since that would have clearly been a lie, she groped for something else. "Make you mad."

Cara reached out and touched my arm. I felt some of my tension relax.

"I don't know what to do with you," I said in a softer voice.

"Just let me go to the club with Mia. I'll find out something that will help, I promise. I know this wasn't very smart, but I'm really good at getting people to tell me stuff." She blurted the words with a great deal of sincerity and energy.

I thought about it for a long time. Pete and I *did* need some fresh information. Also, I was pretty sure that Mia wasn't dangerous.

"Fine. But don't overplay your hand. I'll only be a phone call away tomorrow night."

Her eyes lit up.

"Call me about an hour before you meet with her," I said firmly.

"I will."

After a few more assurances from her and some more stern warnings from me, she was driving away and I was left to wonder if I was making a huge mistake.

"You did the right thing," Cara said.

"I don't understand her. She's a grown woman, but she acts like she's twelve half the time." We started back to the house.

"She does seem a little… immature."

Back at the house, I showered and changed clothes. At ten minutes to seven, I heard the rumble of a diesel engine coming up my driveway. When I stepped out on the front deck, I could see an Army-green MRAP tactical vehicle grinding its way toward the house. Pete's head was sticking out of the hatch on top.

"Is this cool or what?" he shouted.

"Where the hell did you get that?"

"It belongs to my friend, A.J. He and his hunting buddies bought it a couple of years ago."

A.J. waved at me through the small metal port in front of the driver's seat. I had to admit that the little boy in me was impressed. Cara joined me on the deck and couldn't contain her laughter.

"Climb on up, groom boy," Pete said.

"Can't I just use the door in back?"

"Yeah, no, it doesn't work real well. They've been meaning to re-weld the hinges on. Just climb up."

I waved to the still-chuckling Cara, then did as instructed. Inside I found Darlene and Hondo. Both of them looked like they'd already had a drink or two.

"I'd offer you a beer, but I'm not sure what the open container law is in an MRAP," Darlene shouted over the roar of the diesel engine as A.J. picked up speed on the main road heading back to town.

When the vehicle finally stopped, I climbed through the hatch to find that we were parked in front of the old Woolworth's building on the square, though it hadn't been a retail store for more than a decade.

"The owner has been fixing it up as a party venue. We got a great deal on the rental by doing some of the work for him," Pete said with pride as he stuck a cowboy hat on my head. I reached up to take it off. "Don't be a party pooper."

With a theatrical sigh, I left the hat on. Pete, Darlene and Hondo pushed me through the door and into the party. A small cheer went up. As my eyes adjusted to the dim lighting,

I saw a couple dozen deputies and old friends.

"More are coming," Pete assured me.

Shantel and Marcus were sitting in the middle of the room, drinking fancy island drinks.

"Vikki is a pretty good bartender," Marcus said, holding his glass up and pointing to a twelve-foot bar set up in one corner of the room. Behind the counter was Vikki Price, a trooper with the highway patrol.

My eyes narrowed when I recognized the back of a man grazing at the buffet table. "You invited Eddie?" I asked Pete. I had to raise my voice to be heard over the '80s and '90s pop that an unseen DJ was blaring.

"Hey, he's a friend. I thought you might be feeling nostalgic for your old CI. Especially since your new relationship is bit rocky."

"She's not my CI, but you have a point." I'd filled him in on Jessie's recent attempt at undercover work on the trip in the MRAP.

I looked up to see Julio Ortiz walk in. He made a beeline for me.

"I wanted to give you this before the party got started," he said, holding out a business card. I took it, wondering what this was all about.

"My brother-in-law sells insurance." I must have made a face, because Julio quickly said, "No, nothin' like that. He has his own company and was the president of the Florida state association a couple of years ago. He testifies before the insurance commission all the time. I told him where I was going tonight and he asked for you to call him. He said a married man should have life insurance for his family."

I felt a hand on my back. Pete had joined us. "Julio's right. A year into my marriage, when Sarah was expecting, I got my first life insurance policy. Time to think about some of that grown-up stuff, buddy." He looked at Julio. "I didn't know your brother-in-law was a big time insurance guy. Lot of money in that. You got another card?"

I left Julio and Pete talking insurance while I wandered

off to another group of friends. Buying life insurance seemed much too heavy to think about right then.

I had to admit, the evening was more fun than I thought it would be. Pete had invited a handful of friends from high school that I hadn't seen in years. I was happy that they managed to keep the embarrassing stories to a minimum. I did have to remind Pete and Darlene several times of Dad's warning about compromising photos on social media.

About eleven o'clock, I felt all the drinks I'd had settle over me. I'd managed to edge my way out of the limelight and was watching everyone drink, dance and tell tall tales of law enforcement, but now my head started to swim and I decided I needed fresh air. I managed to escape without anyone seeing me.

Outside, the air had turned damp and chilly. I looked up and saw the glow of the streetlights reflected off of low-hanging clouds. Even with the cool air, my head still felt a bit mushy, so I decided to take a walk. I made it halfway around the square before I caught sight of something that made me choke up. I walked over to the bench and ran my hand across the brass plate that read: *In Memoriam – DEA Agent Matt Greene.*

I sat down on the bench, careful not to sit with my back against the plaque. Matt had been killed in an explosion the previous summer that should have killed me too. A man who had been my enemy and had become my friend had been murdered right in front of my eyes. I felt the weight of fate on my shoulders and put my head in my hands.

"What am I going to do with you?"

I turned and saw Pete sit down on the other end of the bench. He reached out and rubbed the brass plate. "You're the only person I know who can turn a bachelor party into a wake."

"Seeing the bench made me think about all the people who aren't here anymore. I wish my mother could have met Cara."

"Milestones will do that to you. Every time one of my

girls has a birthday, I think about my pop. He was already dying when Jenny was born, but when we let him hold our little girl, he was the happiest man in the world."

"So odd to think that the world just goes on turning."

"Men come and go, but the earth abides. Something like that. Our preacher did a sermon on it one Sunday. Said it was natural. The way the world was created should reassure us that there is an order to creation. I told him afterward that sometimes all I could see was the chaos. He said that we see a child die and think only of the pain, but when we see the sick and old die, we can understand that they are being released from pain. The world is pain. So even the young are being spared."

"Do you believe that?"

"I don't know. I can't imagine losing Sarah or the girls. Maybe it makes sense if I think about me dying before them. I know that would spare *me* a world of pain."

"All I know is that I miss my mom. I can't imagine the grief that Matt's mother must feel."

Pete stood up. "Come on, buddy, the only thing dying right now is your bachelorhood." He held out his hand. I let him pull me up and we rejoined the party.

Two hours later, A.J. parked the MRAP outside my gate. I put my hand on his shoulder and shouted, "I'll get out here! I don't want to wake Cara." I might have slurred a few of the words.

"I think I should escort you up to the house," a very sober A.J. told me.

I put my finger to my mouth and shushed him. "I'm fine," I said before clumsily climbing up the ladder and out through the hatch. Luckily, he jumped out of the driver's door and caught me as I slid off the roof.

"I'm fine," I repeated, not turning to look as I heard A.J. close the gate behind me and start up the vehicle. I was afraid to turn my head, since I was pretty sure I'd trip and fall down if I tried.

At the house, I opened the door as quietly as I could,

hearing only a soft *woof* from the dark bedroom. I stumbled to the couch, dropped down onto it and was asleep as soon as I was horizontal.

## CHAPTER SIXTEEN

I woke up in a fog with someone slapping my face with a warm, wet washcloth. I struggled to open my eyes as the slimy wetness struck me two more times. Then I became aware of a fetid odor accompanying the wet rag treatment. When I finally opened my eyes, I was greeted by a horrid vision.

Mauser managed to lick me two more times before I was able to push him away. "Back, foul creature," I mumbled.

I fended him off with my hands as I tried to sit up. At some point, Cara had covered me with a blanket and now my feet were just getting tangled up in it. I heard her gentle laughter.

"Good morning. Is this something I should get used to? My drunken husband stumbling home in the middle of the night?"

"Ugh, I couldn't do this very often." I held my head in my hands while I tried to clear my thoughts.

"You should eat something."

Somehow I managed to nod my head without it falling off of my shoulders.

I had just started on a bowl of cereal when Cara sat down at the table across from me and grimaced. "I did something I shouldn't have."

My spoon stopped halfway to my mouth. I was still too hung-over to come up with an intelligent question like "What?" so I just looked at her.

"I know I really shouldn't have, but I... You left her phone here and I was bored," Cara said, squirming. "I looked at Beth's Facebook page."

"You didn't log out did you?" I asked, my heart racing.

"No, you'd told me about that. But..."

"What?"

"I think I found something important."

I ate a few more spoonfuls of cereal, then pushed the bowl aside. "I'm listening."

"I took a picture of it with my phone." Cara got up and retrieved her phone from the counter. After a few flicks of her finger, she held it out to me.

The picture was of a post on Beth's phone. I had to expand the photo and shift it around to read it. The post showed a missing flyer for a woman about the same age as Beth. She was a brunette, nice looking with sharp, intelligent eyes. According to the post, she'd disappeared the same day that Beth had been killed.

"She was one of Beth's Facebook friends. Her mother, the missing woman's mother, posted it. Several of Beth's friends have shared it."

"Why didn't this show up before now?" I said, still puzzled by the vagaries of social media.

"It probably did show up in her feed right after it was posted. But then it went dormant and only showed up now because another friend of Beth's commented on it last night."

"That makes a lot of sense," I said, not holding back on the sarcasm. "My head is pounding. Would you bring me a glass of water with four tablespoons of honey and a teaspoon of salt?"

"Seriously?" She looked skeptical, but got up to fix the concoction.

"A friend at the academy sold us on it as a hangover cure. Usually works."

After downing the mix, I copied all of the information off the Facebook post. The missing woman's name was Deanne Greer. She lived in Gainesville and her mother was Lisa Greer. I started to call her, but decided I needed a little fresh air first. Outside, the clouds were low in the sky and a cold mist filled the air. I walked around the house a couple of times, circulating my blood and letting my hangover potion take affect.

"Feeling better?" Cara asked when I came back inside.

"Actually, I am."

"Mad at me for looking at Beth's phone?"

"No. Especially not if it turns out to be important. Of course, we should probably let it be our secret that you saw it first."

I picked up my phone and dialed Mrs. Greer.

"Who is this?" she asked.

"I'm Larry Macklin, an investigator with the Adams County Sheriff's Office," I stated as firmly as I could with my still delicate head.

"Have you found Deanne?" Her voice was filled with a mix of hope and dread.

"No. I'm sorry, but I'm investigating a couple of murders up here in Adams County. I'm trying to determine if your daughter's disappearance could be connected."

"I see," she said, sounding like she didn't see at all.

"The flyer you posted on Facebook showed up in the feed of one of our victims. Your daughter and our victim were friends."

"What's her name?"

"Beth Robinson."

"Beth? Yes, I think Deanne met her in college," she said, sounding dazed. "You said she was murdered?"

"Mrs. Greer, do you have anyone else there with you?" I asked, fearing for her health.

"My husband is here." Her voice was very distant.

"Maybe I should talk to him."

"No!" she shouted. "No, if it has anything to do with Deanne, I want to hear it."

"I'm afraid I'm going to be asking more questions than answering them. I'll tell you what I can, but you have to understand that it's an ongoing investigation."

"I'll tell you anything if it will help bring Deanne home." Her voice had regained its strength.

"Tell me about your daughter's friendship with Beth."

"I don't know much. They met when they were both students at FSU and I think they still keep in touch."

"They see a lot of each other?"

"Not that I know of. But every year Deanne goes up to Tallahassee for some of the football games, so maybe they've seen each other then."

"Do you know anyone named Elizabeth Collins?"

"What? You mean Beth? But..." Of course she was confused.

"No. I mean another person named Elizabeth Collins."

"No... I don't think so. Another Elizabeth?"

"We've had two victims in the last month whose maiden names were both Elizabeth Collins."

"How odd."

*You got that right*, I thought. "Tell me about your daughter's disappearance."

"We text back and forth a lot, but last Wednesday morning we talked and she seemed upset about something. I asked her what, but she was kind of evasive. Not like her at all, so after we hung up I got to thinking about it. I tried to call her back, but there wasn't an answer. Later, I got a text that said: *Don't worry if you don't hear from me for a while.* That's all it said. I texted back and tried calling over and over, but she never answered me."

"You contacted the Gainesville police?"

"She lives outside the city limits, so I filed a report with the Alachua County Sheriff's Office. They've tried to help. I really think they have."

"Did they ping her phone?" I asked and heard her mom start to cry.

"That's the worse part. They found her phone on the side of the road. How could that happen?"

"I'm going to contact Alachua County. I'll also be back in touch with you. I'm afraid we'll have a lot more questions for you."

"That's fine. At least I feel like I'm doing something. I've driven all over the county looking for her or her car."

"It would also help if you wrote down anything else you can think of about the relationship between your daughter and Beth Robinson."

Lisa assured me that she would. I told her I'd be in touch and hung up.

"Disturbing," I said to Cara.

"You think all of this is tied together somehow?"

"My gut tells me it has to be."

"How does Elizabeth Collins fit in?"

"They were all at FSU at the same time. I think that's important. Right now, that's the only thing all three women have in common."

"Are you going to call Pete?" Cara asked.

I looked at my watch. "Almost eleven. Damn it, I was hoping to wake him up. It would serve him right." I put my hand to my temple.

"He didn't pour the alcohol down your throat," Cara pointed out.

"You weren't there," I said, tapping his number.

"Just the man I wanted to talk to," Pete said, sounding wide awake. "A fellow found a body out in the woods. Not too far from your place."

I got a sinking feeling in the pit of my stomach. Pete told me where he was.

"I'll be right there."

"Why'd you call?"

"I'll tell you when I get there," I said, wondering if they'd found the missing Deanne Greer.

Pete and Julio were parked in a field about a mile from my house. The sky was still overcast and the mist was almost thick enough now to be called light rain. I walked over to where they stood leaning against their cars.

"Crime scene isn't here yet?" I asked, surprised.

"We wanted to get a good look before they showed up. I'd just found the body when you called," Pete explained.

"Who called it in?"

"Farmer's kid. He was hunting hogs. Planning on having a barbeque for Easter," Julio said.

I thought that Pete and Julio seemed strangely... uninvolved. Maybe unemotional would be a better way of saying it. I chalked it up to them having spent most of the night drinking.

"Where's the body?"

"Over there. About twenty yards just inside that tree line, there's a swamp and the body is half submerged," Pete said, looking up at the sky.

"The team from the coroner's office will love that. You guys coming?"

"We've seen it. Besides, we don't want to muck up the crime scene any more than it is," Julio said.

I felt like I'd walked into the middle of *Invasion of the Body Snatchers*. Both of them were acting so weird. If my brain had been working better, I would have had more questions for them.

I walked across the soggy field and entered the woods where Pete and Julio had indicated. Once inside, I spotted the area that Pete had described. Water was dripping off of the oak limbs as I walked over to the small pond filled with cypress trees. Between the trees themselves and the cypress knees jutting up out of the water, the pond only had a small, clear area in the middle that was open to the sky.

I kept my eyes to the ground as I walked, knowing that this was perfect water moccasin habitat. As I got closer to the water, I could see something sticking above the surface near one of the cypress trees. Sure enough, ten feet from where I stood, I saw the body of a young woman. She had brown hair and unblinking eyes. Half of her body was hidden behind a large cypress tree. The Spanish moss hanging down created a scene straight out of a Southern Gothic movie.

I kept staring at the woman and something rang false. The eyes. They shouldn't have been there. If the body had been in the water even a half day, various critters would have already eaten away at the eyes. Looking closer, the skin color was all wrong too. It shouldn't have been so even.

"Damn them!" I said, loud enough that Pete and Julio should have been able to hear me back at the cars. I turned and stomped out of the woods.

"Not funny!" I shouted at the two idiots who were laughing their asses off. They had to support themselves on the hoods of their cars to keep from actually falling to the ground and rolling around.

"Is this some stupid continuation of the bachelor party?" I asked with as much ire as I could muster.

Pete was waving his hand, trying to catch his breath. "No…" More laughter. "…Really…" He could hardly catch his breath.

"I expect this sort of thing from him, but I hoped for more from you." I aimed this at Julio, who wasn't having any more luck than Pete at getting control of himself.

"No, no, don't blame him." Pete wiped at his eyes. "He got the call. I heard it and met him out here. It was a farm kid, fifteen years old. He really did think he'd found a body. I wouldn't have pulled our little prank on you, but we'd just realized what it was when you called." He fought off another attack of laughter. "I couldn't resist."

I was calming down a little now, knowing that they had been dragged out there on a fool's errand too.

"Yeah, ha, ha!" I said.

"The kid said he wouldn't have been so easily fooled if

there'd been any other trash around. They've had people dumping on their land in the past, but to find the mannequin that far from the road? Nothing else around and on a day like this. I really couldn't blame him." Pete wiped at his eyes again.

I nodded. I tried to stay mad, but it was wearing off.

"Sorry, man," Julio said, catching his breath.

"I thought you both were acting strange," I said.

"I could hardly keep a straight face," Pete admitted.

"Wait till you hear what I learned from Beth's Facebook feed. You'll know what I was thinking when you told me you'd found a body."

I told them everything, except the part about Cara discovering the post. It wasn't that Pete or Julio couldn't be trusted or that they'd even be upset. But the fewer people who knew, the better. Some day in the distant future, I didn't want a defense attorney to make a big deal out of the fact that someone other than law enforcement was examining evidence. By not telling Pete and Julio, they would never have to lie about it.

"We need to find out everything we can about Deanne Greer," Pete said, completely sober now.

"I'll look into her disappearance. Under our arrangement, you're investigating Beth's murder, Darlene has Elizabeth's case and I'm looking for a connection. The way I see it, this comes under the heading of a connection between Beth and Elizabeth's murder."

"I don't see that… exactly. How does Deanne's disappearance tie Beth and Elizabeth together?"

"I admit it's a bit more of a hunch than anything else, but Deanne and Beth were friends and they went to FSU at the same time as Elizabeth. All three of them at school together. All three of them being murdered or disappearing within a week of each other…" I let it hang.

"Yeah, I see your point. What about you, Julio? You're a newly minted investigator."

"I'm not in the big leagues yet. I was just covering this,"

he waved his hand toward the mannequin, "because y'all were taking the day off."

"Which does bring up the question of what you're doing working today?" I asked Pete.

"Believe me. If I've got a headache, I'm better off coming into work than staying at the house with Sarah and the girls. I love them, but there's always some sort of drama. Some very loud drama."

"Speaking of women, since Jessie's meeting with Beth's friend tonight, I'll call her and have her keep an ear out for any mention of Deanne. Now, one of you two call the kid and tell him to fish the mannequin out of the pond. I'm going back home."

"We'll call you if we find any more bodies," Pete said, and I showed him my middle finger as I got back in the van.

As soon as I pulled out on the road, I realized there was something else I needed to do. I turned toward the office. On the way, I called Jessie and told her about Deanne. I wanted her to see if Beth had ever mentioned her to Mia. I also thought that it might help to reinforce for Jessie how dangerous the situation was.

Mentioning Deanne seemed to have the opposite effect. Jessie seemed even more excited about her upcoming meeting with Mia.

Sighing to myself, I said, "I'm headed to the office to pick up a tracking device. I want you to keep it with you at all times."

"Excellent!"

"I'll swing by your place in half an hour."

"Do you know where I live?"

"You think you're the only one who can stalk someone? Already scoped out your place."

I collected the equipment from the office, then pulled into her driveway. Before I was out of the van, she was already coming down the driveway to meet me.

"Is the van for, like, doing undercover work?"

"It's for hauling moose," I said dryly. "Here is your

tracking device. You'll need to put it somewhere on your body. A purse won't cut it. If a bad guy grabbed you, your purse might not go with you. Understand?"

"Neat," she said, looking at the small device.

"Don't lose it."

Our vice squad used the devices regularly, so they were in charge of keeping track of them. Pun intended. Protocol would have had me asking their sergeant if I could use it, but I was skipping that step because Sergeant Malcolm Yates was a bit of a jerk. He would have made me tell him all about the investigation and how the tracker was going to be used. I didn't want to bother explaining what I was going to do with the device. I just needed to have it back by Sunday afternoon.

"We're going clubbing, so my clothes will be sort of skimpy. It's small, but…" She looked thoughtful.

I looked at the dreary sky. "Wear a jacket."

"Yeah, that might work."

"But, and this is a big but, if you put it in your jacket, you can't take it off."

"How's that supposed to work?"

"You'll have to figure it out. But it won't do any good if you put it in your jacket and it gets stolen, or you get snatched when you aren't wearing it."

"I guess you've got a point."

"No one said this was going to be easy."

"Don't worry. I'll get it done." For the first time, I saw grit in her eyes and thought she just might be up to the challenge.

"I want you to remember what the bottom line is. Be careful. Nothing is worth you getting hurt. Understand? Now, I'm going to follow you to Tallahassee, so I'll be just a phone call or text away if you get into any trouble. Got it?"

She nodded.

"And I know about the arrest," I said.

When I'd run the background check, I'd learned that she'd been pegged with a cocaine charge when she was nineteen. She'd been in a car with two other girls and an older guy. The coke was found in plain sight in the console between the two front seats, so everyone in the car was charged with possession. The amount was large enough to make it a felony, but since it wasn't her car and she'd only been a passenger, she was able to plead down to a misdemeanor

"I screwed up. There was more stuff before I turned eighteen," she admitted. "But that was the one that really made me think about my life." She looked at me with a slight tilt of her head. "You still going to let me meet with Mia?"

"You think Eddie's record was clean? It's what you do from this moment on that matters to me."

"I'm doing this 'cause I really want to be a cop," she told me. "But I figured with the misdemeanor on my record, I don't stand a chance."

"We'll see. It's not an insurmountable problem," I told her.

We turned on the tracking device, and I made sure that the app on my phone was working before I headed back home.

# CHAPTER SEVENTEEN

As soon as I walked in the door, I left a message for the Alachua County investigator who was working on Deanne Greer's missing person case.

"Look," Cara said, showing me her laptop. On Genie's Facebook page were several photos of Jimmy looking victorious. He'd taken first place in the discus throw and, in one of the pictures, Dad was holding his hand up in the air. I swear I could see tears in Dad's eyes. *Good for you*, I thought, happy for both of them.

Deputy Aaron Harlow called me back quickly. I'd met him more than a year ago when Cara's father had been caught up in a murder investigation.

"What's your opinion?" I asked him now.

"Her car is still missing. That fact alone makes it harder to classify as foul play. I'm sure you know of cases that seemed for sure an abduction or murder, then two months later the victim showed up none the worse for wear."

"Yeah. We had a fellow up here a few years ago who went missing. All signs were that he'd been murdered, but then he showed up down in Key West. I hear what you're saying, but I want your gut reaction."

"I looked through her house. There's nothing out of

place. Her mother looked through all of Deanne's personal belongings and couldn't give us a definite answer whether anything was missing. So she might have packed a bag, jumped in her car and headed out for a road trip. Only one thing sent a shiver down my spine. We found her cell phone on the side of the road. It was still on. Looked like it had just been tossed out the window of a moving car."

"But that's something a person running away from their old life might do," I countered.

"True. You asked for my gut. I'd say that Deanne left the house on her own. What happened from that point on, I can't say."

"You checked CCTV." I made it a statement, not a question. I knew that Gainesville and Alachua County had a high number of college students. Checking CCTV when one of them went off the rails was standard operating procedure.

"Hours and hours of tapes. We spotted her car several times. From the images, it looked like she was driving, though that doesn't mean much."

"Can I come down and look through her house?"

"If her mother gives you permission. We aren't treating it like a crime scene. There just isn't anything to indicate that it is. I did have a team go in and dust for prints, as well as pick up some hair and other items for DNA testing. Of course, we won't do any testing until there's actually proof that a crime has been committed."

I hung up feeling like a trip down there would probably be a waste of time. I'd wait and see what Jessie learned from Mia before thinking about any road trips.

At eight o'clock, I drove into Calhoun to pick up Jessie's tracking device. I didn't have to track her all the way to Tallahassee since she'd already told me where she was meeting Mia, but I didn't want to take any chances on losing Jessie *or* the expensive device.

Their plan was to go to a club near the FSU campus called The Beat. Jessie parked in the municipal parking garage. I chose a spot on the street nearby and watched my phone as a little blue dot went from the garage to the club. It stopped on the street outside for about ten minutes before merging with the building on the map.

*So far, so good*, I thought and sat back to drink a Coke and eat some chips while I stared at the small light. An hour passed before the dot moved out of the club and headed west. The parking garage where she'd left her car was to the east. Choosing not to panic yet, I figured Jessie and Mia had simply decided to move on to another venue.

My phone rang with a call from Darlene.

"You're on speaker phone so I can watch the tracker while I talk," I said loudly to the phone in its holder on the dash.

"You checked out a tracking device?" Darlene's voice sounded surprised.

"Yeah... sort of," I said as the dot moved closer to campus.

"You didn't ask vice then."

"They just would have come up with some sort of stupid hoops for me to jump through."

"So how's it going, James Bond?"

"No red flags yet, but the test will be in the pudding."

"You're mixing your metaphors."

"Thanks for the editorial critique. Have you made any headway with the Elizabeth Collins case?"

"That woman had to be the most introverted, boring person on the planet. Hubby finally coughed up her phone records, but they didn't reveal anything interesting. She did almost nothing but go to work and come home. The only upside is that any break in the pattern stands out. She made a trip out of town about four months ago. On her credit card statements, I can tell that she stopped for gas at the Busy Bee at the Live Oak exit on I-10, then it looks like she headed for St. Augustine. She paid for a couple of meals there. Most curious was the amount of the meals. They were both for more than one person could possibly have eaten."

"A date?"

"From the look of it, I'd say it was more than two people, but it's hard to be sure. If you buy drinks, two people can rack up a pretty large bill."

"True." The dot had settled on a bar near the campus. The place had been there for decades, probably since before Elizabeth, Beth and Deanne had all been there. "I'll get with Pete and see if there's any chance Beth Robinson visited St. Augustine around the same time." *And Deanne Greer*, I thought. *It would be a solid link if all three women were there at the same time.*

"Let me know what he finds out."

"Did you hear about the dirty trick Julio and Pete played on me?" I asked and heard Darlene fail to suppress a laugh.

"Sure did. I'm just pissed that they didn't call me in to watch. I also heard about the missing person."

"I was getting to that. I'll see if she was in St. Augustine too. Text me the dates."

We killed a little more time with office gossip while I watched the blue light glow over the bar.

"I know you're keeping me on the line 'cause you're bored," Darlene said, "but I've got to go. Hondo's coming over after his shift."

"Fine. Abandon me. I'm used to it."

I spent another hour watching the dot until at last it started back toward the parking garage.

I texted: *Give me a call.*

When the dot reached the garage, my phone rang. "I got stuff." There was excitement in her voice.

I looked at my watch. "Meet me at the IHOP out on the parkway."

Half an hour later, we were seated in the IHOP with an eclectic Saturday night crowd.

"Can I have a full stack of pancakes?" Jessie asked, looking at me over the top of the menu.

"Is your information worth it?" I challenged her.

"I got stuff."

"Have the pancakes."

As the waitress walked off with our orders, Jessie smiled. "Mia can drink."

"You all finished up pretty early, considering."

"She went off with this skeezy guy. I tried to talk her out of it. Couldn't do it."

"What about Beth?"

"She flirted with Dr. Forsyth."

"How far did it go?"

"Mia thought they might have had a fling about five years ago. Dr. Forsyth and Beth went down to some convention or seminar in Orlando together. When they got back, they were acting real strange for a couple of months before things settled back down."

"Strange?"

"Like secretive. Like maybe they were hiding an affair."

"But not anymore?"

"Right. Mia said she thought it was just like a coming together... she called it synergy. Forsyth was having marriage trouble and Beth was too. So boom! Mia said it couldn't last 'cause they weren't compatible."

"Didn't you say she'd told you earlier that Beth was having sex with someone at the office? Currently? Even Eddie said that Beth had mentioned dating a co-worker."

Jessie paused and looked uncomfortable. Her eyes drifted down at the floor and then up at the ceiling. "It's kind of... different."

"What's that mean?"

"According to Mia, Beth and Glenn were having sex."

"Who?"

"Glenn Webster, the other hygienist."

I had to think for a minute because it seemed so incongruous. "The little guy? He seemed..."

"Gay. Yeah, that's what I thought too. But Mia says she's seen him with guys *and* girls. Beth told Mia that it was nice to be with a guy who was... gentle and not very demanding. Sort of helped her to get over losing her husband. Like she still wasn't ready for a relationship that could go somewhere.

At least, that's what Mia thinks."

I still couldn't quite picture Glenn as Beth's lover, which might have had more to do with my somewhat narrow world view than with reality. *Another talk with him could be enlightening*, I thought.

"What about Mia? Did she really care about Beth or were those crocodile tears?"

"No. She's pretty tore up. Every time she mentioned Beth, she started gulping her Long Island Iced Teas. I kinda felt responsible for her going off with that guy 'cause she'd drunk quite a bit. Mostly because I kept bringing up Beth."

"Did you also bring up Deanne Greer?"

"Yeah… that didn't get any kind of reaction. Like she'd never heard of her."

We paused as the waitress brought Jessie's pancakes and my grilled cheese.

"How did you get her to talk without tipping your hand?" I asked after I'd taken a couple of bites.

"I told her I'd met Beth once and that she was the one who suggested I come to Dr. Forsyth." Jessie poured half a bottle of syrup on her pancakes.

"Congratulations! You just used the number one tool of law enforcement—lying," I said with a smile.

"I really want to be a cop," she said with heartbreaking sincerity.

"Have patience, young Jedi. What else did you learn?"

"Do you really think I can get past the misdemeanor thing?" Jessie pushed the issue.

"Do you not understand what the word patience means?" I said, irritated.

She filled her fork with pancakes and submerged them in the syrup pooled on her plate before stuffing them in her mouth.

"Did you learn anything else?" I asked with a softer tone.

Her eyes lit up again. "Sometimes Beth would get weird, sort of poetic."

"Like how?"

"Mia wasn't very clear. She'd had a few drinks before she mentioned it."

"Tell me what she said."

"Beth would talk about the seasons of the sun."

"What?"

"That's what she said, the seasons of the sun."

I pulled out my phone and Googled "seasons of the sun." "Seasons *in* the Sun? Was that it? There was some song back in the '70s called that."

"No. At least that's not how Mia put it. Like I said, she'd had a few drinks by then."

"What else did Beth tell Mia about seasons of the sun? What was the context?"

"Beth told her once that she was going to meet the other seasons of the sun, or something like that. Just weird. That's what Mia said. She said that Beth sounded kind of dreamy and faraway when she said it."

"Was this before a trip?"

"A couple of years ago. But, yeah. Beth got into a tiff with another person at work about some days off and when Mia asked her what the big deal was, Beth said she had to go meet the other seasons of the sun. Made it sound like a make-or-break kind of thing. Dr. Forsyth had to decide who got the time off and he sided with Beth."

"That gives me something to think about," I muttered. I made a note to ask Beth's mother about it.

"Not bad?" Jessie asked as she made more of the pancakes disappear. I assumed she meant her CI efforts and not her pancake-eating skills, though I was mildly impressed with both.

"You earned your pancakes."

"What do we do now?" she asked eagerly.

I took a deep breath. "*We* don't do anything. I'll let you know what's going on, as much as I can. And if, hear that word, *if* something else comes up where I think you might be useful, I'll let you know."

I saw the look of disappointment on her face. "You can

trust me," I reassured her.

Jessie shrugged.

"Tell me what you think seasons of the sun might mean." For some reason, I found myself wanting to make her feel better. I didn't think I'd ever met anyone who wasn't on drugs who had more dramatic mood swings.

"I don't think it has to do with some old song," she said with a thoughtful expression.

"Agreed."

"Seasons. Winter, spring, summer and fall."

"All you have to do is call?" She gave me a blank look. "Another old song. Forget it. Maybe you were right when you said she was being poetic. Someone might say that they were going to meet summer if they were going to the beach for a vacation." I felt myself being drawn into the puzzle.

"But would you say you were meeting all of the seasons?"

"No," I agreed. I Googled "four seasons." "There was a band called the Four Seasons. I've heard their songs on classic rock stations. There's an expensive hotel chain... And there was an iconic restaurant in New York until recently. Maybe Beth was going to New York to meet someone at the Four Seasons. That might be a big enough deal that she would insist on the time off," I said. Actually, that made some kind of sense.

"Maybe," Jessie said doubtfully.

"When did you say this happened?"

"Mia said a couple of years ago. But she was getting a bit fuzzy by the time we started talking about it, so she wasn't real specific."

Another thing to ask Dr. Forsyth about. Since it involved Beth getting time off from work, there might have been a record of it in her personnel files.

"Do you want me to follow you back to Calhoun?" I asked and got an eye roll for my effort. I did walk her out to her truck.

I got home a little after one. Cara had tried to wait up for me, but I found her napping on the couch. The animals, including Mauser, were all flaked out on the floor around her.

"I didn't want you to think you had to sleep on the couch again tonight," Cara said with a drowsy smile.

"I'd definitely prefer to sleep in our bed. Thank you."

"We could do separate beds until the honeymoon. That would make it much more special," Cara suggested.

"If you want to go the traditional route, then you should go stay with your parents until the wedding."

"Now you're getting mean," she said, standing and pulling me into a hug. "How about we just do some adult stuff now and let the honeymoon take care of itself?"

I gave her a long kiss in answer.

## CHAPTER EIGHTEEN

"You look restless," Cara said as I stared out the living room window. Saturday's heavy mist had finally cleared, leaving the air cool and dry.

"I can't decide what I want to do." I'd already called Pete and Darlene and filled them in on Jessie's meeting with Mia.

"Kick back and enjoy a beautiful Sunday afternoon," she suggested.

"You're the one cruising the Internet on your laptop," I pointed out.

"Touché." She snapped the computer closed and got off the couch to join me at the window. "So what are our choices?"

"Go talk to Beth's mother and look through her house, or drive down to Gainesville and talk to people about Deanne's disappearance."

"Beth lived in Tallahassee, right?"

"Yes."

"It's a beautiful day. Why don't we take Mauser and Alvin to Tom Brown Park, then afterward maybe you could meet Beth's mom at her house?"

"You don't mind waiting in the van?"

"You'll have to ask Alvin and Mauser about that. I can't

promise *I* won't come in the house," she said with an impish smile.

"I can work with that. I should take some time to plan my trip to Gainesville anyway. If I went down there today, I might not have a chance to meet with everyone I need to."

We herded the dogs into the van and headed to Tallahassee. Not surprisingly the park was full of folks enjoying an exceptionally beautiful spring day.

"Don't even think about going in there with the other dogs. You aren't mature enough," I told Mauser as we walked past the fenced-in dog park.

As we walked, Mauser attracted the usual number of gawkers and fans. It always amazed me how other people with friendly, well-behaved dogs would make a fuss about the monster mutt whose main claim to fame was being the size of a cow.

"You're too tough on him," Cara scolded me.

"Say that when he's pulling *your* arm off!" I said as he hauled me toward a pair of Boxers he wanted to meet. The Boxers and their owner dodged the approach and sped up their pace to the dog park.

"Look at Alvin. He just smiles and pants. Sniffs a few bushes and trees. Doesn't make a spectacle of himself," I said to Mauser.

"You don't fool me one bit. I've seen the little smile that creeps across your face when someone compliments Mauser. I think you like the attention as much as he does," Cara said, staring me down.

"I don't know what you're talking about. He goes home this evening and no one will be happier about it than me."

"You big liar. I caught you sitting on the couch yesterday, with him sitting next to you while you rubbed his ears. It went on for an hour."

"Self defense. Like playing music to Cerberus."

We walked a huge circle through the park and wound up back at the van with two tired dogs. I called Shelly Collins and explained that I wanted to look through Beth's house.

She sounded sad and tired, but told me it wouldn't be a problem. She'd be able to meet us at two. My watch told me that we had an hour to kill.

"Ice cream," I said softly. Cara turned to me with narrowed eyes while Mauser's head instantly popped up through the gap between the van's front seats. He was already drooling. "He heard me."

"You're evil. You know I can't gain too much weight before the wedding," Cara groused.

I rolled my eyes. "Your weight hasn't varied more than a pound or two the whole time we've been together."

"Little do you know. Get thee behind me, Satan, and don't push."

"Whatever. Mauser, Alvin and I are going for ice cream. You don't have to get any if you don't want."

She punched me in the arm. "Bastard," she said affectionately. "A small cone won't be too bad, I guess."

"A win for the dark lord."

"And it's Sunday. You're going to hell," she informed me.

One small cup of cherry-vanilla, one giant waffle cone of birthday cake and two doggie sundaes later, I drove to Beth's house on a bit of a sugar high. It deflated quickly when I saw Shelly Collins in the front yard, admiring the azaleas.

"Beth always loved the flowers. She bought this house with the insurance money she got from Dominick's death."

"He died of pneumonia?" I asked. I thought I'd seen that in one of the reports Pete had given me.

"That's right. It was so sad. They went on a camping trip up to Hard Labor Creek State Park in Georgia. He was already feeling sick, but didn't want to spoil the trip. On the second day, she took him to the hospital, but it was already too late."

"How's her son doing?"

"Breaks my heart. I've tried to explain it to him the best I can, but I can tell he doesn't want to believe it." She paused. "Neither do I. The truth is, I'm only holding on because of him and my faith. Maybe once we hold the funeral, it might help."

"Has the coroner's office called?"

"Yes, and they were very nice. She's at the funeral home now. We've scheduled the service for Friday."

There was an awkward pause.

"I'd like you to meet my fiancée," I said in an effort to improve the mood. Shelly followed me over to the van where I introduced Cara. Mauser couldn't be left out of the attention and stuck his head out of the window, drooling down the side of the van. For a moment, Shelly smiled.

"When Beth was growing up, our backdoor neighbors had a Great Dane. He would come over to our house and get in Beth's play pool during the summer. They were great friends." She wiped at the tears that started to fall from her eyes.

"Cara, do you want to come in with us?" I asked.

She looked at Shelly and I could see that the woman's heartache made her uncomfortable. She shook her head gently. "I'll stay out here with the pups."

"Pups?" Shelly asked, which led to another round of introductions as Cara put Alvin on her lap so the woman could pet him.

"I should get started on the house," I said.

We went up to the front door and I pulled away the crime scene tape while Shelly took out her key. Inside were the usual signs that Shantel and her team had been through the place. They hadn't done a full work up, since it was unlikely that a crime had been committed in the house, but they'd fingerprinted the common surfaces, door handles, countertops and any obvious objects that were in plain view while Pete had searched the house.

"What are you looking for?" Shelly asked.

*Good question*, I thought. "I'm not sure. But there are a couple of reasons I wanted to look at Beth's house. We've recently received some new information, so something that didn't seem important the first time might jump out at me in light of what we've learned. Plus, we always like to have another investigator look at crime scenes. We all have different experience and knowledge. What one misses, the other might see."

The house was small, only about twelve-hundred square feet at the most, with two bedrooms and two baths. The floorplan was open and simple. All of the furnishings looked broken-in and homey. However, something seemed to be missing.

"Deputy Henley said that it would be okay for me to gather up Tyler's toys and things and take them over to my house," Shelly said as though she had read my mind.

"That's fine."

As I went from room to room, what hit me the most was the normality. Beth had left this house, fully expecting to come back. There was mail on the counter and a few rinsed but dirty bowls in the sink. The laundry basket was half full. The bathroom had all the half-used shampoo bottles, bars of soap and toothpaste tubes that you would find in any home. It wasn't until I entered the bedroom that my heart skipped a beat.

In the corner of the room, just to the right of the bed and the nightstand, was a large painting. The canvas was divided into four quadrants, each of them depicting a different season.

"The four seasons," I said softly, walking over to look at it more closely.

Shelly must have heard me. "Beth's had that painting for years," she said from the doorway.

The canvas was stretched over a frame of one-by-twos. I pulled the painting away from the wall and saw that the back of the frame was covered by more canvas. However, one corner wasn't tacked down. Going on instinct, I lifted the edge and saw a pen, the nice kind that someone would use when they were writing something important. I pulled on a pair of rubber gloves that I'd stuffed in my back pocket, then carefully pulled the pen out.

"Will you look at that!" Shelly exclaimed.

"Can you think why your daughter might have had hidden this here?" I asked.

"Not for the life of me." Her voice was puzzled.

I carefully set the pen down on the nightstand, then went back out to the van to retrieve an evidence bag from the stash of supplies that Dad kept there. After checking in with Cara, I went back to Beth's bedroom and went over everything.

I opened all of the drawers, looked under the bed and inside the pockets of her clothes in the closet, anything I could think of. The only other items of interest were in her jewelry box. I found pairs of earrings and a few necklaces that held images of the sun, including an elaborate gold pendant with a diamond in the middle of the sun's face. They all made me think of the sun in the four seasons painting. Beth had talked about seasons of the sun. She owned jewelry depicting the sun. *Is the jewelry another reference or just a coincidence?* I wondered.

I didn't find anything else, so I put the room back together as best I could.

"Did your daughter ever mention anything about the seasons of the sun?" I asked Shelly, who seemed emotionally exhausted.

"I... don't think so. Is it important?"

"It's just a clue. Whether it means anything or not, I don't know. She went on a trip a few years ago and mentioned to a co-worker that she was going to meet the seasons of the sun. Do you remember the trip?"

"Beth loved to drive. She'd go all over the place visiting friends. Now that you mention it, I do remember her saying a few things that struck me as odd. Though with Beth, she was so... exuberant that it wasn't unusual for her to start talking about something or someone I'd never heard of."

"What in particular struck you as odd?"

"She would say something like 'Winter told me,' or 'I better ask autumn.' Never said it directly to me, just something she'd mutter to herself. But that was Beth. I never thought much of it."

"How often did she do this?"

"Only once in a while. Maybe a dozen times altogether."

"Do you know a friend of Beth's named Deanne Greer?" I asked.

Shelly looked thoughtful. "Vaguely. I think they roomed together in college, but I haven't heard her name in years."

I asked a few more questions, but Shelly didn't have anything else to offer. I had to be careful not to force her to remember something she couldn't. More than one investigator had unintentionally created false memories in a witness.

Deciding the house had told me all it could, I was headed for the front door when we heard a knock at the back door. Shelly and I looked at each other. I remembered that Beth's friend, Bob Harper, lived nearby. Maybe he'd come over to see what was going on. But why would he go to the back door? Habit? I walked through the kitchen to the small utility room.

The solid wood door had a simple lock on the knob and a chain lock that wasn't attached. Not much in the way of security. I unlocked the door and went to swing it open, but the door seemed to be stuck. I pulled harder, then heard wood splinter as part of the frame near the door knob gave way.

"I didn't think that looked right," Cara said from outside the door. "Sorry, but I got out to take a walk and when I saw the back door was… messed up, I thought I ought to let you know."

"What happened here?" Shelly asked, concern in her voice.

I looked closer and could see where someone had tried to drive a couple of screws into the frame in an attempt to repair the damage.

"Looks like someone jimmied the door open, then tried to patch it." I turned to Shelly. "Was it like this the other day when you were here?"

"I'm sure it wasn't. When I came to pick up Tyler's things, I came out this way to get his Tonka trucks." She pointed toward a sand pile about thirty feet from the back stoop.

"This looks like something a homeowner would do as a temporary patch to secure their home," I mused. "I've never seen a burglar try to put the door frame back together."

"I didn't see anything missing," Shelly said.

I wondered about the "four seasons" painting. Had someone broken in the back door in order to retrieve something else hidden behind that print? If so, why had they tried to patch the door back together?

"I don't think they were trying to hide the fact they'd broken in," Cara said, echoing my thoughts.

"No. The first time anyone tried to open the door, it would be noticed. Crazy. These are star-head screws, so they probably used a battery-operated screwdriver to put them in. What burglar would carry one with them?"

"And bring the screws," Cara added.

I looked around to see if there was a shed or anything in the backyard where the screws and tool might have come from. Nothing. And the house didn't have a garage. It was very odd.

I took some photos of the damage, then we did our best to secure the door and I put the crime scene tape back up.

"I'm going to send our team back out to take more fingerprints," I told Shelly.

"I think that's a good idea," she said earnestly.

I looked at the door. "I'll send someone out to fix that too." I would talk one of the maintenance guys into riding over with Shantel. Shelly Collins didn't need to worry about the door too.

Finally on our way home to Adams County, I asked Cara, "Would you text Dad and see if they've gotten back home?"

The answer was *yes*, so we swung by to return Mauser to his owner. He had a jubilant reunion with Jimmy, who wanted to take a picture with the dog and all his medals. Jimmy put the medals around Mauser's large neck, making it look like the dog had cleaned house at both the Westminster and Crufts dog shows.

After promising to meet with Dad first thing in the morning to update him on both the investigations and my bachelor revelries, we finally got home. Alvin barely managed to eat before collapsing on the floor, snoring loudly.

"Admit it. The house seems empty now," Cara said.

"The lunkhead does fill up a room," I agreed, though I would never concede that I missed the goofball.

We had a quiet evening. Cara read while I did some online research into the missing Deanne Greer. I didn't come up with much. Deputy Harlow had sent copies of some of the reports, but most of them contained only basic information. Nothing connected up with our victims. Convincing Dad that I needed to drive down to Gainesville on company time was going to be high on my agenda when I met with him in the morning.

# CHAPTER NINETEEN

Halfway to the office on Monday, my phone rang. I didn't recognize the number. My first response was to let it go to voicemail, but then I remembered the hang-up call from a week ago. I answered, but there was no response. I took the phone out of its holder on the dash and pressed it to my ear so there was no chance I'd miss anything.

"Is this the person who called last week?"

Still nothing. With the car running, I couldn't even tell if there was breathing on the other end.

"Does this have to do with the murders of Elizabeth Collins and Beth Robinson? Is Deanne Greer involved?"

This time I heard a sharp intake of breath.

"Deanne?" I took a shot in the dark and waited.

The person didn't hang up.

"Does this have to do with the four seasons?"

I heard another gasp, and then the dull pulse of the dial tone.

"I guess that answers that question," I grumbled, putting the phone back in its holder. I didn't see the point in calling back right away.

Pete and Darlene were already comparing notes when I got to my desk. Remembering that Dad wanted to see me first thing, I looked at my watch. I was running early, so I took the time to fill them in on the odd phone call and my visit to Beth's house.

I told them about the painting and the jewelry, then held up the pen in its evidence bag. "I found this hidden behind the painting."

"And someone broke into the house?" Pete asked.

I showed him the pictures I'd taken.

"It was the craziest thing. I even called Beth's friend Bob on the way home, thinking that he might have gone over to check on the house and seen the door broken and secured it. No dice. He said he hasn't had the heart to go over there at all."

"On top of this, you got another mysterious phone call," Pete said. "I'm feeling like a fifth wheel."

"He's right, slick. If you're going to be hot-dogging it, we'll just turn both cases over to you and go about our business," Darlene said with a wave of her hand.

"Ah, guys, don't let your feelings get hurt. I'm sure some strange stuff will happen to you too."

"I've managed to all but eliminate Elizabeth's husband as a suspect. I found neighbors on both sides of his house with security cameras that covered the street. He didn't drive anywhere after he got home on the night she was murdered," Darlene said.

"I talked to folks at the main library in Tallahassee where Beth volunteered. Well loved, got along with everyone and no one remembers anybody creeping on her," Pete reported.

My phone buzzed with a text alert and I saw that it was from Dad: *Where are you?* It was only five minutes past eight.

"Look, I'm so important I'm getting texts from the boss. See you kids later," I said to Pete and Darlene, then headed toward Dad's office at a pace that was several clicks faster than casual mode. I didn't want him in a bad mood before I'd even gotten there.

As soon as I walked into his office, Dad looked at me and then at his watch.

"I was briefing Darlene and Pete," I told him.

"Glad to hear you weren't late to work. You just forgot who the boss is."

My first thought was *Who looked after your mountain of a dog this weekend?* but I was smart enough not to say it. Instead I asked, "Bad morning?" and averted my eyes. I didn't want him to think I was challenging him.

"Fine so far. But I've got budget issues to deal with all day. We're months away from the new fiscal year, but we're still waiting on some of the state funds we were promised as reimbursement for the costs we incurred due to the hurricane." He looked up at me. "Sit."

An invitation from him to sit was always a good sign.

"You know I don't need to hear the details of the investigations. All I want to know is if you've found a solid link between the two cases, and are there any serious persons of interest identified in either case?"

"No and no. I know that Darlene and Pete are following a number of leads, but I think they would have told me if they had anything solid. There's also been a new development." I proceeded to tell him about the disappearance of Deanne Greer.

"Can you link it with either of the other cases?"

"Only by coincidence at this point. She was friends with Beth Robinson and disappeared the same day Beth was killed."

Dad leaned back in his chair and looked out the window. Normally, he made decisions quickly and, amazingly, they were almost always right. He'd told me once that, early in his law enforcement career, he'd taken a year and performed a little experiment. The first half of the year, he'd taken his time and made his decisions very deliberately, doing whatever research he could before he made them. The second half of the year, he'd just gone with his gut instinct. At the end of the year, he'd learned that he made more right decisions when he didn't overthink things and second-guess himself. Plus, he found that he was happier and more relaxed. Today, he didn't seem to be following that rule.

Finally, he turned back to me. "I think you're right. The missing woman is worth looking into. Having said that, I can't authorize the travel or time for you to go to Gainesville on the department's dime."

"But you'll back me up. I mean, you're authorizing me," I made air quotes around the words, "to go to Gainesville and talk to whoever I need to."

"Correct." He also made air quotes and glared at me.

"I have some personal days."

"Above and beyond what you'll need for the wedding and the honeymoon?" he asked, surprising me with his almost fatherly concern.

"I do."

"So how was the party?" he asked, signaling the end of the conversation about the investigations.

"So far, nothing on social media," I said cheerily.

He frowned. "You think that's a joke?"

"No, I don't. I know that you already spend plenty of time you don't have responding to the crap that people upload."

"Damn right. As if there weren't enough problems these days."

"Seriously, Pete did a great job. Everyone had a good time."

"Before the wedding, I want us to talk," Dad said ominously, then dismissed me. "Good luck in Gainesville."

*Want us to talk? What the hell was that about?* I wondered. *Maybe I can avoid it.*


I made sure to line up all of my interviews in Gainesville in advance. I didn't want to be down there for more than a day, especially since I was taking my own time and money to do it. I met with Lt. Johnson and filled him in on what I was planning to do.

"Not the right way to do things," he grumbled, sitting

rigid and staring daggers at me.

"I would much prefer to be on the payroll."

"No one's fault but the damn bean counters. The department should have the money it needs to thoroughly investigate our cases."

"I couldn't agree more."

"Guess you have no choice. Your leave is approved," he said and waved me out.

I was almost to the door when he asked, "Have you had any luck with that hit-and-run?"

I turned around, surprised that he would ask. Johnson normally gave us a couple of weeks before he started asking about a case.

"I've pulled security camera footage. Randy Spears offered to look through it. I thought I'd check in with him this afternoon."

"That's fine." Johnson looked slightly embarrassed, something I'd never seen. "I only asked because my wife's nephew was one of the young men who was hit."

"I didn't know that. What's his name?" I asked, trying to remember the names of the teenagers involved.

"Andre Norris. Sorry, I shouldn't have mentioned it. No special attention." He turned back to his monitor.

"I'll be sure to keep you in the loop," I said.

"That will be fine," he said softly, staring straight ahead at his screen.

I headed for my desk, shaking my head. Someone should have told Johnson that Calhoun was too small of a town to take things like protocol so seriously. No one else in the whole county hesitated to ask for special favors.

I got a text from Pete: *On to something—Ha!*

Hoping it was something that would bust both murder cases wide open, I called Deputy Spears. "Have you had a chance to go over those videos from the hit-and-runs?"

"I'm halfway through. I'm making notes of all the cars and people I see as I watch them, so it's taking a little time."

"Perfect. In the long run, it will save a lot of time if

there's anything there we can use."

Of course, sometimes it was more important what *wasn't* on camera. If a suspect claimed to be at a certain place at the time of a murder, but video footage could prove that he wasn't, then bingo!

"You're making a note of each tape and the time stamp, right?"

"Duh. Give a guy some credit."

"Thanks, Spears." I started to say goodbye, then mentioned, "Did you know that one of Lt. Johnson's nephews was a victim?"

"No. Which one?"

"Andre Norris."

"I remember him. Nice kid. Seventeen, I think. He had a slight concussion and a few other minor injuries. He was pretty shook up. Seeing him and the boy with the broken pelvis pissed me off. I'd really like to catch the dirt-bag who hit them. I get off the road in a couple of hours and I'll get back on those tapes."


I got home before Cara and was thinking about what to have for dinner when she came bursting through the door, looking a little frantic. "Less than three weeks!"

"What?" I asked without stopping to think.

"The wedding! It struck me about three o'clock this afternoon that our wedding is less than three weeks away. There's still a ton of stuff to do." She was as stressed as I'd ever seen her.

"We've been working on everything. It'll be okay," I said calmly. Apparently that wasn't the right tone to take.

"You don't know that!" Her eyes had a crazed look in them.

I thought of Sarah's words of wisdom and took a deep breath.

"Get your planner and we'll go over everything," I said, wanting nothing more than to have dinner and get ready for my road trip tomorrow.

"Okay. Yeah, you're right." She sighed heavily and grabbed her big planner from the counter. We spent the next hour double-checking the timeline and making a list of all the people we still needed to follow up with.

"I feel a little better," Cara said afterward, giving me a hug.

"I'll call everyone on my list on Wednesday," I promised.

"What about tomorrow?"

I explained about my trip to Gainesville. I didn't point out that I'd mentioned it to her on the phone earlier that day.

"Okay. I guess that will be fine." Cara gnawed on one of her fingernails.

"We'll make this work," I assured her as I got up and started rummaging in the refrigerator. It was eat or pass out at this point.

"I know. It's just freaking me out a bit. The funny thing is, it's more about not disappointing other people."

"And that's what keeps you from falling into the bridezilla category," I said, reheating some meatloaf and green beans.

"You're being rather sweet about the whole thing. I've told a couple of people at work how much you've helped out. You've gotten some major boyfriend credits."

*Thank you, Sarah*, I said to myself. "It will all be worth it if I get to spend the rest of my life with you."

"Now you're just being sappy." She laughed.

"I'm not sappy, I'm hungry," I said, grinning and shoving meatloaf into my mouth.

## CHAPTER TWENTY

The traffic on I-75 was awful, with spring break in full effect. I just barely managed to get to Gainesville without actually pounding my steering wheel into a different shape. It was a credit to how well built the steering wheel was.

Aaron Harlow met me at the door of the Alachua County Sheriff's Office. The handsome young black deputy shook my hand firmly. *You were made for public relations*, I thought. *Or maybe for sheriff.*

"Like I told you on the phone, I'm not one hundred percent sure that the Greer case is related to ours."

"Hey, information is never a bad thing. I was glad you called. Let's go back to my office."

Once we were seated, he passed over a folder.

"There isn't much in there that I didn't already share with you. We've identified a couple of people who could be involved if this turns out to be a criminal case."

I flipped through the paper in the file.

"There's a former boyfriend, her cousin and a guy who lives in the same neighborhood who's on the sex offender registry," Harlow continued. "Of course, no one is suspected of anything at the moment."

"These are the names we've gathered from our two

murder investigations." I handed him a piece of paper where I'd copied down the main characters and most of the peripheral individuals from the two cases. "Do you recognize any of them?"

Harlow studied the list as I looked over the Greer file. In the end, there didn't seem to be any obvious connections between them except for the fact that Beth Robinson and Deanne Greer knew each other, went to college together and were currently Facebook friends.

"One of our victims took a trip to St. Augustine about four months ago. Do you know if Deanne went over there around that time?"

"You think they were all meeting there?"

I shrugged. "It's a possibility."

"Her mother is collecting credit card and financial information for us. We're concentrating on recent activity. Our priority is finding where Deanne Greer is now."

"I understand that. I'm meeting with her mother at noon."

"She's pretty shaken up. When I saw her, there was no doubt in my mind that something dramatic had happened to cause Deanne Greer to go missing."

We talked about the possibilities and the probabilities.

"The bottom line is that we're looking at a great big question mark. Until we find her car or some other evidence, we don't have any clear trail to follow." He stood up. "I'm sorry, but I've got to head to a meeting."

He walked me out to my car.

"If you'll share anything you have that you think might help us out, I promise to do the same," Harlow said, giving me a firm handshake.

Deanne Greer's house was located five miles from the Gainesville city limits. The area had been built up with a number of subdivisions called Deer This and Turkey That. Deanne's old farmhouse must have been there long before the first subdivision had ever been envisioned.

Lisa Greer was waiting outside her daughter's house. While the houses weren't similar at all—Deanne's was an old, two-story frame house and Beth's was a small starter home built in the '80s—I couldn't help but feel a sense of déjà vu at seeing the forlorn mother standing in front of a house that had held happy memories, but was now only a reminder of her loss.

Lisa Greer was effusive in her thanks as I introduced myself.

"I'm grateful to anyone who can help. I just don't know what else I can do."

"I'm sure you're doing everything you can. Deputy Harlow said that you were gathering all of Deanne's financial papers?"

"I've got a lot of it. What was in the house, at any rate. But getting access to Beth's accounts without her to authorize it is next to impossible. Even with a police report, they won't give me anything. They need a death certificate or a court order. I don't mind telling you, I just lied to them. Told them I was Beth. That's gotten me past a couple of them and their stupid bureaucratic security." She stuck out her chin. "I guess I've broken some laws, but I don't care."

"I won't be arresting you," I said, smiling a little. If I was missing, Lisa was just the type of person I'd want hunting for me.

"Here, I'll show you the house," she said as we walked up onto the front porch.

"Did Deanne live here alone?"

"Sometimes she had renters or had friends staying over. Some years she had a regular boyfriend. I didn't want my husband to buy her this house, but he couldn't help indulging her. I always said she was spoiled, but not spoiled rotten."

The house was in good shape and well kept.

"I saw in the reports that she worked from home?"

"That's right, she did consulting work. I don't really

understand all of it, but she had a degree in nursing and several years' experience working in nursing homes. People hired her to look into abuse charges and that sort of thing. My husband could tell you more about it. If you want to talk with him, you can follow me back to our house. He was in a car accident two years ago and doesn't get around very well. This has ripped his heart out. Before he got hurt, he would have been tearing the city apart to find Deanne."

As if on cue, her phone rang. I could tell from her half of the conversation that her husband was calling to find out if I'd arrived and what she was learning.

While she talked to him, I walked around the house. The rooms were all tastefully decorated with period antiques. The place had a dollhouse quality to it. Fragile.

"Have you cleaned the house since she disappeared?" I asked when Lisa was off the phone.

"No. I haven't touched a thing."

"Has anyone else been in here?"

"She hasn't had anyone staying with her since last fall."

"Does she change the locks when someone moves out?"

"My Deanne is meticulous about security. She always has the locks and the security code changed."

I looked around the room and, sure enough, there was a motion sensor and I could see a security camera.

"But you didn't turn it off when we came in?"

Lisa held up her phone. "It's an app. I'm the only other person right now who has the code. I turned it off when I got out of the car."

"Has anyone checked the security cameras?"

"Yes. They show her working at her computer the morning she disappeared, and doing normal household things. The cameras are only on the first floor and just in the common areas."

"I'd like to have a copy of the footage from that day."

"Of course. Everything seemed so... normal that Deputy Harlow didn't see any need to restrict access to the house. There just isn't anything that makes it look like anything happened here. About mid-day, she went out and got in her car. I say that, but you can't see it. She keeps the car in the carriage house and there isn't a camera out there. But the exterior camera picks her up when she leaves the driveway. You can see her in the driver's seat and there doesn't appear to be anyone else in the car."

"Is her bedroom upstairs?"

"Yes, you can go on up. There are three bedrooms and a bath upstairs. When Deanne first moved in, there were four bedrooms upstairs. She converted the fourth bedroom into a very nice bathroom," Lisa said, following me up the mahogany staircase.

Deanne used one of the bedrooms as an office. Everything was neat and tidy. "Has anyone looked at her computer?" I asked, looking at the desk.

Lisa seemed uncomfortable. "I don't know what to do about that. I don't have the password, and I'm afraid to take it to someone. I doubt it would do any good. Deanne was very security conscious and doubly so about her computer. You see, with the work she did, there were HIPPA laws to consider and the cases sometimes involved lawsuits. So the files she worked with were very... sensitive."

"I understand. I just wonder if she might have seen something on the Internet or gotten an email from someone that set in motion the events leading to her disappearance."

"Nothing like that would be on that computer. She had one of those, what do you call them... just a screen?"

"A tablet."

"That's it. She did all of her personal emails, Internet and whatnot from that. The computer was only for business."

Deanne had obviously been a very cautious person. *So what went wrong?* I wondered.

The next door I opened led to the spacious master bath. Everything in the room was as neat and tidy as the rest of the house, so it was impossible to tell if anything was missing. I opened a cabinet and saw that Deanne had been prescribed medicine for anxiety.

"Does Deanne see a psychiatrist?" I tried to make it sound like a casual question rather than an accusation.

"From time to time. She gets... worked up. Something gets in her head and she just can't shake it. Even when she knows it's not important or not a real threat. The drugs help her stay focused. Of course, she didn't like the way they made her feel. I understand most people feel that way. So she'd only take them when her anxiety got out of hand."

I looked at the prescriptions. They were all out of date by several months. I shut the cabinet.

"You might want to check and see if she's picked up a new prescription in the last month." If she had, then she'd apparently taken it with her when she left. Maybes and ifs were all I was finding.

"Is this where her roommates would live?" I asked, opening a third door into what appeared to be a guest room.

"No. When she had guests, they'd stay here. There's a nice little apartment over the carriage house. That's what she rented out."

The last door led to Deanne's bedroom. I was reminded again of a dollhouse. The room would have fulfilled the dream of many an adolescent girl. There was a large four-poster bed with a frilly canopy, a dresser with a wrap-around mirror and shelves full of stuffed animals, Breyer horses and books.

I walked slowly around the room, trying to take everything in. At the dresser, I opened the drawers and looked through the neatly organized cosmetics. To the side of the dresser was a beautiful carved jewelry cabinet that stood five feet high and was a foot-and-a-half wide.

"Do you know if any of her jewelry is missing?" I asked as I looked carefully through the rings, earrings, bracelets and watches.

"I wouldn't know. There's so much."

I thought I had looked through the whole jewelry case until I noticed that the side opened up. It folded back, giving Deanne a place to hang necklaces. I noticed several that hung toward the front. They were of various designs, but they all had one thing in common. The name "Autumn" was engraved on all of them.

"Are these hers?" I asked Lisa.

She moved closer and squinted into the case. "Yes. In fact, those are some of her favorites."

"Was Autumn a nickname?" I asked, puzzled.

"I guess you could say that. She loved fall. Once she told me she wished it could be autumn all year round."

That's when I realized that many of the paintings in the house depicted fall scenes. One of the four seasons. And Deanne was in love with autumn. Was it a coincidence? I felt like I could almost reach out and touch the elusive connection between the three women. That's when it hit me. Two women murdered, plus one missing, equaled three. Four seasons. Could the four seasons represent four people? Our three women, plus one more? Maybe the fourth was the mysterious woman caller, or maybe the caller was Deanne. And if it was Deanne, what game was she playing?

"Do you have any video of your daughter? Or a recording?" I asked Lisa.

"I've got a movie we took at my husband's birthday last year." She took out her phone and started scrolling through it. "Here it is." She held the phone out to me.

The video was already playing. Mr. Greer, looking in very poor health, tried to smile as a cake was brought out to him. Deanne, who I recognized from the missing flyers, carried the cake and made happy talk as she set it down on the table and patted her dad on the shoulder. Lisa came into the picture carrying plates with silverware and napkins stacked on top. I wondered who was doing the filming.

I listened to Deanne and tried to decide if hers was the voice I'd heard on the phone, but I hadn't really heard enough to make a firm conclusion.

"Thanks. I just wanted to get a feel for her."

"I should post it on Facebook. It makes her… come alive." There were ominous undertones in her voice.

"We'll find her," I assured Lisa, hoping that I wasn't promising more than I could deliver.

"Thank you."

I made one more pass around the inside of the house before going outside and checking all of the doors and windows to see if the person who had broken into Beth's home had tried to break into this house too. Everything looked secure and untouched.

"I'm going to see Boyd Fleming," I said as we reached the cars. Fleming was the old boyfriend that Deputy Harlow had mentioned in his files.

"He's such a nice young man. He and Deanne dated years ago, but they've stayed friends."

## CHAPTER TWENTY-ONE

I met Boyd Fleming outside of Shands, the University of Florida's teaching hospital, where he worked as a nurse. He was blond and muscular, with an open and friendly demeanor.

"We can go inside if you want," he offered.

"I'm fine out here." The weather was pleasant, and I figured sitting outdoors would be less distracting for him than being inside the hospital. "Why don't you start by telling me a little about your relationship with Deanne?"

"We met at a nursing seminar in Atlanta. That was about ten years ago. We hooked up right away. You know what it's like. We found out we were both from the same area and had some interests in common. I was very attracted to her. Not just her looks, but her… vulnerability."

"What do you mean by vulnerability?"

"She would have anxiety attacks and kind of freak out. Most of the time, they weren't much worse than most people have from time to time. But every once in a while she'd have a bad one. I was pretty good at calming her down."

"How long were you all together?"

"Two years, something like that. Only lived together for a year. We rented an apartment and, when the lease was up, so were we."

"Why'd you break up?"

"We got on each other's nerves. That sounds trite, but it's the best way I can explain it. Sharing an apartment with Deanne was difficult. She was very protective of her stuff. Maybe you could call it obsessive-compulsive, I don't know. But if I moved something and didn't put it back where it belonged, I'd catch hell for it or, worse, she'd give me the silent treatment. There were days on end that she wouldn't speak to me, and I had no idea what I'd done. Funny, I think what drew me to her also made it impossible to live in the same house with her."

"How's that?" I asked, trying to understand Deanne and their relationship.

"It was my fault. I got to where I didn't want to upset her, so I became over-protective. Later she told me how annoying she found it." He shrugged.

"Was she happy with the breakup?"

"Relieved. I think it stressed her out more than me."

"What about you? Were you okay with the separation?"

"Absolutely. Neither of us blamed the other. I mean, she was really stressed. She wasn't using her anger to manipulate me. And she knew that what she was asking of me, never touching or moving anything in the house, was unreasonable. On the other hand, I came to understand that I was smothering her. The night the lease was up, we went out and celebrated."

"And stayed friends?"

"Best friends."

I thought that Boyd didn't seem as upset as he should have been that his best friend was missing, possibly in danger or even dead.

"When was the last time you saw Deanne?"

"The day before she disappeared. She wanted to drive down to McIntosh and look at an antique desk. I've got a truck, so she asked me to drive down with her. It's about thirty miles south of here."

"Did she buy the desk?"

"No, the way it was put together, the dovetailing or something, made her think it was more modern than the dealer said it was. So we came back to town and had dinner at the Steak 'n Shake before I took her home."

"Did you talk or text with her after that?"

As soon as I asked the question, I saw his eyes look quickly to the right and left. "A couple of texts," he finally said.

"Can I see them?"

With no hesitation, he pulled out his phone, scrolled through some texts, then handed it to me. They started the night before Deanne disappeared.

Her: *Thanks bro for dinner. Kisses.*

Him: *No prob.*

On the following day, they continued.

Her: *How's the coal mine?*

Him: *Dark and deep today.*

I looked up. "Coal mine?"

"That's how we referred to the hospital. I know that sounds bad. It's just a joke. You know, going down in the coal mine to work. That sort of thing. Just being silly."

"You sound like you weren't having a very good day."

"It was pretty awful. We lost a boy who'd come down with a staph infection. He'd been admitted for a broken leg. They had to put in a plate and screws. A relatively simple operation, but he got an infection and went down quickly. It was a low moment for me."

I went back to the texts.

Her: *You need a shoulder?*

Him: *Maybe later. Just need to survive the next six hours.*

Her: *You got this. You're my hero.*

That was the last text she'd sent him. I flipped back through some of the other texts between them, usually several messages per day. All of them supported his assertion that they were good friends. I handed the phone back to him.

"Have you been helping Mrs. Greer put up flyers?"

"Whenever I'm off work. I took two days off right after Deanne disappeared to help look for her."

Boyd still didn't look as upset as one would expect. However, I knew better than to go by some metric norm of behavior. People's reactions to stress covered a whole spectrum of behaviors. There were people who became calmer when the shit hit the fan, only to break down days after a crisis. Other people were great liars and could mimic any of the classic emotions well enough to fool an expert. I could think of many examples of law enforcement going down the wrong rabbit hole because they misread someone's reaction.

"What do you know about the four seasons?" I was hoping to catch him off guard.

He looked at me and didn't say a word for a ten count. "Like what? Are you talking about a place?"

"Or people."

"I don't understand."

"Why does Deanne have several necklaces with the word 'Autumn' on them?"

I saw a look of relief cross his face. *Why? Because with that question, I just told him that I don't know much about the four seasons.* I gave myself a mental kick in the head for being so obvious.

"Fall is Deanne's favorite time of the year. You should see her house and yard at Halloween. Now that I think about it, Halloween is the only time of the year that she throws caution to the wind and goes a little wild, decorating the yard and making the house look spooky."

"You can't think of any other reason for her to have jewelry with that name?"

"I told you, she likes fall. What else did you think?"

I ignored his question. "Where do you think Deanne is?"

"I don't know," he said flatly.

"Has she met someone else? Could she have gone out of town for a liaison?"

"I doubt it. She hasn't really dated in a year or more. I've been trying to get her to come out of her cave a bit more. But the last relationship seemed to be the straw that broke the camel's back. After that breakup, she's given up on finding someone she can live with."

"Or who can live with her?" I said, needling him.

"That too," he acknowledged.

Thinking of the strange calls I'd received, I asked, "Does she have any other phones?"

"Like a work phone?"

He was in the classic answer-a-question-with-another-question mode, which was often a sign that a suspect felt they were on shaky ground.

"Or a burner phone."

"A what?" I saw in his eyes that he knew exactly what a burner phone was. So I just looked at him and let the silence grow. He didn't dare ask me again because he knew that I knew that he knew.

"Oh, like druggies and prostitutes use?" was the best he could come back with.

"I think they like to be called sex workers now," I said snappishly. I was getting pissed off that the man who claimed to be Deanne's best friend was playing games with me when her life could have been on the line. Did he already know that she was safe?

"Are drug users pharmaceutical addicts?" An edge had crept into his voice.

"Listen to me," I said sternly, giving him my best don't-screw-with-me stare. "If you have information that could help us locate Deanne, and you don't share it with me right now, at some later date you could find yourself charged with any number of serious crimes, ranging all the way from obstruction of justice to accomplice to murder."

This made a small dent in his armor and knocked him back on the defensive.

"I don't know where she is and I would never do anything that might endanger her," he said, returning my stare.

"You're a nurse. I bet you get patients all the time who think they know how to do your job. How often are they wrong? I'm the expert here. Not you. I strongly advise you to tell me what you know and let me decide what's the best way to protect Deanne."

For almost two minutes he sat there and didn't say a word. At any moment, I thought he might blurt out what he was hiding, but he never did.

At last he said, "I'm done answering your questions," and stood up.

I pulled out one of my cards. "Think. If you decide to do the right thing, give me a call."

He stared at the card, then hesitantly took it and turned back to the hospital.

*I'll be seeing you*, I thought as I watched him walk away.

On my way home, I received a call from Zeph Roberts.

"Deputy Macklin, Mrs. Roberts," she said, obviously assuming that I'd remember her from the CPA firm. The ice in her voice, I remembered. "I wanted to let you know that we've found a rather... odd file on Elizabeth's computer."

"Not one of your accounts?"

"Obviously not. This looks like some work she was doing for herself."

"What's odd about it?" I asked, knowing that if she got too deep into the math, I'd be lost.

"From what I can tell, it's research Elizabeth was doing into someone's business practices. What you might find most interesting is that the business was crooked."

"Crooked how?"

"The figures show that what the business reported ran contrary to estimates that Elizabeth was able to make."

"I don't understand."

"I'm sure that, as a police officer, you've seen someone whose job couldn't support that person's lifestyle. When that's the case, you would expect to find that the person is either accumulating debt or has a hidden source of income. This is similar. Elizabeth appears to have uncovered someone whose business was a front. Like a pyramid scheme."

"But the person wouldn't have let her look at their books?"

"If you know where to look, you don't have to look at their books to know a business is a scam."

"Who are we talking about?"

"I don't know. Elizabeth was being very discreet. She used abbreviations and code names."

"If she knew that a business was operating a front for a scam, why would she keep it quiet?"

"I think she was being cautious. Destroying a business, even one that's bent, has consequences. If she got involved in a high-profile investigation, it could have even affected our business. Also, she'd probably be sued by whoever was running the business just as a matter of course. I can imagine all of that could be very... disturbing for someone who guarded her privacy as much as Elizabeth."

"I see what you mean. Can I get a copy of the data?"

"Of course. You'll have it in your email by the end of the day."


The next day, I brought Darlene and Pete up to speed on my trip to Gainesville and the phone call from Ms. Roberts.

"Pete, didn't you mention you were working on a lead?" I asked him.

"I might have been overly optimistic. I've got a meeting tomorrow with a guy who knows a guy. I shouldn't jinx it by talking about it."

Pete was being sincere. I'd seen him like this before. He looked like a guy who was going up to bat at the bottom of the ninth with two men out, and he could be the winning run. He might knock one out of the park or he could strike out and lose the game.

"Suit yourself," I said, dying to know what he thought he had.

"I want to change my job in all of this," Darlene said. "Elizabeth is the saddest victim I've come across in a long time. Doing a forensic workup on her life has just left me feeling dead inside. I don't think the clue to the mystery is going to come from her, even with this strange set of figures Roberts sent over. Other than the one account I was able to find that showed the trip to St. Augustine, I don't have anything else. She even shredded her receipts. There are still a couple of credit card accounts that I'm waiting to see after the companies accept our warrant, if they even will. One of the people I talked to told me that most customers choose their company because of their privacy policies and the bank of lawyers they use to back it up."

"Interesting," I said, not meaning to sound annoying, but knowing that I was.

"Interesting if you aren't the one spending all day working your way through phone trees," Darlene shot back. She was a woman of action. Having to deal with corporate institutions from a distance wasn't her strong suit.

"I've been thinking… there's one thing that these women had in common. Beth and Elizabeth both had very strong personalities. I think I'd say the same for Deanne."

"Beth was very outgoing. Very caring. I've had a dozen people tell me that she would go out of her way to help anyone who needed it," Pete said.

"Elizabeth was a bit of a kook, but there's no doubt that she was a brilliant accountant," Darlene allowed.

"And Deanne was almost a borderline obsessive-compulsive personality who was a bit paranoid on top of that."

"So what does it all mean?" Pete asked.

"I don't know," I admitted.

"Maybe their peculiarities brought them together," Darlene suggested.

"They were all in college together. Maybe they met there, bonded over their unique personalities and became friends." A thought was coming back to me.

"They could have just as easily become enemies as friends," Darlene said.

I remembered the idea I'd toyed with the day before. "They met at FSU and became friends. Friends known as the four seasons. So where is the fourth season?"

Darlene and Pete stared at me.

"So now we have another missing person?" Darlene sounded incredulous.

"I know. This is a house of cards that I've built on a foundation of pure speculation."

"Wow. That sounded great. Whose quote is that?" Pete asked.

I gave a slight bow. "That's all me."

"It's also all true. If they did have some secret group, they've managed to keep it well hidden."

"Whatever might have been hidden behind the painting with that pen could fill in a lot of the gaps," I said.

"Do you think Deanne or your mysterious Woman Number Four broke into Beth's house?"

"Or the killer," I said.

"Or one of them is the killer and broke into the house," Darlene said. "You were just talking about them all having strong personalities. I'd say volatile is another adjective that could describe them."

"I won't say you're wrong."

I was following up on my other active investigations when Deputy Spears stopped by my desk after he got off patrol.

"I watched all those tapes and wrote down information on the cars and pedestrians on film. I started two hours before the first hit-and-run that damaged the car and went two hours after the incident with the young men." He handed me a spreadsheet. "I'll email you the file in a bit."

I looked at him with a newfound respect. "You realize this is better than if I'd done it?"

"I... was just being thorough," he said, sounding a bit embarrassed.

"Anything suspicious?"

"I've identified five cars that were driving erratically and ten more that appeared to be speeding. Unfortunately, it was dark the entire time, so it's impossible to tell what color most of the vehicles are."

"I've got the lab working on paint samples from the car that was hit. You've identified fifteen probables. How many vehicles altogether?"

"A hundred and fifteen cars over four hours, captured on eleven cameras spanning a two-square-mile area," Spears recited like a student during an oral exam.

"Okay, I'll look at them first thing tomorrow. We won't know anything about the paint chip for at least another week or so."

"The wheels of justice grind slowly or something like that," he said.

"Slow and steady wins the race."

He chuckled and left me with his spreadsheet.

## CHAPTER TWENTY-TWO

Early on Thursday, I gave Lt. Johnson an update on the fifteen cars we were focusing on for the hit-and-runs.

"Do you have plates?"

"We have complete plates on four, partial plates on three and nothing on the other eight. Most of the cameras are privately owned and aren't set up to capture the plates of cars on the road."

"Have you checked the body shops?"

"We're working on that now. There are two official shops in the county and four shade-tree operations. I also asked a friend who knows the business to check out the ones in Tallahassee."

"That's a long shot anyway. You'd have to be an idiot to take a car that was damaged in a hit-and-run to a body shop."

"The only way you can do it is to have another accident on purpose to cover up the previous damage. I read about a guy who hit a kid on a bicycle. Two days later he ran his car into a tree."

"That's pretty smart. If you can hide the car for a day or two."

"This guy kept his in the garage until he took it out at

night to have his accident. The only reason he got caught was because the body shop guy was a friend of the family whose boy was killed. He noticed some hair and blood on the back side of the bumper when he removed it."

"Luck. I hate to rely on luck to solve cases." Johnson's eyes got a faraway look. "Of course, you only have to be on one battlefield to learn pretty quick that luck is the only card worth having." I glanced at the photos on the wall of Johnson's old unit in Iraq and could only imagine what he was thinking.

After leaving Johnson's office, I went back to my temporary office in Shantel's lair to update my notes with everything I'd learned during the trip to Gainesville. I wasn't able to scrounge up another white board, so I taped large sheets of paper to the wall to start organizing the information on Deanne Greer.

I heard the door open behind me.

"And you said you weren't moving in," Shantel huffed.

"I *feel* like I'm moving in."

"Who's the other woman?"

I told her about Deanne Greer.

"I had a little chick clique when I was in school," Shantel said. "We called ourselves the Bad Girls. You know, like the theme song from *Cops*. We were all studying criminology. Our group was kinda fluid. One of us would have a heavy load of classes or get a boyfriend and not be around for a couple of months. So we'd pick up some naïve freshman who looked lost to fill in the group."

"Y'all sound scary."

"We'd have eaten your skinny ass up, son!" she said with a grin. "Nah, we were really more of a study group. Shared information on all the classes. Which teachers to take and which ones to avoid. Now don't get me wrong, we'd party at the end of the semester, but we were all paying for our education by the sweat off our brows. Not a one of us was being spoon-fed money from our parents."

"So what do you think?" I said, waving my arms around

at the white boards and files.

"They're connected."

"Why do you say that?"

"Too many coincidences. Also, the two murders have a staged feel to them. Like someone wanted them to look dramatic."

I looked at Shantel, impressed. "That's a good point. I wasn't conscious of it, but now that you mention it, it's been bothering me too. Burying Elizabeth under the mulch at the nursery so she'd be discovered by the first customer to come along. Then throwing Beth off of the bridge into a creek while leaving her car parked alongside the road. They both have a theatrical air to them, as though they were being staged for an audience."

"Or sending a message," Shantel suggested grimly.


By that afternoon, Pete's date with his hot lead had completely slipped my mind. I was now almost as caught up in the countdown to the wedding as Cara, and spent a bit of time working on my list of phone calls. It didn't help that we were also fielding calls from friends and relatives about hotels, schedules and gifts.

I was driving back from an interview with a witness to an assault and battery when I got a call from Pete.

"Ha! Who's the man?" he shouted.

"Let me guess, you are."

"You got that right, sonny boy. Where are you?"

"Headed back to the office."

"Perfect. Meet me in your war room."

Twenty minutes later, I walked in to find Pete pacing up and down with a huge smile on his face while Darlene sat in a chair, looking exasperated.

"Thank goodness! The lotto winner here wouldn't tell me a thing until you showed up," Darlene complained.

"I didn't want to have to repeat myself." Pete's good humor was unaffected.

"So tell," I encouraged him.

"You deserve some of the credit," he said, as excited as a kid unrolling a treasure map. "Remember when Julio came up to you at your party and gave you his brother-in-law's card?"

I nodded vaguely, though I didn't have a clue where the card was now.

"Over the weekend, I got to thinking about motives for Beth's murder. Love, revenge, fear, hate and the big enchilada, money. Beth didn't have any money. Not to speak of. I asked her mother about life insurance, but she wasn't aware of any. There wasn't any paperwork or evidence of any premiums paid out except for house and car insurance. No go.

"But that card made me think. I'd heard about people taking out insurance on other people without them knowing it. So I thought, hey, Julio is hooked up. Just to cover the bases, I decided to contact his brother-in-law and see if he could find out if there were any policies written on Beth. He called me back sounding funny, said he was out of town and couldn't meet with me until this morning." Pete stopped to take a breath. He'd been pouring out the story like someone in an auctioneer's contest.

"He found something?" Knowing that Pete was no fool, I was interested to see where this was going. Darlene was literally on the edge of her seat.

"Not just something. The gold ring that binds them and the murders all together," he said, waving at the women's names on the boards.

He paused for dramatic effect, but Darlene and I were too caught up in the story to give him a hard time about building suspense.

"An insurance policy that names four women as beneficiaries."

Both Darlene and I uttered a few choice expletives.

"Give us the details," I urged.

Now Pete sat down and took out a small notebook. "I

wrote it down because it's pretty complicated," he said, flipping through the pages. "One of his friends remembered Elizabeth Collins contacting him about an insurance policy about three months ago. She wanted to take out a life insurance policy on four women, including herself. The policy would pay out to the survivors and into a trust. The trust was for any children whose mother had died. So, for example, if Beth died there would be a one-million-dollar payout. Half would go to the surviving women and the other half would go into a trust fund for her son. If, on the other hand, childless Deanne were to die, half of the money would go to the surviving women and half would go into a trust for the other women's children.

"What she wanted was more complicated than anything this guy handled, so he referred her to a man named Nigel Whalen. I talked to Mr. Whalen and he said that Elizabeth had explained how the women were all unofficial godmothers of each other's children. The point being that if one mother died, the other women would be there to help the children out. Plus, of course, the children would have the trust fund."

"How was the trust set up?" I asked.

"The surviving women would administer it. Let me tell you one of the most interesting clauses in the policy. If more than one of the women died before the policy paid out, then the money wouldn't go to the family of the deceased but rather to the surviving women." Pete was almost vibrating with excitement.

"Let me get this straight," Darlene said. "Since Beth died before the insurance company paid out for Elizabeth's death, then both shares will go to Deanne and a fourth woman?"

"Does the policy cover murder and suicide?" I asked.

"Murder is covered and suicide is covered after six months," Pete said. "Pretty standard."

"By the way, quit burying the lead. Who is the fourth woman?" Darlene demanded.

"Shannon Carrol. Trust me, I have the full details on

Shannon." He looked smug. "So you see the possibilities?"

"If something has also happened to Deanne, then this Shannon person gets one-and-a-half-million dollars," I said.

"Plus control of the trust for the other half. And she has a boy of her own."

"That is one big greenback motive." Darlene whistled.

"Sounds like even more of a motive when you get the background on Shannon Carrol," Pete said. "Her maiden name was Shannon Grzesik. She was born in Mobile, Alabama and attended Florida State University at the same time as our other women. She studied pre-law and graduated in the top of her class. That is about the end of the happy Shannon story. She was accepted to the University of Florida's law school, but dropped out after a year. Not long after that, she had a son out of wedlock."

"Any idea what happened?"

"Alcohol. She had a DUI in Gainesville shortly after dropping out of law school. She went to rehab while she was pregnant with her son. She stayed clean for a while, then bounced off and on the wagon a few times with some more trips to rehab. Then she met a man named Barry Carrol. He was stationed at Naval Air Station Pensacola. A top NCO, he was in charge of ordnance. His responsibilities shifted during his service, but the gist is that he oversaw the ordnance that went onto combat aircraft. They married and Shannon, her son and Barry were a happy couple for about five years. He had a couple of deployments, but everything seemed to be fine until he injured his back in an accident. Something to do with the job. He got a medical discharge. Unfortunately, somewhere along the line he got hooked on painkillers and other drugs. Three years ago he was arrested for prescription fraud. Shannon got pulled over a year ago and was arrested for possession. The son is currently living with his grandparents." Pete set his notes aside.

"Wow," was all I could think to say.

"Where is she now?" Darlene asked.

"Barry and Shannon have somehow managed to hold

onto their house in Pensacola. I've already asked the Pensacola police to check it out. They said the house looks like it's been rented out to an unsanitary zoo to house their primates. No one was home when they went by and, according to the neighbors, they haven't seen the Carrols for almost a week. They told the officers that it had been a quote, blessed week of silence, unquote."

"So…" Darlene said, an expectant look on her face.

"That's why I kept this under wraps," Pete said, pausing again like a magician preparing his audience. This was Pete's moment of glory, so I waited patiently for the rabbit to appear.

"I know where they are," Pete revealed. "A report of a stolen credit card had already been filed, naming Shannon as the prime suspect. Do I even need to say that neither Barry nor Shannon have working credit cards?"

"We could have deduced that," Darlene muttered.

"Shannon had a job at a Waffle House in Pensacola until she didn't show up a week ago. A co-worker's credit card disappeared around the same time. And where, might you ask, has this credit card been used? Pelican Island."

"Oh, anywhere but there," I groaned.

Dad and I had royally stirred up things in the area last summer. And while we'd solved a series of murders, our meddling had resulted in the local sheriff being replaced. I was afraid that there were more than a few deputies who hadn't appreciated our help.

"The card was used to rent a unit at the Seascape Trailer Park. I've already made sure that no one informs the park owner about the card so no one else flushes our love birds."

"Have you contacted the sheriff's office down there?" I asked.

"No. My thought is that we should just go down there for an interview. No reason to involve your friends in the sheriff's office over that. The only problem is I don't know exactly which trailer they're in."

"If you didn't contact the park's owner, how do you

know that they used the card to rent a trailer instead of something else, like a boat?" Darlene asked.

"Well... I might have asked Sarah to call up and pretend to be from the credit card company. She told them she just wanted to confirm that it was a legitimate purchase. Flimsy, yes, but it worked. She even got them to chitchat with her for a few minutes, but she couldn't come up with a good reason why the credit card company would need to know *which* trailer they had rented."

I started clapping. "All of this." I waved my hand at his notes. "I'm very impressed." Darlene was clapping now too. Pete took a theatrical bow.

"You're the coach; what's the game plan?" I asked.

Pete cleared his throat with a look of embarrassment. "You may have noticed that, as compelling as the facts are, we have zero evidence. Therefore, a delicate approach is called for. All three of us go down there. One of us knocks on the door while the other two block the roads out of the park. The knock on the door is very polite, simply suggesting that Shannon and Barry might want to know that two of Shannon's friends are dead. They are only material witnesses, blah, blah. Then all we have to do is talk them into coming up here for an interview. Once they're here, Pensacola will charge Shannon with credit card theft, fraud and anything else they can think of. If they can get into their house with a warrant, I'm pretty sure they can find something to charge Barry with as well. We might even hit the jackpot down at Pelican Island if we can get a look in the trailer or Barry's truck."

"And since, like you said, we're only going down there to interview them, then there's no reason why we'd have to let the local sheriff's office know we're in town." I really didn't want to deal with deputies who had an axe to grind.

"Exactly. But I think you're worrying about nothing. Those guys are probably happy you forced Sheriff Duncan out," Pete said dismissively.

"He's right." Darlene's tone suggested that she thought

just the opposite.

"Yeah, what could go wrong?" I muttered.

Two hours later, we were sitting in Dad's office so Pete could explain the case and our plan to both him and Lt. Johnson.

"I don't like playing in someone else's sandbox without making them aware of it," Johnson said, frowning deeply.

"There were definitely some hurt feelings last June, but if everything is done discreetly, I don't see the harm. Of course, if things get out of hand, y'all will be knee-deep in a very nasty septic tank," Dad told us.

I looked at Darlene and Pete. "We've thought about that. If Shannon and Barry do anything stupid, we'll just back up and keep them under surveillance. If they run, we'll follow at a distance. If they just stonewall us, then we'll watch them and contact the locals, acting all surprised like we really did think the Carrols were just witnesses."

"And what if they come out shooting?" Johnson asked.

"We'll do what we have to do and take our punishment like the big men and women we are," I said.

"I don't think they'll do that. Run, absolutely. Hole up, possibly. But these are drug addicts. They've been drug and alcohol abusers for years. At this point, they're mentally impaired. My best guess is that they'll come with us thinking they can outsmart us. This whole scheme suggests that they're overconfident in their ability to fool the cops," Pete said.

"That's why only one of us is going to knock on their door. A single investigator looks like the cops are fishing around, not sending a raiding party," Darlene said.

"You said they're overconfident. What I see are two killers who are desperate," Johnson said.

Dad turned to him. "I can tell you aren't comfortable with their plan. What would make it work for you?"

Johnson looked thoughtful. "My biggest concern is that, when the trailer door opens and Bonnie and Clyde find out that the guy in the suit is a cop, they'll start shooting."

"I wasn't going to wear a suit," I said unwisely.

Johnson ignored me. "Even if they don't kill Macklin, they could escape and go on a spree. They fire on a cop, they'll know that all the rules are out the window. So my suggestion would be that you take four people down there. Darlene and the fourth person cover the two exits from the park while Pete, from a distance, covers Larry with a rifle."

It wasn't a bad idea. Pete was the department's designated sniper. I'd be much safer with him at my back. Plus, he'd also be in a position to stop them from escaping from the trailer if all hell broke loose.

"Who do you suggest as the fourth man?" Dad asked Johnson.

"Someone mature. I hate to send another one of my investigators. Our caseload is becoming critical. However, I would be comfortable with Ortiz backing them up."

"Done," Dad said. "Tomorrow?" There were nods all around. "Pete's in charge. You will inform me if anything goes wrong. Immediately. I'll need to get the damage control rolling fast. Try to keep this clean. In and out. Now get what you need and brief Julio on the plan."

Our faces were solemn as we walked out of the office, hoping we weren't getting ready to jump naked into a nest of fire ants.

"This sounds dangerous," Cara said after I explained the plan to her that evening.

"It could be." I wasn't going to lie to her. She frowned at me and chewed her lip. "I'm being honest."

"I'm not sure I want you to be. What kind of danger?"

"Mostly the unknown kind." She gave me a look. "I'm not trying to be funny. The most dangerous part about it is that we don't know these people. Most of the time, when we're going to interview or bring someone in around here, we have a good idea of their history so we can pretty accurately judge how they're going to react. A guy who's never been violent probably won't be violent and vice versa. No guarantees, but it holds true most of the time."

"You don't know anything about these two?"

"Pete has talked to some of the cops in Pensacola who've had run-ins with them. The word is that they're your typical druggies. Nonviolent on the whole. Of course, if they're pumped on the wrong drug, they might put up a fight. The thing is, they've never been in this kind of trouble. If we're right, they've already killed at least two people and now they're on the run. Criminals that aren't on their home turf tend to be more dangerous than when they're in their own neighborhood."

"That makes sense. But why do you have to be the one to knock on the door?"

I already regretted giving Cara the details.

"It just worked out that way." I said. "Pete will be covering me. If there's any sign of danger, he'll take care of it."

"No one down there knows you're coming?"

"I think it's better that way. I'm positive there are deputies who resent what we did last summer. Pete decided to go ahead and call the owner of the trailer park to let them know we'll be coming, and to get the trailer number."

"Can you trust the owner?"

"There's no sign of any connection between him and the Carrols. Besides, if he did tell them, then they'd just be gone. We decided it was a risk we have to take. If we just show up there tomorrow and someone sees Pete with a rifle or notices Julio and Darlene blocking the exits, they might raise the alarm in the middle of the operation, making a tough situation worse."

"Operation. I don't like that word. It makes it sound like you're soldiers or spies or something."

"I've got good people watching my back. All of us are aware of the danger, which is the first step to prevent anything bad from happening. You know when cops get hurt? When they least expect it. We know this isn't a routine traffic stop." I pulled her in for a hug.

"I know. I think the wedding has me on edge, and this just seems like bad timing." She returned my hug fiercely.

"I'll call you as soon as we're done. But don't worry if it takes a while."

The rest of the night was tense as both of us dealt with our own nerves about the coming day.

## CHAPTER TWENTY-THREE

Julio was vibrating with excitement as we loaded up the cars at six o'clock on Friday morning. Getting there early was an important element. Most bad guys weren't early risers, so waking them up would give law enforcement an edge. We weren't raiding the Carrols, but it still wouldn't hurt to catch them off guard and a bit groggy.

"We got everything?" Pete asked. We were going down in two cars, Pete and me in one and Darlene and Julio in the other. We were all wearing our tactical vests. I had on one of the newer, less bulky ones so as not to scare the bad guys, as well as some extra Kevlar to cover my more vulnerable parts. It was a little awkward and uncomfortable, but I wasn't taking any chances.

It was a ninety-minute drive down to the coast on a perfect spring morning, clear and cool. The drive through the miles of longleaf pines in the Apalachicola National Forest was beautiful, though the closer we got to the coast, the more evidence we could see of Hurricane Marcy's destructive path. There was the smell of smoke in the air, which usually meant that the park service was conducting prescribed burns to keep the longleaf habitat healthy and vibrant. This year it just meant they were burning storm debris.

Little did we know that the drive down was going to be the highlight of our trip. I knew we were screwed when I saw the unmarked but unmistakable cop car parked in front of the office at the Seascape Trailer Park.

"Bad news," I said.

"Damn! I thought the owner sounded a little funny on the phone yesterday."

We'd left Darlene at the main entrance while Julio drove around to the back gate. I thought about calling them and giving them a heads-up that the plan might get rather fluid, but decided Pete and I should go on in and see how bad it was.

The guy behind the counter was pushing seventy and looked nervous in his pastel polo, flower-print shorts and sandals. A deputy was standing at the counter and turned to look at us as we walked in. He was wearing a suit, but had his gold star hanging on his belt.

Pete walked up to the desk, ignoring the deputy, who was built like a Mack truck. "Are you Arnold?"

"That's right. I guess you're the fella who's been calling about number twenty-two."

Pete showed him his badge. "I'm Pete Henley, an investigator with the Adams County Sheriff's Office."

"I know you said not to tell anyone, but I got to thinking, what if you weren't who you said you were? Maybe you were even drug guys or mafia or something and were going to hurt the guests. I just thought I ought to call our sheriff and see if this is all above-board. You know?" Arnold looked like he expected Pete to reach across the desk and hit him. Pete didn't, but I wanted to.

The deputy just stood there, watching and listening with a smirk on his face.

Pete turned to him. "Pete Henley," he said, sticking out his hand.

"Don't know who you are," the deputy said, turning to look at me. "Him I know. He has a real bad habit of coming into other people's jurisdictions and taking a shit. Not this time."

"We just came down here to interview a witness," Pete said in a firm but friendly tone.

"Bullshit. You think we're a bunch of country bumpkins? I looked into all of this after Mr. Randle called us. I've talked to Pensacola PD. I got the whole story."

I could see Pete trying to come up with a way around this muscle-bound roadblock. I'd later learn that the deputy, Freddie Mullins, had been a captain under the old sheriff. Dad and I had cost him a considerable cut in pay and authority. Word was that the new sheriff had wanted to fire him, but hadn't been able to for political reasons.

"Let us talk to the Carrols. If they don't have any information we can use, we'll be on our way," Pete said, trying to be reasonable.

"Yeah, you can talk to them after we arrest them for using a stolen credit card. I've got backup on the way. Y'all are welcome to stand back and watch us do our job."

I could see Pete working to control his anger. For a minute I thought he was going to argue with the goon, but Pete wasn't stupid and he was also less likely than me to hit his head against a brick wall, so he just kept his mouth closed.

We went back outside and leaned against our car as we waited. I called Darlene and Julio while Pete stewed in fury and self-recrimination.

"I shouldn't have called last night. Damn it!" He muttered a number of obscenities under his breath.

"It is what it is," I told him as we watched a marked truck pull up. Two deputies got out, armored up as if they'd just come from a no-knock raid in Iraq.

"That seems like overkill," I murmured to Pete as the men clumped up to the office in their combat boots and body armor. Each carried a short-barreled rifle, while their vests were loaded down with at least six magazines each.

Five minutes later, they came back out of the office with

Deputy Mullins in the lead. "Stay back. Any interference and I'll have you arrested for obstructing justice." He spat the words at us as he walked by.

We waited until they were twenty yards ahead of us before falling in behind them. The Keystone Soldiers got looks from some of the park's early risers.

Trailer number twenty-two had an eight-by-eight-foot deck at the front door. As they got closer, I saw Mullins signal to the man on his right to circle around to the back of the trailer. *At least they got that much right*, I thought.

Deputy Mullins walked onto the deck and up to the door. He waited while Robocop stood off to the side before he knocked. They waited. More knocking. More waiting. When the door finally opened, I could tell that the woman was drunk, even from a distance.

Mullins talked for about ten seconds before the woman started screaming. Robocop reached around from beside the door and grabbed her wrist. He yanked her out of the house and threw her down on the deck before flipping her over and squatting down on her back. He was struggling with her hands, trying to grab them so he could cuff her.

"He'd have an easier time if he wasn't wearing all that body armor," I observed.

Pete just grunted.

Mullins moved to help his partner, apparently forgetting that there were supposed to be two people inside the trailer. As soon as his back was to the door, a man came charging out with a baseball bat and swung for the outfield fence. The blow caught Mullins on the arm. Pete and I could hear the bone snap from where we were standing. If the bat had made contact with the deputy's head, he would have been dead before his body hit the ground. As it was, he just crumpled to the deck and screamed.

Barry moved over to the other deputy, who had looked up when Mullins screamed. His helmet saved his life as Barry slammed him with the bat. The man yelled and fell over, clutching his face with both hands. I could see blood smeared across his hands.

Pete and I were already on the move as Barry helped Shannon up, then ran across the deck, holding the bat ready to swing at anyone who got in his way. I saw Shannon reach down and grab something, eliciting more screaming from Robocop.

Pete and I were on a collision course with Barry, who had seen us coming. He growled and held up the bat as he came down off the deck.

"Drop it!" I heard Pete yell. Pete already had his gun in hand and was pointing it at Barry, who either didn't see it or just didn't care.

I was clearing my holster when I saw what Shannon had grabbed from the deputy. She was gripping the short-barreled rifle and raising it to her shoulder. Barry and his bat were between Pete and Shannon, so Pete couldn't see that she had a rifle. I had a fraction of a second to decide whether to shoot her or not. There was really no decision to be made.

Training took over. Lining up the shot and pulling the trigger was all muscle memory. I'd been trained to aim for center mass and I'm sure that's what I did. Whether because she was moving or because I jerked the trigger, the shot went high and to the right, catching her in the shoulder. I'd learn later that the bullet fragmented, with the copper jacket coming within a fraction of an inch of entering her heart while another piece of lead bit into her throat. She went down.

The sound of the shot caused Barry to turn toward me. Pete hit him like a city bus, taking the man down to the ground hard. When he tried to slam Pete in the head with the bat, Pete slugged him with his pistol, ending the fight.

Robocop Two came running into the front yard just in time to see the end of the fight. I'd say this for him: he was quick on the radio, ordering up ambulances and backup.

Breathing heavily, I re-holstered my gun and dropped down beside Shannon Carrol. My mind was racing. I'd been to several classes where we'd practiced treating gunshot wounds. I'd even had to help out at a couple of crime scenes when victims or suspects had been wounded. But I'd never had to deal with a person that *I* had shot. My vision was blurring and I found it hard to concentrate.

Finally, someone pulled me away. I heard someone say, "He's in shock," not realizing that they were talking about me. Why would I be in shock?

"Let's go over here," Pete said, dragging me to another trailer where we sat down on the steps. "Remember, don't answer any questions but the very basic ones. They'll want to debrief you. Just tell them you'll come back in a couple of days and give a full report." Pete was making full eye contact and speaking very firmly.

I knew that any witness who'd been through a traumatic experience needed a few days to recall the events in their proper perspective. The tunnel vision that occurred when the shit hit the fan could cloud a person's recall for days after the event. By waiting, you saved yourself the trouble of having to explain why you gave one account of events immediately following and then a completely different one a week later.

"How bad is it?" I asked Pete.

"Snotty the deputy isn't going to be able to use his right arm for months. From what I could see, the bone looked crushed. Pretty sure the SWAT guy has a serious concussion, but they'll know more when they get him to the hospital. Shannon is alive and, assuming nothing shifts too dramatically, she'll live. They're planning to airlift them both to Tallahassee." He paused. "You saved lives today."

"I don't know. The rifle's safety was probably on. I doubt she knows enough to take it off."

"Maybe it was, maybe it wasn't, but she was a clear threat. You stopped the threat just the way you're trained to do. If there is any criticism to be made, it's that you didn't fire another round. A determined attacker could have still been a deadly threat. You made two decisions. One to stop the threat. Second, you chose not to end her life."

"When I fired that first shot, it was intended to kill her." I felt very conflicted about this shooting. I'd shot at plenty of suspects before, but it had always been under an exchange of fire. This was different. My mind was telling me that Shannon hadn't posed a serious threat. That she couldn't operate the rifle and, even if she'd managed to get off a shot, the odds were that she wouldn't have hit anything. However, that was all Monday morning quarterbacking. The reality was that there'd been an angry suspect with a deadly weapon in her hands who could easily have killed all of us.

A man in a much nicer suit than what Mullins had been wearing walked over to where Pete and I were sitting. "I'm Major Scott Hill. This is a mess." He didn't sound accusatory.

"I'm Pete Henley and this is Larry Macklin."

"I remember you," Hill said to me. "Lot of changes around here since last year. Most of them for the good. Of course, we haven't gotten rid of all the bad apples. You should have contacted the sheriff. If you had, we'd have made sure you were given proper support."

"We didn't know until—" Pete started to argue. Hill held up his hand to stop him.

"I got the full story. I understand why you all chose the path you did. Mistakes were made and people got hurt. There are folks in our department who'd love to see you locked up in our jail," he said to me, then obviously saw the look on my face as I was unable to stop my anger from rising. "Don't worry. I don't think it will come to that. While Deputy Pratt may not remember what happened, his bodycam was running the whole time. Hopefully it picked up the shooting. Also, as much as Mullins is an ass, he isn't a liar. He'll never admit that his meddling led to this, but he won't lie about what he saw. Now, I'll need your gun." He took out a pair of gloves and an evidence bag. "We'll also need to do a paraffin test of you hands. Both of you."

The fact that he was taking my gun and doing paraffin tests actually made me feel better. It meant that Hill wasn't a fool. Protocol would be followed.

"I'll give you a complete statement in a couple of days," I told him.

"That's what I would expect," Hill told me as he sealed the bag holding my gun. I hoped I'd get it back someday.

"Our office will want the results of the tests," Pete said to Hill, who nodded.

It hadn't occurred to me until that moment that I'd have to undergo an officer-involved shooting investigation from our internal affairs department.

After Darlene and Julio had been questioned, they joined Pete and me as we watched the wounded being picked up by helicopter.

"This couldn't have gone much worse," I said gloomily. I was starting to think clearly again. "Oh, hell, did you—"

"Talk to your dad? Yes. He wants to meet with us when we get back to Calhoun," Pete said.

"Looking forward to that," Darlene said with a heavy dose of sarcasm.

"I was just guarding the back gate," Julio said.

"Go ahead and jump off the ship, rat man," Pete said, chuckling darkly.

At that point, I remembered I needed to call Cara, though I didn't want to. I told her just enough to let her know that the whole operation had gone balls-up, fending off any questions until I got home. Her voice was full of concern for me, which just made me feel worse. This was the last thing she needed to worry about now.

Once the helicopters and ambulances were gone, Hill walked back over to us.

"You," he said, pointing at Darlene, "may accompany our forensic team through the trailer and the search of the suspects' car to determine if there is any evidence related to your cases."

I didn't have to ask why he picked Darlene. She and Julio were not involved in the shooting, therefore they wouldn't be a part of Hill's ongoing investigation into the assault on his officers and the shooting of a suspect.

By four o'clock, we were sitting in Dad's office, looking like a group of students sent to the principal's office for bad behavior.

Pete gave a very succinct account of the affair. When he was done, Dad sighed and rubbed the bridge of his nose. Lt. Johnson just shook his head.

"I want all of you to write up a report and have it on my desk by noon tomorrow. You," he pointed at Pete, "will detail what went wrong and what actions you and your team could have done to prevent this monumental screw-up."

"Yes, sir," Pete said, averting his gaze from the intensity of Dad's green-eyed stare.

"And *you*," Dad said, glaring at me, "are suspended with pay until Major Parks is finished with the internal affairs investigation into the shooting. During your suspension, you will receive counseling."

Lt. Johnson looked poleaxed. The criminal investigations division already had a backlog of cases and losing me for God knew how long wasn't going to help. Concerned over the budget, Dad had suspended overtime except in extreme emergencies.

Dad turned to Darlene. "Was there any useful evidence in the trailer or vehicle?"

"I photographed several dozen items and Major Hill's forensic team collected them. Hill said they'd be in touch with you to work out the details. The items included several burner phones, clothing and a copy of an insurance quote that detailed what Pete learned from the agent. I also requested DNA and fingerprints from the suspects."

"The insurance documents are good. That proves the suspects knew about the policy and the opportunity for them to benefit from the deaths of the other policy holders. Did Hill seem open to us interviewing the suspects?"

"Yes on Barry Carrol. He said we could interview him in regard to the murders and as part of our internal investigation into the shooting. Of course, interviewing

Shannon will depend on her recovery from the gunshot wound." She glanced at me.

"Johnson and I have agreed that you will take over the investigation into the murders. Pete can assist you, but he's not to have any contact with the Carrols until the investigation into the shooting is concluded," Dad told Darlene while shooting me another frown.

After more glares and guilt trips, we were finally dismissed.

Cara met me at the door and gave me a long, hard hug. I was numb, but tried to return her affection.

"I guess it would be stupid to ask if you're okay." I nodded. "Do you want anything for dinner?"

"No. I… we…" I was restless and angry. "We shouldn't have let that buffoon railroad us!" Emotions that I'd tried to keep a lid on finally tore at me. Like a swimmer caught in a rip current, all I could do was go with them or drown.

"It's all right," Cara said, concerned and uncertain what to say or do.

"We just fucked up. From the moment we got down there. Three people could have died. Luck was the only thing that saved them. Pete and I were just standing there like idiots watching the whole thing go down. If we'd moved faster, I wouldn't have had to shoot Shannon Carrol. I killed her!" My rage was intense.

"She's dead?" Cara's hand flew to her mouth.

"No, no, but not because I didn't intend on killing her. When I pulled the trigger I… meant for her to die." I started pacing the room in agitation.

"You've shot at people before."

"When they were shooting at me. This just… seems different. When I went over to her and saw the blood flowing from her shoulder, I felt… I don't know how to describe it… helplessness, maybe. I just felt lost."

The rational part of my brain knew that I was pushing my

own emotional buttons, like a person who can't stop picking at a scab. I'd held it together all day, but now my id was taking over, exposing all of my frustration, self-loathing and pain. When I thought about Cara and how she shouldn't have to put up with my emotional breakdown, I just felt worse.

It was a bad night. Cara tried to comfort me, but I kept erupting into fits of anxious fury. Around midnight I finally convinced her that it was safe to leave me alone. Hugs and whispered assurances sent her to bed and gave me some time alone to calm down.

I tried to watch TV, but turned it off after fifteen minutes. I opened my laptop, which held most of the case files on the two murders. Had the Carrols been responsible for them? And where was Deanne Greer? Those were the two questions that needed to be answered as soon as possible.

I wanted to go into the office and study the white boards and the paper files. I had my keys in my hand before I realized that I couldn't do that to Cara. If I left in the middle of the night after the evening we'd had, she'd worry the entire time and wouldn't be able to sleep. I sat back down at the laptop.

When I could no longer understand what I was reading, I collapsed on the couch and my body shut down.

# CHAPTER TWENTY-FOUR

I opened my eyes and saw the cool blue light of morning coming through the windows and was surprised that I'd actually slept. I heard Cara making coffee in the kitchen. The vet clinic would be open this Saturday and she was already dressed in her scrubs. When she noticed that I was awake, she kneeled down beside the couch.

"Are you going to be all right?" she asked, laying a hand on my chest.

I took her hand in mine. "Yes."

"I can take the day off."

"No. I'll be fine. Besides, you guys are always busy on Saturday." I wanted her to go to the clinic and leave me by myself in my emotional mud wallow.

Cara leaned over and kissed me. Finally, after a few more promises that I was fine, she headed off to work. I considered getting up off the couch, but found myself dozing again.

My phone woke me up just after nine.

"How you doing?" Pete asked.

"I'm surviving. I was up half the night trying to decide if Shannon and Barry are our killers."

"You weren't the only one. Darlene went back down

there last night and interviewed Barry. He's messed up. Mentally. She said he couldn't come up with an alibi for either of the murders. He also said that he thought the insurance information had come in the mail last week or the week before, but he couldn't be sure."

"Any chance they still have the envelope it came in?"

"Darlene made sure that the house in Pensacola is sealed. The cops over there said that it didn't look like anything had been thrown out in a decade, so she's going to ride over there and search the place today or tomorrow." I wondered if Dad was going to let her make the trip on the department's dime.

"Did Barry give an excuse for why they took off from Pensacola and were hiding out on Pelican Island?"

"He claimed that after Shannon learned about Beth and Elizabeth, she went off the deep end. Boozing and taking drugs while the paranoia grew. Finally, she was wigging out so bad that they just ran."

"What do you think?"

"Maybe, maybe not." In Pete's voice I heard an echo of my own self-doubt.

"Whether they are murderers or not, they're certainly material witnesses. We were justified in going down there and questioning them."

"I know. We just screwed up when we let that jackass take over."

"We made a mistake, that's for sure. Let me know what Darlene finds out," I said, suddenly wanting to end the call.

"I'll have her call you."

The rest of the weekend was torture. All I wanted to do was curl up in a ball on the couch, but for Cara's sake I pretended to feel better and help out with some of the wedding preparations. When I got the chance, I would open up my laptop and obsess over the case reports.

Darlene called on Sunday afternoon.

"Their house was a cesspool." I couldn't hold back a small smile. Darlene was the first person all weekend who hadn't started the conversation by asking how I was. "You should have been there to crawl through all that crap with me."

"Find anything useful?"

"Never found the mystery envelope. Did find some receipts that date from around the murders. We'll have to try and work out the timeline and conduct a boatload of interviews to follow up. Most of the receipts are for fast food joints. I've called a couple of them, hoping to catch them before they erase over security footage. What have you found out?"

"What do you mean?"

"Cut the crap. I know you've been pouring over the files. I would be."

"You caught me. There's something there, but I don't know what. I want more information about the insurance policy."

"Shannon is conscious. I've talked to Major Hill and he said they're planning on a formal interview on Monday. He told me I could sit in."

"Let me know how that goes."


I felt a little better on Monday. At least the weekend was over and some progress could now made on the shooting investigation. Sure enough, my phone rang at five after nine.

"We need to schedule an interview," said Sergeant Martin, who was with our department's internal review board.

"Sure. Anytime."

"Wednesday then." Martin was a no-nonsense guy. I liked him.

"Done."

"Meet us in Major Parks's office at nine o'clock."

Almost immediately after I hung up with Martin, Major Hill called and asked if I could meet him that afternoon.

"We're interviewing Mrs. Carrol at Tallahassee Memorial

Hospital at one o'clock. I could meet you at your office at four. This will be a formal interview covering the targeting of Shannon Carrol as a suspect, and the shooting that resulted from the arrest."

"We targeted her as a material witness, but we did not attempt to arrest her," I said, feeling my face flush.

"You'll have ample opportunity to give your side of the events. Of course you know that you can have a lawyer present."

"I know that I don't *have* to answer your questions," I said.

There was silence from the other end of the line.

"But I'll be glad to speak with you and explain our position. I'll see you at four."

"Good."

At least that gave me a reason to get cleaned up and dressed.

Full of nervous energy, I went into the office at noon and headed back to my improvised war room to go over the evidence again and stare at the white boards. I ran into Shantel coming out of the evidence vault.

"Son, you shouldn't leave the county. You get out there in the real world and Mother Shantel can't protect you." She gave me a big hug. "I'm glad you were there to back Henley up. I'd miss that teddy bear."

"Not our proudest moment."

"You can make all the plans you want, but in the end God's in charge. Seems to me He was looking after you all pretty well."

Once in the small office, I put up another sheet of paper with Shannon's name on it. I didn't have to make connections between the victims anymore. We knew that they were all friends. The big question was: how many more pieces were missing?

Looking through the files of what we'd learned so far, I came up with a few questions. Who had started the women's strange club? What were the relationships between the four women? I texted my questions to Darlene, hoping she'd have a chance to ask them during her interview with Shannon.

The insurance policy was also bothering me. Why had they done it? Whose idea had it been? Who was supposed to pay for it? I texted these questions to Darlene as well.

Then I called Pete. "Do you have a copy of the insurance policy?"

"I do."

"I'd like to see it."

"It came in this weekend. It should be in Beth's file."

I went to the box and found the file. Inside were copies of the policy. "This doesn't have any signatures on it."

"He just sent the Word document or whatever."

"I'd like to see photos of the original signed document." The document they'd sent had the insurance company's name and phone number at the top. *I'll give them a call*, I decided.

"Don't contact them until you've been given the all-clear from internal affairs," Pete said, as if reading my mind.

"Since when did you become such a rule follower?"

"I try not to screw up a case more than once. We've done enough damage on this one. Let's give things a chance to settle down."

"Sure," I said noncommittally.

"If you want, I'll call the agent and see if I can get him to send it over."

"That's a plan I can get behind."

I hung up on Pete to take a call from Lt. Johnson.

"I've got a psychiatrist for you to talk to," Johnson said without preamble.

"I don't really think—"

"This isn't negotiable. Your dad wants it and I'm ordering it. I think this guy could do you some good. You have to talk to someone," Johnson argued.

As much as I didn't want to talk to a psychiatrist, I also didn't want to piss Johnson off any more than he already was. He would have considerable input when it came to putting me back on active duty.

"Sure," I said.

"I'll text you his contact information. I told him to expect your call." Johnson hung up and the text followed two minutes later.

I sighed. *Maybe his schedule will be full for the next week or two*, I thought as I dialed the number.

My call was answered by a sweet-sounding receptionist. "Mr. Macklin, Dr. Prier already has you booked for Wednesday at one."

"I… thanks."

Apparently Johnson had already worked it out with the good doctor. I consoled myself with the thought that maybe this meant I was on the fast track to getting back on duty.

I spent another couple of hours staring at the files and making notes before giving up. I swung by my desk to look at the mess I had waiting for me when I was finally allowed back to work. On top of a pile of reports was the list of vehicles Spears had made up for the hit-and-run case.

I glanced at it and was getting ready to walk away when a make and model jumped out at me. There was a partial plate and the letters looked familiar. Kicking myself or not noticing it before, I dropped into my chair and used my phone to pull up the BOLO on Deanne's car. It was the same make and model. Spears had listed the car on the tape as light-colored, while Deanne's car was grey. I flipped through the paperwork. In addition the spreadsheet, Spears had printed copies of each still from the videos. I found the one I was looking for. The last three letters on the plate were all I could see: STRN. Deanne's personalized tag read: BESTRN. I didn't need a doctorate in detection to know that this had to be Deanne's car. Why was it here? Had she been driving it? I decided to sit on the information for a little while until I had a clearer idea what it meant.

Still excited by my discovery, I headed to the conference room to meet with Major Hill.

I got home at seven. When I saw the apprehensive look on Cara's face as I walked in the door, I felt guilty for the state I'd been in all weekend.

"How'd everything go?"

"Good. They're comfortable with the bodycam footage and Mullins's and Pratt's testimony."

"You knew you didn't do anything wrong," Cara said, taking my hand and squeezing it.

"Even if there were things that bothered them, I think their men did enough dumb shit that they don't want to rake me over the coals too much," I said, being honest.

"So what does this mean for the internal affairs review board?"

"Without Hill or their sheriff demanding charges, Major Parks and the review board aren't going to push it. They'll want me to see a counselor, which Lt. Johnson has already taken care of. Beyond that, I don't think they'll make me jump through too many hoops before letting me back on duty."

"That's great," Cara said with forced happiness. She could tell that I still wasn't at peace with the shooting.

"It is. I want to be able to wrap up the two murder cases."

Cara bit her lip.

"What?" I asked.

She still didn't say anything.

"Come on, you can talk to me. What's wrong?" I pushed, putting my arm around her.

"Do you want to postpone the wedding?" she asked quickly.

For a moment I didn't know how to respond. "No. No, of course not. Look, I know I've been acting like a jerk. I'm just...upset. We'll work through it." Then a thought occurred to me. "*You* don't want to postpone it, do you?"

"No. But I just want it to be... right. I want us to be able to enjoy it," she said, tears forming in her eyes.

I kissed her, then whispered in her ear, "Everything will be fine," willing myself to believe it.


Around eight, I couldn't wait any longer and texted Darlene to see how the interview with Shannon had gone. She called back ten minutes later.

"Enjoying your vacation?"

"That's just cruel."

"Don't sweat it. You'll be back swinging a six-shooter in no time," Darlene said in what passed for her sympathetic voice.

"How'd the interview go?"

"Interesting. She was quite talkative. Waived her right to a lawyer. Not surprisingly, she claimed she was a victim. You know the routine. Didn't murder Beth or Elizabeth. Hadn't been near Adams County in years. She sounded convincing. Unfortunately for her, most of her alibi consists of lying around her house in a drug-induced stupor. To her advantage is the three-hour travel time between Pensacola and Calhoun. That's a six-hour round trip, not counting how long it might take to commit the murders. Of course, her alibi is complicated by the fact that there are two of them. Barry could cover for her and vice versa. I think it's going to be very difficult for her to prove that she or Barry couldn't have killed those two women."

"Did she explain the relationship between all of them?"

"I don't think I could have stopped her. I could tell that there was a lot of nostalgia where their relationship was concerned. Remember, that time in college was probably the last time Shannon's life was on track. Beth and Elizabeth met first. It was the coincidence of their names that brought them together."

"We know Elizabeth wasn't exactly a social butterfly."

"Shannon said that if it hadn't been for the name and meeting Beth, Elizabeth might have gone through all four years at the university not talking to anyone."

"And Beth was the opposite of Elizabeth."

"Exactly. Once Beth got to know Elizabeth, she couldn't let her just curl back up into her cocoon. I think Elizabeth brought out Beth's nurturing side. Since they both hated the dorm, they decided to rent a house. That's when they met Shannon and Deanne. The four of them realized at some point that they were all a bit… odd and formed this clique. It was Deanne who came up with the four seasons thing. Beth was summer because of her outgoing, sunny nature and Deanne was autumn because she was a bit flighty and scared of everything. They thought Elizabeth was spring because she had so much potential, like the bud of a flower waiting to open. Finally, and I could tell she wasn't really happy about it anymore, Shannon was winter."

"Why was that?"

"She told me that, even then, there was some darkness in her soul. She did the Goth thing in school and was often depressed. Not that you have to be depressed if you're a Goth. I had friends in school who went very dark, but weren't depressed."

"Thank you, Madam Black, for that PSA."

"Anyhow, Shannon did suffer from depression. It was in college when the drinking started, too."

"I can see why she wouldn't like being called winter."

"Shannon said it didn't bother her at first. Like the Goth clothing, she embraced the darkness. It wasn't until she couldn't get out of the gloom and depression that it began to eat at her."

"With the money being dangled out in the air and a festering resentment over being pigeonholed as winter, maybe that was enough to give her the excuse she needed to hatch a plan to kill them."

"A strong argument could be made for that," Darlene said.

"What do you think?"

"With someone who's that impaired after years of drug

and alcohol abuse, it's very hard to read them. They can be entirely sincere one day about their love for someone, while doing horrible things to that same person the next day. Being an addict means you've spent a lot of time lying. When we talked to her, she was able to portray herself as a friend who would never hurt the other three. But who knows?"

"What about the insurance?"

"She was a little fuzzy on that. They would get together a couple of times a year. The four of them had decided in college that they would keep their group a secret, like a mini version of Skull and Bones or one of those other stupid college groups. So they'd make up a story for friends and relatives before sneaking off to meet somewhere. This last time it was St. Augustine.

"During the weekend, the women with kids started talking about their concerns for their future. Particularly since all of them had some sort of relationship issue. Someone, Shannon didn't remember who, came up with the idea that they would all act as godmothers for the children. That way, if something happened to one of them, the others would be there for the children. That all went over well. According to Shannon, it was Elizabeth who brought up money. How would they take care of the kids without money? Finally, they decided to take out an insurance policy and Elizabeth agreed to arrange it."

"Don't you have to get a physical and all that to get a life insurance policy?"

"For most of them you do, and this one wasn't an exception. All of them submitted to a physical. Shannon laughed when she admitted that her health and history caused the policy to cost about twice what it would have without her in the mix."

"So she *did* know about the policy?"

"Shannon claims she knew they were getting the policy, but she thought only the kids were beneficiaries. Not surprisingly, she told us she was pretty drugged out the weekend they met and only had a sketchy recollection of the details."

"Did she remember signing anything?"

"She thought she had."

"What else came out in the interview?"

"Hill focused on the shooting. Shannon claimed she was going to use the gun as a club, not that it matters much. You can certainly beat someone to death. Two things were clear from talking to her. One, she intended on doing as much damage to everyone there as she could and, two, she was heavily impaired at the time, meaning that she couldn't have exercised control over her impulses."

"How did Major Hill react?"

"We talked on the way out. I think he was satisfied that the shooting was justified."

"That was the impression I got when he interviewed me."

I decided to tell Darlene about catching Deanne's car on the surveillance video.

"That puts a little different spin on things," she mused.

"If I'd looked at the video earlier, we might have taken a different approach to Shannon and Barry."

"I see what you mean. If we have evidence that Deanne was in Adams County around the time of the murders, then she becomes a person of interest."

"Deanne has the same money motive as Shannon."

"But she doesn't have all of the baggage Shannon has."

"Probably not. But who knows. Maybe there's a secret gambling habit or a man we don't know about. I sensed that her friend was hiding something."

"Well, hell," were Darlene's words of wisdom on the situation. "I guess I'll take that hit-and-run on my plate too and move Deanne up higher on the suspect list. You need to get yourself reinstated as soon as you can. I'm good, but I can't do everything by myself."

I didn't sleep well that night. The shooting was still eating at me. I spent half the night arguing with myself. I kept telling myself that it was as good a shooting as one could hope for, given all the circumstances, but my contrarian self wouldn't let it rest. It kept repeating every negative thought I could come up with. I forced myself to stay in bed, knowing that if I got up and paced the house I'd just screw up Cara's chances of a decent night's sleep.

# CHAPTER TWENTY-FIVE

I spent most of Tuesday fielding calls from the deputies covering my other cases. Having to take the time to bring them up to speed was irritating. I wished the brass would just let me do my job. I understood why they wouldn't want me out in public with a gun, but I could have manned my desk and wrapped up what I could by phone. But I knew that wasn't going to happen. Suspension was suspension, and cases couldn't be put on the back burner just because the investigator assigned to them was suspended.

Wednesday's meeting with the review board finally came and felt like a formality. Major Parks had talked to Major Hill, who had informed him that there were no plans to bring any charges against Pete or me. Once that was established, I knew the board just wanted to go through the motions so they could say they had investigated the matter and had a full file folder to prove it. The meeting ended with them telling me that it could be up to a week before they came to a decision. More covering their asses and giving it some time in case anything changed.

Pete and Darlene met me for lunch at Deep Pit.

"This all feels very unsatisfying," Pete said after he'd finished half his sandwich.

"The food?" I asked, knowing that wasn't what he meant.

"No, the sandwich is amazing. I mean the Collins and Robinson cases. I feel like we've managed to snatch defeat from the jaws of victory."

"I'll be honest. Something isn't right about this. Shannon and Barry might have done it, but I'm not convinced. Especially not with this video of Deanne's car in the area." Darlene had told Pete about the hit-and-run angle.

"If you've committed a murder, you might be driving erratically enough that you hit a parked car. But then the question is, are we still saying that the two hit-and-runs are related or not? Maybe it was just a coincidence that they happened so close together." Thinking about all of the variables was driving me nuts.

"I've prioritized finding Deanne. I did a briefing this morning to patrol about Deanne's and Elizabeth's cars. I can't help but think that if we can find either one, we'd be making some major strides in the investigation," Darlene said.

"I don't know what to make of the hit-and-run angle, but I agree that finding Deanne is key," Pete said.

"Maybe she's our killer. We could have gotten it all turned around. She might have been running from what she'd done and it was Shannon who was scared and went into hiding," I suggested.

"Since there was nothing conclusive in the interview with Shannon, I'm going down to interview Barry again tomorrow. If we don't get something we can use from him, I don't see how we can press charges," Darlene said.

"We need evidence that links them to at least one of the crime scenes," Pete agreed.

I chuckled grimly. "On the bright side, because of the messed-up way things went down on Pelican Island, there are enough other charges against Shannon and Barry to keep them in jail for a while."

"Which gives us time to dig up something. Maybe we'll get a DNA match from something left on the bodies or in

Beth's car." Pete was trying to sound optimistic.

I looked at my watch. "I've got to go. I have an appointment with my psychiatrist." I gave them what I hoped was a sardonic grin and they both wished me luck. Shootings and their aftermath just weren't that much fun to joke about.

I started to walk away and then stopped and turned back to Pete. "Did you remember to ask the insurance guy to send a signed copy of the policy?"

"I did."

"I don't think it's come through."

"I'll check with him again."

I reached Dr. Prier's office in Tallahassee with fifteen minutes to spare. It was in a row of brick medical offices on the east side of town. Feeling awkward and uncomfortable sitting in the waiting room, I filled out the reams of new patient forms. Just as I handed them back in to the receptionist, a woman with sharp features and brooding eyes came out of the inner office and the receptionist informed me that it was my turn.

Dr. Stephen Prier sat in a leather wingback chair that was just big enough for him. It wasn't that he was fat; he was just massive. He could have convinced anyone that he was a retired professional wrestler. He stood up and took my hand in his bear paw and shook it firmly.

"Mr. Macklin. Have a seat." He indicated the twin to his chair that was placed just a little farther than knee-length away from his.

"Dr. Prier, I appreciate you seeing me so quickly."

"Johnson made it sound like a priority."

"Have you seen Lt. Johnson professionally?" I asked.

He smiled. "You know better than that. Let's talk about what brings you here to my office." His voice was deep and soothing.

I proceeded to describe the shooting. Then I hesitated, but figured I might as well get my money's worth and went on to describe how conflicted I'd felt since the event.

"A restless night or two after shooting someone is not unexpected. In fact, I'd be concerned about anyone who shot a person and *didn't* feel some remorse."

"There's an… anger. Or maybe anxiety is a better word for it. I haven't been this unsettled since a friend of mine was killed on duty."

"Tell me about that and also what else is going on in your life," the doctor said, making notes on a tablet he'd taken from a table beside his chair.

I told him about witnessing Matt's death before describing my life in general.

He looked at me with steady, unflinching eyes before speaking. "I think you're channeling some old emotions left over from that horrific experience last July, as well as some of your anxieties about the changes that are taking place in your own life, into this shooting. Like my wife likes to say when I'm catastrophizing an event: no one died. The person you shot is recovering. Your actions very well might have saved lives. You know this… here." He tapped his head.

"You really think that's why I'm so… upset?"

"You mentioned that you recently visited the spot where Matt was killed. That was bound to dredge up some raw emotion. As for wedding anxieties, everyone has them. Again, I would be more worried about you if you *didn't* have concerns about a decision of that magnitude. You said you love your fiancée. That prevents you from openly admitting your fears and doubts over your relationship and the marriage. So instead, your unconscious mind looked for an outlet and found it in the shooting. Very natural. You're proving that you're a normal person with feelings that are completely rational. I can prescribe something to help you with your anxiety or to help you sleep, if you'd like. Beyond that…" He shrugged. "Get married and give it a little time. I'd like to see you back here after your honeymoon. If things have changed for the better or for the worse, we'll make adjustments."

"That's it?"

"If you want, I can schedule you for two sessions a week and tell your bosses that you should be on disability leave. But that wouldn't be honest. Now, go forth and think about what I've told you. I believe that if you examine your feelings, you'll find that what's happening to you emotionally has more to do with past trauma and fears about the future."

I didn't know what I'd expected. Had I wanted him to tell me that I was broken? *No, I didn't*, I told myself and stood up.

He shook my hand. "Larry, relax. If anything comes up that you don't feel you can handle by yourself, I have an after-hours number where I can be reached twenty-four seven."

I left feeling surprisingly better.

I spent the following weekend with Cara, working on last-minute wedding chores, including a few final details for our honeymoon in Savannah. But every so often, I slipped in a few minutes to review the murder files again. And when we stopped at the nursery to check on the flowers for the wedding, I even talked Cara into driving back to the mulch pile where Elizabeth's body had been found.

On Sunday, I realized that Pete still hadn't sent me a copy of the signed insurance policy. At first I'd just wanted it out of curiosity, but now I was beginning to wonder if there was a reason the insurance agent wasn't sending it.

On Tuesday, I got the welcome call from Major Parks telling me that the review board had cleared me. Ten minutes later, Lt. Johnson was on the phone telling me he expected me at work as soon as I could get there.

The first thing I did when I got in was to check with Pete about the insurance policy. He still hadn't received it, so I called the agent, Nigel Whalen.

"Really?" he said after I'd introduced myself and told him we still hadn't received the copy of the policy. "I've sent them a couple of times."

"Are you faxing them?"

"Yes." He read off the number, which matched the department's fax machine located in dispatch.

"We still don't have them. Look, why don't you take pictures of the policy or scan it and email it to me?"

"Sure, no problem."

"Also, I'd like to come in and talk to you about your meeting with Elizabeth Collins."

"I actually met with her on several occasions."

"When would it be convenient for me to come talk to you about those meetings?"

"I'm pretty jammed up right now. How about next week?"

"I'm getting married this weekend, and I'll be on my honeymoon next week."

"Congratulations. Just give me a call when you get back, and I'll make some time for you."

"I'd really appreciate it if you could fit me in this week."

"I don't see how."

"I understand. I'll look forward to getting your email," I said and gave him my address.

"What did you think of Nigel Whalen?" I asked Pete after I hung up.

"He seemed very busy. Top-of-the-line office. His assistant looked like he made more money in a month than I do in a year."

"Where's his office?"

Pete gave me an address in Tallahassee that wasn't far from Dr. Prier's office.

"Did you run a background on him?" I asked.

"You're just pissed off because you haven't gotten that policy," he joked. "No, I didn't run anything. It's my understanding that insurance agents undergo a basic background check to get their license."

"I think you're right. I just want to dig a little deeper."

"Knock yourself out."

That night, Cara and I were sound asleep when my phone rang. I was back on regular duty, so it could have been any number of cases that I was involved with.

"Yeah, Macklin here," I said, which was the best I could do at four in the morning.

"You shot her," said the woman's voice on the other end of the phone.

"Who?" I was still trying to clear the fog out of my head.

"Shannon!" the voice screamed.

I was wide awake now.

"Is this Deanne?" Silence. "Talk to me. I didn't want to shoot her. Please just talk to me. We can work this out." I was expecting her to disconnect the call, but she didn't.

"Did she kill Beth and Elizabeth?" she asked, surprising me.

"Do you think she might have?"

For a while there was more silence, then she said, "She always kinda scared me." Her voice sounded tired.

"She can't hurt you now. Both she and Barry will be in jail for a while."

"Did she do it? Is that why you shot her?"

"I shot her because she had a gun and posed a threat to others. You would be helping us out if you came in and told us your story. Your mother is very worried about you."

"I was afraid to tell them where I was. I thought whoever was killing us might hurt them to get to me."

"That makes sense. But you can come out of hiding now," I told her, wondering if she was really safe or not. What if Barry and Shannon weren't the killers?

"Okay, maybe. I want to be sure."

"I understand. Just—" I was cut off by the dial tone.

"Was that Deanne?" Cara asked groggily.

"Or someone pretending to be her." *Had* it been Deanne? Was she the killer, and the call just an attempt to fool us into thinking she was innocent? Calling in the wee hours of the morning would have certainly been a clever way to catch me off guard.

On Wednesday, I was finding it hard to concentrate on work as the pressure of the wedding became almost overwhelming. Cara's parents and some distant relatives of mine would be arriving on Thursday, and the rehearsal and dinner were scheduled for Friday. Cara had already taken off from work and never seemed to stop moving. It was helping to take my mind off of the murder investigations, which seemed to have stalled, waiting for new evidence to come forward.

I saw Pete as I was heading out of the office for lunch and he told me that the doctors were planning to release Shannon to Major Hill, and jail, early the following week. Everything seemed to be simmering along and I was determined not to worry about anything but getting married to the woman I loved and going off for a week of blissful not-giving-a-damn.

That afternoon, I was making progress on wrapping up all of my other cases, or at least putting them in a wait-and-see mode, when I saw an email come in from the Whalen insurance company. *Finally*, I thought.

I opened the email and looked at the attachments. Nigel Whalen had sent photos of the policy that looked like they'd been taken by a five-year-old. The last page, which was the only one I was really interested in, had the bottom half cut off. The half that would have held the signatures of the parties and the witnesses. Was this a mistake? I didn't think so. *Fine*, I thought. *He said we can meet the week I get back, so I'll just wait and take him to the woodshed then.*

That night, every time there was a slack in the wedding prep, I'd think about Whalen blowing me off and it made me furious. I was sure that Dr. Prier would have told me that I was channeling other emotions into this one issue. If that was the case, so be it.

"Can you pick up your tux tomorrow?" Cara asked and a

light bulb went off in my head. The tux place wasn't that far from Whalen's office.

"I'll be glad to," I said. She looked at me funny, so I explained about stopping by Whalen's office. "I'd like to take care of that before the wedding so I can stop thinking about it."

"Don't get in any trouble."

"Who, me?"

## CHAPTER TWENTY-SIX

I headed into Tallahassee at noon on Thursday. After grabbing a quick bite of lunch, I picked up my tux and drove over to meet Whalen. I wasn't going to play around. I was just going to show up and make him see me.

Pete was right about the office. Several of the cars parked outside each represented more than I made in a year. There was a very nice brass plate beside the door announcing the establishment as "Whalen Insurance and Investment Agency—Dealing in Specialty Insurance and Investments." While it seemed redundant, it clearly made the point that you shouldn't come in expecting to buy run-of-the-mill auto insurance. Inside was a plush layout that made every insurance agency I'd ever been in look like second-rate used car dealerships.

I could feel my feet sinking into the carpet. The assistant's desk was bigger than those belonging to a lot of CEOs.

"May I help you?" he asked before I'd made it two feet into the spacious reception area.

"I'm here to see Mr. Whalen." I hoped that my tone implied I wasn't going to take no for an answer.

"Do you have an appointment?" asked the smiling young

man. The plaque on his desk identified him as Keech Kinder.

"No."

"Oh, I'm sorry. I don't think he has any openings this afternoon," Kinder said without looking at anything to confirm it. "But if you would give me your name and what you need, maybe we can arrange a time that you can meet with Mr. Whalen." The smile was still there, but looking a little more forced as he evaluated my choice of clothing.

"I don't think that will work," I said, taking out my bifold and showing him my star and ID. "I'm here on a matter of some urgency. In response to a previous request, Mr. Whalen sent me some papers, but unfortunately the photo of the document cut off the part I most needed to see." I made this last sound like a crime.

"I'm sure that we can straighten it out without bothering Mr. Whalen," Kinder said. There was only the faintest hint of the smile on his face now.

"Fine. I need a copy of the signed insurance policy taken out by Elizabeth Collins about two months ago," I told him.

"I'll see what I can find out." I noticed that he hadn't taken any notes. When he stood up and moved to the door, he looked as though he expected me to pounce on him.

At Whalen's office door, he tapped twice and went in. Five long minutes later, he came back out. "Mr. Whalen will be with you in a moment." The smile from earlier had been replaced with a full-on glare. I glared back as I waited.

Whalen's door flew open a few minutes later. The insurance agent stood just a little higher than my six feet and had sleek, dark hair. He wore a blue hand-tailored suit and the smile on his face was infectious. As angry as I'd been before, I still found myself sticking out my hand and giving him a hint of a smile back.

"Deputy Macklin, was there a problem with the photos I sent to you?"

"Yes. I was particularly interested in the signatures on the last page, but the picture you sent cut them off."

"I'm a mess when it comes to technology. I should have let Keech do it. He's a master IT guy on top of all his other talents. Come on back to my office. You said you had some other questions."

He stopped at his door and turned back to his assistant. "Keech, cancel my two o'clock conference call."

Whalen waved me into his spacious office, which looked like a set from *Downton Abbey*. "Please, have a seat. Can I get you something to drink? Hard or soft?"

"I'm good. Do you have the copies of the policy?"

"I do." He grabbed some papers off of his desk and handed them to me.

I flipped through them and, sure enough, the last half of the last page was all signatures.

"Thank you," I said. "And thank you for taking the time to answer my questions."

"No big deal. Shoot," he said, taking a sip of the gin and tonic he'd poured for himself.

"Tell me about Elizabeth's first visit to you."

"She called and talked to Keech first. Gave him a brief rundown of what she was looking for and asked us if we could get her a policy. I told her I could."

"*Get* her a policy?"

"Yes. In this case, I acted as the broker. You'll see on the policy that the actual insurer is a company out of Panama, Trent International. It's a very old insurance company. Like Lloyd's of London, they're willing to write unique policies. I'm one of their agents."

He smiled. "I can see from your face that you don't understand how we work. I'm an agent for a number of different companies and I broker policies. I deal almost exclusively with policies where the value exceeds ten million dollars. The Collins policy is actually below what I would normally deal with, but it's very unique. They would have had a hard time getting a policy like that anywhere else. Besides, when Elizabeth explained why they were doing it, I thought it was a generous thing for friends to do for each other."

"What was she like when she came in?"

"Calm, very earnest and... structured. She knew exactly what she wanted. I liked that too."

"Walk me through the process as it played out with Elizabeth."

"It was all pretty straightforward. When she came in, I'd already done some research based on her phone call with Keech. I laid out the options and she picked the one she thought best suited their needs. At that point, we got all the health paperwork from the women, I wrote up the policy, then sent it to be approved by Trent's home office. Elizabeth came back in and picked up the papers. When she returned a week later, she had all the signatures. All I needed was payment from her for the policy to go into effect. I wish I could tell you more, but the woman was not very talkative."

I knew that to be true. I felt like I was missing something, but I didn't know what.

"I'd like to have a timeline of the transaction."

"Of course, Keech can prepare that for you. I saw in the paper that one of the women named in the policy was shot. Do you think she committed the murders?"

"We don't know yet."

"Very sad. As their agent, I'll have to decide how the policy pays out. Of course, there is a clause in the policy stating that if a death is the result of actions by one of the other parties, then they are excluded from benefiting from it. The sooner Shannon Carrol's guilt can be determined, the sooner a payout can be made." He stood up, indicating that he was done with the interview. I couldn't think of any reason to extend it, so I allowed him to escort me out of the office.

Keech took ten minutes to put together a thorough timeline of Elizabeth's visits to Whalen Insurance. He clipped it all together, along with his card, and presented it to me.

As I drove home, I wondered about Nigel Whalen. I'd been pretty pissed with him for seeming to avoid me, but now he just seemed like a rich, busy guy who didn't really have a lot of time for lowly law enforcement officers. Since I had what I wanted, I decided I could forgive him for his earlier abruptness.

Cara called and said that she would be spending the evening at the motel with her parents, but to expect them to come by the house early Friday morning. I looked up at the roof of the car and gave thanks that they had accepted our offer to put them up in a motel.

At home, I fed Alvin and Ivy and filled them in on their living arrangements for the next week. Ivy wouldn't be too put out. Dad was going to stop by, or send Jamie over, every other day to refill her food and water bowls, as well as clean out the litter box. I didn't think Alvin would mind what we had planned for him either. He was going to stay at Camp Mauser. Jamie would look after them both when Dad wasn't there.

I looked around the house and thought about the fact that in two days I'd be married. It was an odd feeling, as if I was a kid playing dress-up. And I couldn't decide if it felt like a monumental shift or just a continuation of the wonderful life I'd already found with Cara.

"Doesn't matter now how I feel. It's happening," I told Ivy, who nudged my hand and demanded a few more head rubs.


When I woke up Friday morning, I felt like I was riding an express train out of the station. I could hear Henry's and Anna's voices in the front room. Cara was telling them all about the arrangements for Crandall Grove.

I'd told Johnson that I'd be in for half a day, so I got up and took a quick shower. After getting dressed, I put on my shoulder holster. Since Major Hill and crew still had my Glock 17 in their evidence locker, I'd had to put one of my personal guns to use. I'd picked a Colt 1911 that dated from the '70s when Colt gunsmiths had assembled and polished each of the Gold Match pistols. I had several other handguns which would have been more practical, but they failed the test for one reason or another. Either I didn't have an appropriate holster for the gun or enough extra magazines. As it was, the only holster I had for the 1911 was a shoulder holster straight out of a *Miami Vice* episode.

Stepping out of the bedroom, I chatted briefly with Henry and Anna before kissing Cara and heading for the door. "I don't mean to rush out, but I want to take care of a few things before the honeymoon," I apologized.

"The sooner you go, the sooner you can get done. Call me when you're leaving the office. There will probably be some things you'll need to pick up." Cara's voice was high and excited.

"Promise."

I got to the office and was met with smiles and pats on the back. Everyone at the sheriff's office had received an invitation to the wedding and most of them would be there. A couple of presents were already on my desk from guys and gals who had to work.

It was a relief that the only person in the evidence room was a new intern. I waved to him and went into my war room. I was only planning to put the copy of the policy in Elizabeth's folder, but then I decided I wanted to look through her old bank statements to see if the amount and date of the check she'd written for the policy tallied with the information I'd gotten from Whalen. It would only take a minute.

Elizabeth's bank had sent statements with photocopies of all of her checks, though there weren't very many of them. Most of her bank transactions had been by card or automatic withdrawal. However, I thought she might have used a check to pay for the insurance premium. If not, I could still see where she had paid with her card. Except there was nothing. I went through all of her credit card statements that we'd been able to acquire, back to two months before the policy had been signed. Still nothing.

I looked at the folders for a minute. Maybe she'd used some other account that we didn't know about to pay the premium. I supposed it was possible. I took out my phone and called Whalen's office.

"Whalen Insurance and Investments," Keech answered.

I told him who I was and was sure that I heard him sigh.

"I wanted to know how Elizabeth Collins paid the original premium on her policy."

"I'd have to check," he said, but I didn't hear him moving.

"I'd appreciate it," I assured him. I heard him sigh again, but he put me on hold so I assumed he was searching for the information.

Classical music played as I waited and waited.

"Mr. Whalen says that she paid with cash," Keech finally reported.

"I see." That didn't seem likely.

"Goodbye," he said and was gone.

"No. I don't think so," I said to myself.

I went back to the bank statements, looking for checks written for cash that might have been large enough to cover it. I still couldn't find anything.

I kept looking at the checks. Something wasn't right. I took out the policy and looked at it again.

"Damn it!" I said as I looked at the two side by side. I was so intent on them that I didn't notice when the door opened.

"You can't hide out in here," Darlene said. I was so startled I dropped the policy. "Calm down. I've heard of wedding jitters, but I think you're taking it to extremes, Prince Charming."

"Look at this," I said, ignoring her. I picked up the last page of the insurance policy with the signatures and held it next to the photocopies of Elizabeth's checks. "Notice anything?"

"A three-year-old could do a better job of forging a signature," she said with a furrowed brow. "So... someone other than Elizabeth Collins signed that policy."

"And I'm pretty sure I know who." I told her about the runaround I'd gotten from Whalen.

"Why would he want to lie about Elizabeth taking out an insurance policy?" Darlene asked.

"That's the million-dollar question, literally. Maybe he's in cahoots with Shannon or Deanne."

"Keeps the insurance front and center as the motive."

"Obviously he didn't have a copy of Elizabeth's signature to work from," I said, waving at the two very different versions. "Which would seem odd if this was a plan that he'd hatched with someone who was her friend."

"Might make sense if it was Shannon. That woman ain't cooking on all her burners."

"Whalen isn't stupid or disorganized. I can't see him hatching a plan like this and half-assing it."

"Maybe he was rushed."

"That's what I was thinking. He kept stalling me when I wanted a copy of the policy with the signatures. I think he didn't have it and wasn't sure where to get it. When I just showed up at his office, he didn't have much choice so he ad-libbed."

"There *is* another option. Maybe he's telling the truth and the woman who came in and took out the policy wasn't Elizabeth. Whalen wouldn't know that, so he went ahead on good faith," Darlene suggested.

"Than why not just come out and say that? He's seen pictures of Elizabeth since she was killed."

"You said he's got some fancy office selling insurance and investments. He might not want to admit he was taken for a fool."

"That's a fair point. His business depends of people trusting him. If he looks like someone who can be tricked, that would hurt his reputation. Something like that could ruin his business. Either way, we need to pull him in and interview him." I took out my phone.

"Whoa, there. You've got a rehearsal tonight and the main event tomorrow."

I looked at my phone, trying to decide what to do. "I guess I can leave it to you and Pete."

"Not only can you, you have to," Darlene said. "I'll call Pete. We'll go over there this afternoon and talk to him, see what kind of vibe we get off of him. Find out if he's willing to come in on his own for an interview."

"I'll be gone next week."

"Then you'll just have to miss it. I think Pete and I can handle this while you're off doing your honeymoon thing. A couple of draft horses like Pete and I can pull our load and your load too."

"Ah, shucks, Miss Marks, I just hate to miss out on all the fun," I said with a smile.

"I know it's going to be tough on you, spending a week off in Savannah with Cara."

"Call Pete, but remember that if you all go over to Tallahassee, he has to be back in time for the rehearsal."

She shooed me out of the room with a wave of her hand.


"I told you yesterday that you needed to lay out what you were going to wear," Cara told me as I came out of the shower, asking her where my clothes for the rehearsal were. "Lucky for you, I went ahead and pulled everything out." She pointed to my shirt, socks, shoes and suit, neatly organized on the foot of the bed.

An hour later, we were on our way to Crandall Grove. As we drove, Cara checked the weather app on her phone for the hundredth time.

"Looks like we should be okay. Morning clouds and clearing in the afternoon," she told me. The wedding was scheduled for one o'clock.

By this point everything was moving in a blur. There were too many people, too many tasks to complete and way too many emotions to deal with. Luckily, we'd agreed to keep the wedding party small. In addition to Pete as best man, I'd have Jimmy and Tim Akers, an old friend from high school, as groomsmen. Cara's maid of honor was a friend of hers from the clinic, while her two other bridesmaids were friends from childhood.

We all stumbled through the rehearsal, with Reverend Pritchard having to assure us that everything would go smoother on Saturday. I was sure that a wedding of cats would have been easier to organize. But at last we were done and getting ready to move to the Palmetto for dinner.

"Sarah, can Pete ride with me?" I asked, sounding like a ten-year-old talking to my best friend's mom.

"Who is Cara riding with?"

"She's going with her parents so they don't get lost," I told her.

"Take him," she said, giving Pete a push. "I know you all are going to talk business. You should be ashamed of yourself, Larry Macklin. Can't you forget about chasing bad guys for a couple of days?"

"Thank you, Mrs. Henley," I kidded her.

"How'd the interview with Whalen go?" I asked Pete when we were in my car. He'd shown up to the rehearsal at the last minute and, with everything else going on, we hadn't had time to talk.

"I could have brought you up to speed without the car trip. The office was closed when we got there. We tried his phone and went by his house. Nada."

"What's that mean?" I asked as much to myself as to Pete.

"It *is* Friday. The weather is going to be good this weekend. He might have closed up shop early and headed out of town. Or he might still be in town, just not at his home or office. We're just going to have to do some more digging to find him."

I had mixed feelings about this development. On the one hand, the sooner we could get the guy talking, the better. On the other hand, I wanted to be there when he was interviewed.

"I guess there's nothing to do about it now," I muttered.

"I did get an interesting phone call from Julio's brother-in-law. Rumor is that Whalen Insurance and Investments is under investigation."

"For what?"

"He was thin on details. He said they keep investigations pretty hush-hush since a company can be ruined if word gets around. He also pointed out that he didn't know many insurance companies that *hadn't* had complaints lodged against them. Kind of like cops, insurance companies can piss people off.

"Now, forget about the investigation and get married. Darlene and I will do what we can while you're gone, and if we don't have everything wrapped up in a neat package, you can get back into the action when you return."

"Fair enough. I'm officially switching from investigator to groom now," I said with mock seriousness.

"That's the spirit," Pete said and grinned.

# CHAPTER TWENTY-SEVEN

We pulled up to the Palmetto as the sky darkened. The air was damp and a breeze was coming out of the north. I looked around the parking lot. The restaurant was one of only a few in town that was worthy of the name, so there were a number of cars in the parking lot that weren't part of the wedding party. I got well wishes from several people who promised to be at the wedding as I stood at the entrance and waited for Cara and her parents to arrive. Pete and I didn't have long to wait. Henry's truck pulled up, followed almost immediately by Dad's truck and Sarah's car. Cara rushed over and gave me a hug before we all went inside to the private dining area.

Almost two hours later, all of us were full of the Palmetto's excellent food. I leaned back in my chair and took in the image of the extended and slightly odd family coming together to celebrate our wedding. There was a Norman Rockwell meets *The Addam's Family* quality to it that made me want to save the image forever in my memory. It was something I would be able to come back to in the future when I needed to be reminded of what good times looked like.

I had turned the sound off on my phone before dinner

started, so I almost didn't notice when my text alert went off. I felt the vibration and considered not looking at it, but I didn't see what harm it would do to take the phone out to see who it was. Around me, everyone was involved in various conversations. I had been talking to Pete, who'd done a great job of giving a toast earlier, but now his chair was empty after he'd gotten up to relieve himself of the gallon of sweet tea he'd tossed back.

I pulled out the phone, telling myself I'd just glance at it before putting it away again. The message made my heart skip a beat: *Mr. Macklin, I want to talk. I'm in the parking lot. Deanne.*

How did she even know I was here? My wedding wasn't a secret, but the rehearsal dinner wasn't exactly front page news. Could she have followed me? Maybe. I tried to think of all the possibilities. She could have decided that this was a good time to approach me when I would be unlikely to want to make a big fuss. If that was her thinking, then she was right. I couldn't resist going out and trying to talk with her, but I didn't want to get a bunch of other deputies involved.

I would have told Pete if he'd still been seated next to me, but he hadn't returned yet. *Maybe I'll run into him coming back from the restroom,* I thought. I whispered to Cara that I'd be right back and she gave me a quick kiss before I stood up.

I felt the heavy weight of the 1911 sway reassuringly in my shoulder holster as I walked to the door. I'd kept my coat on during dinner so I wouldn't come across like an extra from a bad cop show.

Still no Pete. I wondered what Darlene was doing. I was just about to open the door when a voice told me not to be a dumbass. There were two types of law enforcement officers in the world—those who listened to their inner voices and dead ones. I didn't want to be one of the latter, so I stopped and called Darlene.

"Aren't you supposed to be eating and getting toasted or roasted or something?" she said cheerily.

"I am. But I just got a text from Deanne, or at least it

says it's from Deanne. She wants me to come out in the parking lot to talk."

"Isn't Pete there?"

"I don't want to get everyone riled up."

"I'll be right there. Don't go outside until—"

"No. I'm going out by myself. I don't want to spook her. Just head this way and stay within a block or two in case I need you to follow her, or come charging in to the rescue."

"I don't like it."

"Just stand by. Don't make me regret calling you," I warned.

"Fine. I'll be a block away and let dispatch know we might need backup."

"That's all I wanted. I better go before she takes off."

I opened the door and was hit by a gust of damp, cool air. Everything was quiet as I looked around at the parked cars. The lot was lit by two street lights, but there were half a dozen ancient live oak trees spread throughout the parking area which left much of it in darkness. The pavement formed a quarter-acre "L" shape that ran along the north side of the building and around to the back. On this Friday night, there weren't many empty spaces, with cars and trucks parked everywhere. I walked around the north side of the lot, then started toward the back of the building when I saw a flash of light from a car parked underneath one of the largest oak trees. Was that her? One thing I did know was that it wasn't her car. This one was dark, not grey.

I started toward that corner of the lot, wishing I had my gun on my hip. It was much less conspicuous to place your hand close to the butt of the gun when it was on your side than when it was resting under the elbow of your other arm.

As I got closer, I could see movement outside the dark sedan. I heard a car pull into the lot behind me, but it must have found a spot close to the front door. I heard it stop and the engine turn off as I kept walking. There was no one else nearby. That was good. If things broke bad, I didn't want to have to worry about bystanders.

Another dozen steps and I could see a woman standing nervously beside the car. The car made it so I couldn't see below her chest, so I drifted a bit to the right. Another half dozen steps and I could see her clearly. Her hands were behind her back and she looked like she hadn't had a good night's sleep or a change of clothes for a couple of days.

"Deanne?" I said when I was twenty feet from her.

She nodded.

"You wanted to talk?"

"I think she did, but I caught her first. She won't be saying anything with the gag in her mouth." Whalen appeared from behind her. He held a foot-long Bowie knife that glinted even in the limited amount of light that reached them. "Do anything and she dies."

"I'm not going to do anything you don't want me to," I said, half raising my arms and actually putting me in a better position to draw my gun.

"Better not."

"What's the point of this?" I nodded toward Deanne.

"Of what, capturing her? This was my second attempt. She almost caught me when I killed Beth Robinson. Apparently Beth had told her she'd be meeting with someone who had information about Elizabeth's death and asked her to be there. I guess she was nervous after what had happened to Elizabeth. But Deanne here was late and showed up just as I was getting ready to leave. I chased her through half the county," he said and I looked at the front of his BMW, noticing the dents in the hood. He'd hit the teenagers. "Good luck and bad luck. She never got a good look at me, and I never caught her. Tonight it turned out we both had the same idea. Come here to meet you. She was just unlucky enough to get here first."

"What are you going to do with her?"

"That depends on you. I just want to have a private talk, that's all."

"All you had to do was call," I said, trying not to sound too sarcastic.

As I talked, I edged closer to him and Deanne. This was a calculated risk. Normally it was better to maintain, or even increase, your distance from a threat. However, in this case I wanted to be as close as possible so that if Whalen attacked Deanne, I'd be able to intervene quickly.

I could hear people coming and going from the restaurant. It would not be good for someone to stumble on our little tableau. If they did, events would quickly become unpredictable.

"All of this could have been avoided," Whalen hissed. "That bitch Elizabeth couldn't just take her policy and go, she had to start snooping through my company's business."

Of course, Elizabeth of the Type A personality and the extraordinary accounting skills would have wanted to check and double-check the company she was considering using for a major insurance policy. After all, an insurance policy is only as good as the company that backs it. That's when it hit me. It was Whalen's company that she'd been researching.

"You killed her because she found out you cook your books?"

"It's a little more complicated than that. I'm lucky that a friend told me she was digging into my background."

"And Elizabeth and Beth were very close, so she had to be eliminated too."

"Elizabeth was using Beth as a safety net. When she came to me, she told me I couldn't hurt her because she'd already told her friend. Not so much. It just meant twice the work."

"And you wrote the fake policy to put suspicion on Shannon and Deanne."

"Precisely. Then it turns out you're as much of a snoop as Elizabeth was."

I was only about eight feet from them now. I should have wondered why Whalen wasn't trying to stop me from getting closer, but I was focused on getting to Deanne. My plan was to jump him if he gave me an opening or if he made any move to hurt Deanne. Now that I was this close, I hoped I'd be able to get inside the swing of the foot-long knife he was holding at her throat.

Rapists and other bad guys preferred knives because they intimidated people. Everyone was familiar with the pain of a cut from a knife. It was natural to remember that pain and recoil from it. I'd had some training in how to take an knife away from an assailant, yet knives still gave me the heebie-jeebies.

Whalen was letting the knife move down and away from Deanne's throat.

"What's the end game?" I pushed.

"For you? Or for her? I guess that's for you to decide."

"Why are you here?" I asked and a voice in my head answered me: *He's desperate and he intends to kill both of you.* Realizing this, I couldn't give him too much longer to execute whatever twisted plan he had. But the realization came too late.

He shoved Deanne violently toward me. What I'd failed to notice was that he'd duct-taped her feet together as well as her hands, which were secured behind her back. When he pushed her toward me, she could only stumble and fall.

I had two choices. She was going to fall into me and I could either catch her or toss her off to the side. Doing the latter would mean that she would hit the car next to me or land on the pavement and bash her head against the parking lot.

I should have let her fall while I drew my gun, but I didn't. I broke her fall just as I saw Whalen, knife outstretched, coming at me. Eight feet is too close to stop a determined knife attack if you're tangled up with a woman whose hands and legs are bound together. I knew that I was going to take the knife in my chest or shoulder. I started to let myself fall backwards, hoping that I could keep the blade from plunging into my heart. Even as it was happening, it seemed that I could feel the pain from the last time I'd been stabbed, even before Whalen's blade had reached me.

I heard an ear-piercing scream which, for a moment, I

thought had come from me. But it hadn't. I saw Whalen's mouth open and his body contort as though he was trying to scratch his back.

Miraculously, the Bowie knife dropped from his hand just before he fell to his knees. I gently lowered Deanne onto the ground before scrambling toward Whalen, who was on his knees and trying to reach back over his shoulder. I shoved him to the ground and was rewarded with another screech from the big man. I didn't have any cuffs, but I rolled him over on his stomach. He seemed to be more than anxious for me to turn him over. When I had him face down, I realized why he'd screamed. Sticking out of his back was the top of a green beer bottle.

I looked up and saw Jessie Gilmore sitting on the ground behind him, looking like she was going to throw up.

"What the hell are you doing here?" I asked her and received only a glazed stare in return. "Listen to me! I want you to go over to Deanne and help get the tape off of her. Do it now!"

Slowly, Jessie stood up and walked over to kneel down next to Deanne, who was trying to spit out the gag. "Help her!" I wanted Jessie doing something to keep her from drifting off. She was reacting like a zombie.

I pulled out my phone and called Darlene, telling her to bring in the cavalry, including an ambulance for Whalen, though it didn't look like he'd suffered any life-threatening injuries. Still, he moaned and cursed for the entire five minutes it took for help to arrive.

"That bastard!" Deanne yelled when she'd pulled the handkerchief out of her mouth. "Did you do that?" she asked Jessie.

"I guess. I just..."

We could hear the sounds of sirens headed our way. Deanne hugged Jessie while I called Pete.

"What the hell is going on?" he sputtered, and I realized I could hear him without the phone.

"We're over here!" I shouted.

Pete came jogging over with Dad not far behind him.

"Really, in the parking lot during your rehearsal dinner?" Dad said, shaking his head. I was pretty sure I detected a hint of a smile on his face.

Within minutes the entire wedding party, an ambulance and half a dozen law enforcement cars surrounded us. Cara had pushed her way through the crowd and was hanging onto my arm as I perched on top of Whalen. Darlene loaned me her handcuffs and, reluctantly, I cuffed him with his hands in front due to his injuries. Darlene helped the paramedics move him onto a stretcher, then they cuffed him to the stretcher for good measure before wheeling him through the crowd and into the ambulance.

"I'll ride with him," Darlene said.

"Thanks, but first I want to do the honors." I climbed into the ambulance and informed Whalen that I was arresting him for the kidnapping of Deanne Greer. All the other charges could come later. I informed him of his rights and asked him if he understood them. He spat out a curse which I found very satisfying.

Deanne was refusing to go in the second ambulance. It took several of us to persuade her that she should go to the hospital and spend the night so they could be sure she didn't have a concussion. I had saved her from hitting the ground too hard, but Whalen had knocked her in the head before restraining her. She reluctantly agreed to go with the EMTs. I assured her that someone would be in touch soon. She was our star witness.

"You know, you scared your poor mother to death," I said as I walked Deanne over to the ambulance. "Why did you throw your phone away?"

Deanne looked at the ground. "I panicked. I thought it would make it harder for whoever killed Elizabeth to find me. I regretted it as soon as I did it."

"There's one other loose end I wanted to ask you about. Did you break into Beth's house and steal something?"

"It was the journal that Beth kept of our meetings. I

thought maybe I could find some clues about who was hunting us down. But there wasn't anything useful. Just a few cryptic statements at the end about Elizabeth having problems getting the insurance. I didn't know until tonight the significance of that." She shook her head sadly.

I thanked her as the EMTs helped her into the back of the ambulance.

I found Cara sitting with Jessie, who was in the back of Julio's car, wrapped in a blanket and drinking coffee. I made sure that she was okay and Julio offered to drive her home. I was dying to know why she'd been there, and she would have to be interviewed in the coming days, but all of that could wait.

"See you tomorrow," Cara said, giving her bemused parents big hugs before they drove back to their motel.

I went over to where Dad, Genie and Jimmy were climbing into Dad's truck.

"Wow, that was weird," Jimmy said, shaking his head and laughing. "I hope nothing like that happens tomorrow."

"You and me both," I told him.

"At least you managed not to get hurt," Dad said, as though I were accident-prone.

"I caught the murderer," I protested.

"Not before he caught you," he pointed out. "You owe a lot of thanks to your strange pixie of a CI," he said with a laugh.

Cara and I were a mess in the morning. Both of us had been too keyed up after the night's excitement, let alone with wedding nerves, to get much sleep.

The skies were overcast and a light mist was in the air as we gathered our clothes and hauled everything out to the car. We'd be spending our wedding night at the Grove and had reserved a suite large enough for everyone to dress there beforehand.

"I think we get the award for the most exciting rehearsal

dinner," Cara said as we drove.

"I'm still trying to imagine the string of people following me to the restaurant. I can't wait to sort out everyone's account."

"Jessie admitted that she'd been following you most of this week. She said it was just for practice and that she didn't really expect anything to happen. But when she noticed Whalen pulling in after her, she decided to leave and come back a few minutes later, hoping he wouldn't notice her. I think that was pretty smart."

"Hmmm. She's actually pretty good at it. I never noticed… But if Whalen had figured out that she was following me, it wouldn't have gone well for her. I don't understand that woman."

"She's stubborn. I think you're going to have to accept that she's imprinted on you."

"Great," I said sarcastically. "Just what I need, a crazed little duckling following me around."

"You were lucky she was there last night," Cara reminded me.

"You've got a point," I allowed.

Half an hour before the ceremony, the clouds burned away and a bright spring sun beamed down on the guests who sat facing the gazebo and the lake beyond.

I had just finished shrugging into my coat and stepping outside when I heard a loud *woof*. I turned to see my overgrown furry brother dragging Dad behind him.

"Don't jump up on him today," Dad told Mauser, who wasn't listening.

"Where's Jamie?"

"He had to go to the restroom," Dad said, trying to get an overexcited Mauser to sit.

"I can't believe you brought him."

"I had a dozen people, including your future father-in-law, specifically ask if he was coming." I was sure that was the truth. "Besides, he's got his formalwear on." Dad pointed to the bowtie around the Dane's neck.

"I'm just glad we were able to talk everyone out of the idea of him being the ring bearer," I said, frowning at Mauser, who had finally put his big butt on the ground.

"I've been wanting to talk to you before now, but it's just been hard to find the time," Dad started.

"Dad, I'm sure it can wait," I assured him. I didn't really want to get into anything deep just before the wedding.

"Larry, I just want to say that I'm proud of what you've accomplished. Both in the department and finding someone as wonderful as Cara to share your life."

"Wow," I said, so startled by both his praise and the sentiment that I didn't know how to respond. "Cara *is* special."

"Don't screw this up." His tone made it clear that he was only half joking.

"I tell myself that all the time," I said honestly. This earned me a big smile and a nod from him.

"You ain't as stupid as you look," Dad said. "You better get going," he told me, nodding toward the gazebo where we could see Pete, Jimmy and Tim waiting alongside Reverend Pritchard.

When I stood between Pete and the minister, looking over our friends and family as I waited for Cara and Henry to start down the grassy aisle, I felt a calm wash over me. Never had I been so sure about the path that lay before me.

My heart swelled as Cara approached, her white gown sparkling and her hair glowing in the sunlight as she walked arm-in-arm with her father. Watching her, I understood that I was being given a great gift. Her blue eyes shone with love as she looked at me and smiled. She took my hand and everyone else faded away.

We bumbled and stumbled a little over our vows as Pritchard guided us through the ceremony. When it was over, I kissed Cara and knew that the world was no longer mine. The new world was ours.

Larry Macklin returns in:

# Summer's Rage
## *A Larry Macklin Mystery–Book 14*

# ACKNOWLEDGMENTS

As always, thanks to my wife, Melanie, for her editing skills and support; to H. Y. Hanna for her inspiration, assistance and encouragement; and to all the fans of the series. Larry never would have come this far without all of you!


Original Cover Concept by H. Y. Hanna
Cover Design by Florida Girl Design, Inc.
www.gobookcoverdesign.com

# ABOUT THE AUTHOR

A. E. Howe lives and writes on a farm in the wilds of North Florida with his wife, horses and more cats than he can count. He received a degree in English Education from the University of Georgia and is a produced screenwriter and playwright. His first published book was *Broken State*. The Larry Macklin Mysteries is his first series and he released a new series, the Baron Blasko Mysteries, in summer 2018. The first book in the Macklin series, *November's Past*, was awarded two silver medals in the 2017 President's Book Awards, presented by the Florida Authors & Publishers Association; the ninth book, *July's Trials*, was awarded two silver medals in 2018. Howe is a member of the Mystery Writers of America, and was co-host of the "Guns of Hollywood" podcast for four years on the Firearms Radio Network. When not writing, Howe enjoys riding, competitive shooting and working on the farm.

Made in United States
Troutdale, OR
02/12/2025